WALK WITH Wisdom

A Journey into the Sanctuary of Life

DONNA BLOOM

Copyright © 2026 Donna Bloom

All rights reserved.

No part of this book may be reproduced, stored in a retrieval system, or transmitted in any form or by any means, electronic, mechanical, photocopying, recording, or otherwise, without prior written permission of the author, except for brief quotations used in reviews or scholarly works.

This is a work of fiction. Names, characters, places, and incidents are either products of the author's imagination or used fictitiously. Any resemblance to actual persons, living or dead, or actual events is purely coincidental.

First printing, 2026

ISBN 979-8-9997040-0-9

Independently published

www.WiseMindHypnosis.com

Dedication

For my grandmother Rachel
and my father, Sheldon,
whose love and quiet wisdom live on in these pages.

About the Author

Donna Bloom
Author, Hypnotist, and Coach

Donna Bloom is a Board-Certified Hypnotist, Certified Life Coach, and founder of Wise Mind Hypnosis, based on Long Island, New York. She works with clients locally and worldwide, guiding people to quiet anxiety, strengthen self-trust, and reconnect with their inner calm through personalized hypnosis and mindset coaching.

In addition to her private practice, Donna presents at professional hypnosis conferences and facilitates workshops and corporate lunch-and-learn programs focused on confidence, stress reduction, and mindset development. Her approach blends practical tools with heart-centered awareness. Participants often describe her presence as compassionate, grounded, and inspiring.

Walk with Wisdom marks the beginning of an unfolding journey into the Sanctuary of Life. Through story and imagination, Donna brings to life the inner guidance she has witnessed in her clients for years. It is the quiet wisdom that has always been there, waiting to be embodied and trusted.

She believes meaningful change begins when we pause long enough to listen within and trust what we already know in our hearts.

On a personal note, Donna enjoys long walks in the woods, traveling to interesting places around the world with her husband, playing pickleball, and spending time with her family. She especially adores her grand puppy, Zoey, an adorable Havanese who is the ultimate reminder to play and love unconditionally.

To learn more about Donna's work, speaking engagements, or private sessions, visit

www.WiseMindHypnosis.com

Thank you for your support. It truly makes a difference.

Table of Contents

Chapter 1:

The Girl with the Sparkling Heart

Once upon a time, there lived an ordinary girl born into an ordinary family. Yet from the very beginning, there was something quietly extraordinary about her. She always seemed to know things, truths she felt deeply but could not yet put into words. She was born with an intuitive spirit. It lived within her as naturally as her brown eyes and her sweet, curious smile.

This inner knowing had a way of making everything feel brighter, lighter, and more colorful, like the world simply worked better when she trusted it.

She was a bright, funny girl who appreciated life's simple joys: friends, family, puppies, and the thrill of exploring new places. Just as much, she cherished the comfort and quiet of her bedroom, with its soft purple carpeting and space to dream. Her vivid imagination helped her dream up all kinds of stories and enjoy fun adventures with her sisters and friends.

And yet, she was not entirely ordinary.

This girl was born with something special, a gentle sparkle in her heart. A sparkle that quietly illuminated her life and guided her even when she didn't realize she was being guided. It helped her shine in subtle ways, offering reassurance, direction, and a sense of calm she didn't yet understand. Her heart sparkled and always had.

Her name was Lark.

Her parents noticed that special sparkle the very day she was born. They saw it in her eyes, in her presence, in the way she arrived already carrying something wise and tender within her tiny body. They gave her the very fitting name Lark, believing that one day she would learn to fly freely. They had a strong hunch this child would grow to be adventurous, carefree, and deeply authentic. This could allow her spirit to rise and her heart to shine brightly into the world.

At fourteen years old, Lark was learning that growing up was not always easy. Her emotions sometimes felt unpredictable, rising and falling without much warning. Her mind was busy; constantly thinking, wondering, and worrying. There were days when her thoughts seemed to pile up faster than she could sort through them.

She worried if she was smart enough, pretty enough, thin enough, or funny enough. So many questions swirled through her mind, often leaving her feeling overwhelmed. Sometimes her constant thinking made her irritable or uncertain, instead of her usual cheerful self.

School was where her overthinking showed up the most. Lunchtime and recess, moments meant for ease and laughter, often felt uncomfortable instead. She often compared herself to others and was overly concerned with their opinions. Those moments confused her, especially because they didn't match how she felt when she allowed her imagination to sparkle.

When she tapped into her creative side, Lark felt calm and at ease. In those moments, her mind softened, her body relaxed, and everything felt just right. She sensed that familiar inner knowing again, the one that had been there her whole life. During these times, she trusted herself and felt connected to something steady and reassuring.

What puzzled Lark was that she didn't know how to make those calm moments last. She didn't yet have the words to describe this inner connection or understand why it seemed to come and go. She only knew that something wise lived within her, patiently waiting for her to take notice and trust her inner wisdom.

Lark was the oldest of four sisters. The twins, Rebecca, who everyone called Becca and Grace. They adored Lark and followed her everywhere, even as they tested her patience daily. The twins were energetic, expressive, and often very loud, filling the house with movement and chatter. They weren't troublesome, exactly—they were just *extra.*

Several years later, baby Hope arrived and completed the Roberts family. Hope was quiet and sweet, with a calm presence that seemed to soothe everyone in the family. At just four years old, she was content to observe and was happy with whatever attention came her way. She laughed easily, smiled often, and had a natural ability to go with the flow. Hope was, quite simply, hopeful.

Though Lark sometimes felt overwhelmed by the noise and responsibility, she secretly loved being the oldest. The role felt familiar; it fit her perfectly. Being first came with expectations, but it also came with a sense of purpose. Deep down, Lark sensed that she was meant to lead, and being the eldest felt like gentle preparation for something important to come later in life.

These thoughts drifted through her awareness like soft whispers, comforting but easy to miss. Her sisters envied her oldest-sister privileges, especially having a room of her own while the twins shared a room. Hope, still too young to care, happily occupied her small room without complaint.

Lark carried her worries, her responsibilities, and her quiet wisdom all at once. She didn't yet realize how much strength she already possessed or how her sparkling heart was guiding her, even now.

And though she didn't know it yet, everything was about to change.

Lark and her family live in the small, mountain town community of Casper, nestled deep within the trees in an enchanted forest. *It is truly a wonderful place to grow up*, Lark thought. There are many places in nature to explore, small nooks for reading or conversing, and so many areas to enjoy peaceful moments. The neighbors are friendly and supportive. Everyone in town always seems to have a warm smile or a kind word. Visitors love to enjoy the beauty and solitude of this storybook town. There is a warm, welcoming vibe to the town and a strong sense of community. The people are happy and love tradition, customs, and doing things the same way for generation after generation.

Lark's family has lived in Casper for three generations. Her parents are proud of the roots her family set in this town, and everyone fondly knows the Roberts family. Then again, everyone knows everyone here! Lark loves this fact and could not imagine living anywhere else… or could she?

Sometimes she dreams of growing up and moving to a great big city, where she will meet talented authors and artists, eat foods from all around the world, and be anything she desires. Lark secretly dreams about becoming a published author of children's storybooks. These thoughts are both inspiring and terrifying! *How can two types of opposing thoughts be true at the same time?* Lark thinks quietly to herself. These types of unspoken thoughts and intuition fill Lark with a sense of effortless calm. She relishes the times when her mind is steady and still. It feels as if she is connected to everything and everyone. All things are possible. These are the moments when Lark is at her best, carefree and engaged fully with life.

And then there are those other times and other thoughts! The dreaded cycle of worry, doom, and gloom that seemingly comes out of nowhere. It's like *bam, here I am, your new friend and companion, here to come along for the ride to keep you safe.* Lark detests those days and struggles to shake them off. And if truth be told, it's worse during the days before her friend, her monthly period, arrives. If being a teenager was not bad enough, enduring intrusive thoughts adds a whole new level of challenges, especially with her friends at school.

The worrisome thoughts plague her good-natured mind. With Lark's same sense of inquisitiveness, she is baffled why her mind can feel so noisy, like a TV that won't turn itself off. Secretly, Lark ponders if others have the same mental chaos in their minds. *Do my friends struggle with this very same thing?* Even though she is curious, she is afraid to ask for fear of embarrassment and shame. Maybe they will think I'm weak and won't want to be my friend.

Despite Lark's emotional struggles, she enjoys her life very much. She has a small group of wonderful friends, a nice school with great teachers, caring parents, and friendly neighbors. It is an idyllic life. There are always activities and gatherings of friends and family. There is always something to do to keep busy on the weekends and even after school.

Lark and her three besties, Gwen, Ashley, and Nikki, frequently like to hang out on Main Street by Sullivan's Ice Cream Shop. Sullivan's has been around forever, as far as the girls are concerned. Her parents remember it as a luncheonette where they used to serve egg creams (a strange beverage with milk, chocolate syrup, and soda water) and sell comic books. Now it was an eclectic coffee bar that has the most delicious ice cream on planet Earth. This place really was popular and famous, and many travelers would make this a destination stop when visiting Casper. The ice cream was made at a local creamery and was always fresh and delicious. And Main Street is bustling with small shops and restaurants. It's the place to be and be seen.

Gwen only lives a few blocks from Main Street, so her house was pretty much the go-to hangout before heading into town. She and Lark met on the first day of kindergarten, and they clicked right away. Gwen could be a little moody and had a habit of pushing sweet, go-with-the-flow Lark around when she felt like it. But Gwen was also the fun one, the kind of girl everyone wanted to be around. Better to be in her circle than on the outside of it. She met Nikki and Ashley in second grade through Girl Scouts, and after that, the four of them were inseparable.

When Lark is not busy with her friends or sisters, she loves quiet time alone in her room, especially after school. She seriously loves her alone time. Even though she lives in a small town, social media is a big source of enjoyment with her friends. All the threads and chats do take a toll on her mind. As a typical teen, she feels it's her responsibility to read and respond to all threads, snaps, and chats. As a matter of fact, Gwen gets quite testy when friends don't reply right away. Lark thinks it's a nice reprieve that her parents do not allow cell phones at the dinner table, and then after eight in the evening. Mom values family time, and the dinner table is for family and food only. So, Lark has the perfect excuse to disconnect at dinnertime.

Lark has a wonderful evening ritual of moon bathing. She loves the glow and the mystique of the moon. This evening was a ten out of ten, though the temperature was cold. Tonight, as she stepped out into the family's backyard, she immediately felt a sense of awe! She peered up at the velvety black sky and delightfully noticed all the twinkling stars. The moon was full and illuminated the sky with silvery light and a radiant aura of orange bands. She silently wondered how many stars are in the solar system, in the vast expansiveness that seems to go on forever. She breathed in the cool evening air, which brought her peace and solace. She heard owls hooting far, far up in the trees. She loves her alone time to think and to be still.

Lark is a thoughtful soul. On this night, she slowly began to contemplate, *I wonder what else is out there.* She has a deep yearning for more, to expand beyond the charm and simple life where she is being raised. *But what could that be? How will I know?*

With that notion, she said goodnight to the creatures of the night, went inside, kissed her parents, and went upstairs to go to sleep.

Chapter 2:

A Life-Changing Dream

Even though Lark struggles with worry, she truly loves her life and all that she will experience in the days, weeks, and years to follow. She is curious by nature, and deep down, she has a hidden desire for more. She does not want more things like trinkets, clothes, or accessories; she just wants emotional growth and more access to the *spirit in nature*. She feels it deep inside, intuitively knows it is there, but she needs to know for sure and wants to see everything in plain view. So where did this yearning spark come from? How does Lark know about such things? Where did all this intuition come from? Why does she yearn for more? Some refer to Lark as an old soul. She always thought it was odd that Grandma called her an old soul on more than one occasion. Then, when Mom used the same expression last week after a deep conversation, Lark took notice of that term. Who is an old soul?

Well, all this curiosity magnified with a dream. A dream one night that would change everything. Unbeknownst to Lark, this dream would disrupt her life as she knew it in a mysterious, magical way. This dream would be the start of a magical set of adventures where Lark would meet an intuitive guide who would teach her how to connect with nature and, more importantly, her inner calm and authentic self so that the worrisome thoughts can be a thing of the past.

It was a cold fall night, and the wind was howling outside Lark's bedroom window. The moon was full and glistening with a silver, glowing light. Lark was snuggled up under the warmth of her covers, and she began to imagine the warm, sunny days of spring and summer when she could be outside playing and exploring and be swept up in her own world of imagination.

The sound of the wind lulled her into a sound slumber. Her body was relaxed and her mind calm. She needed sleep, glorious sleep, to reset from the day. She drifted deeper and deeper into a sound, restful sleep. She remained comfortably still and content. She was completely at peace.

And then, as if by magic, there she was at the entrance gate to a magical garden. Lark took a breath and felt her heart sparkle and illuminate. The gate slowly opened as if inviting her to enter. Lark felt even more at peace; she was completely relaxed and serene and felt a sense of unconditional love.

It was at that moment that Lark noticed something or perhaps someone. The figure appeared to be an older woman, but not like her mom or grandmother. This woman appeared different to Lark, almost ethereal. She had a unique pendant around her neck, a shining amulet with four colorful stones. The elder figure bowed her head and welcomed Lark home. The two stood there in silence for several moments, though it seemed like hours. She took her thin hand and motioned for Lark to enter this mystical realm. And then Lark remembered; she remembered, well, everything. She remembered this place, which felt like home. It was not quite a place but rather a feeling of unconditional love. This love was and is multidimensional; it's as if it shone with brilliant colors, beautiful flowers, aromatic scents, comforting, serene music, and an absolute lightness embracing her spirit and her true essence of self.

The elder woman simply smiled, no words, just a smile and a heart that exuded unconditional love and acceptance. She was like no other person Lark had ever encountered. Her eyes were wide and bright. Looking into her piercing eyes was like looking into a bright blue sky full of possibilities. Her hair was a unique combination of white and turquoise blue, with waves and ripples. It reminded Lark of the tranquil Caribbean Sea in which to float and dream. Her nose was straight and unusually long, with the cutest, delicate nostrils. Her ears were simple and decorated with earrings created in nature to amplify her hearing and perception. What struck Lark the most was her mouth and simple smile. Her lips were pursed closed gently, as if to speak only with loving words.

There was a simple shawl around her shoulders with the same flowing colors as her hair. It provided warmth and comfort. Her dress was also simple and contoured her body so delicately. Right in the middle of her chest was that same beautiful crystal that sparkled brightly. And then there were her hands. Just to look at her hands was awe-inspiring. Her hands seemed to float with her body in the air. Anything she touched would surrender into a peaceful, serene state.

Lark noticed birds of all colors chirping behind her in a cheerful way. She did not utter one word to Lark in her dream, for there was no need. Lark felt a sense of love, like nothing she had ever experienced. She knew she was both sleeping and dreaming, and had no desire to return to a waking state. Lark felt like she was in heaven. She knew she was dreaming the dream of all dreams and felt calm and peaceful. She wanted to bottle this feeling forever. She wanted to stay, to explore, and to know more about this woman. Lark was in total bliss.

Beep, beep, beep went the sound of her alarm clock to rouse her from her deep slumber and get ready for school. And then there was the sound of the twins awakening from their sleep, hungry and ready for breakfast. Lark rolled over in her bed, still in a state of absolute bliss. She wondered if her dream could possibly be real. Was this a fabrication of her imagination or real? And what really is real?

Lark took another breath and vowed to always remember this elder woman and the wonderful dream. She quickly pulled her journal from her nightstand and attempted to sketch the figure of the woman in her dream. This was the most fascinating dream she had ever had in her whole life, and she wanted to capture every detail, aspect, and the essence of this mystical woman. She furiously wrote down everything she could remember, and the simple act of writing jogged her memory with many details. She secretly hoped every night and in every dream, she could return to where *she* lived in that enchanted garden. It was certainly a magical and mysterious dream.

Chapter 3:

Time to Explore

After school that very day, Lark wanted time alone to clear her head. The dream from the previous night consumed her thoughts all day during school. She was distracted in class and found it troublesome to focus on the lessons. She attempted to recall the details of this woman and tried once again to draw her inside one of her notebooks. However, her sketch did not do her justice. She was so baffled by the dream. Sure, she had strange dreams before, but this one was different on so many levels. It was fantastic and a great escape from reality.

Lark was happy she made it through the long day. Now she was ready to be outside and enjoy the solace of the beautiful autumn day. She dashed into the house, threw her backpack on the floor of her room and quickly changed out of her school clothes into something more comfortable. She grabbed a snack and a quick drink before hurrying out the door. She told her sisters, Becca and Grace, she would be home before sunset. Luckily, they were just old enough to stay home alone while Hope was in day care.

The beautiful thing about living in Casper was all the nature nestled within the thriving community. Within a mile of her home were the most glorious trails set amongst the backdrop of trees with mountains in the background. The paved paths lead to gorgeous scenery, trails, and even picnic destinations. Every inch of this place was picture-perfect.

This day was especially brilliant as it was a warm fall day with bright blue skies. The trees were in full autumn bloom. Lark could not decide which color she liked the most. She simply admired all the different varieties of trees with the yellows, the oranges, the greens, and the reds, and even some magenta leaves adorning the trees. She slowly stopped at the beginning of her favorite trail with complete gratitude and adoration of nature's beauty. It filled her with the same peace as her vivid dream the night before.

She slowly started her adventure, allowing only her steps and the nature surrounding her to fill her thoughts. Lark was completely present in the experience. She purposefully looked up into the sky and noticed the abundance of trees. Gorgeous, colorful trees and so much magnificent scenery. Looking up at nature was more gratifying than looking down at a screen. This gave her a new sense of peace and inner calm, which was a welcome relief from the chatter of her thinking mind.

At just fourteen, Lark was wise in her own right. She instinctively knew that life only happens in the present moment. The past is already gone, and tomorrow is nothing more than imagination. How fitting, she mused, that the very word "present" means both this moment and something wonderful waiting to be opened, a true "gift."

Lark breathed in the warmth of the fall air and continued to marvel at all the trees and the shapes and colors of all the different leaves. They all amazed and dazzled her imagination.

As she continued to walk, she felt a sense of inner and outer bliss. She was very much aware of her feet taking each deliberate step. She felt the warmth of the sunshine gracing her hair. Lark was grateful for her health, her family, and her ability to be among these mystical and magical trees.

Lark was about twenty minutes into her walk and her own mindfulness experience when she approached a beautiful, small, thin tree. It was adorned with golden oval-shaped leaves. They were so delicate-looking, and the leaves had a touch of whimsy about them. Each leaf glistened with what appeared to be sunshine.

Lark got closer and decided to stop and simply admire the delicate tree, and as she did, she could almost hear the tree speaking to her and welcoming her to the sanctuary. As Lark allowed herself to become completely quiet, enthralled, and enchanted, she was able to see more and see deeper into the depths of the trees. Many of the other trees seemed to have a variety of colors she had never seen before. The leaves were so colorful and alive. There was something in the air that had a settling feeling. There was a sense of equilibrium, optimism, and peace. As Lark continued to simply be among the trees, she could almost intuit the trees speaking directly to her heart, filling her with guidance. Yet no words were spoken. It was a sense of presence, a sense of simply being without anything to do. It was a real gift!

Lark wondered if this place always existed and if others knew about it. And why others did not speak of it. She wondered whether all forests and trees were like this one. Lark had so many questions. But when she started to think, her mind started to race. She noticed she could no longer feel the mystery and serenity of this place. It was as if it all disappeared into thin air, and as much as she tried, that feeling slipped through her hands like water.

And there it was, that old familiar voice in her mind, that constant companion that made her doubt herself. *BUT…what if that voice is correct and I am hallucinating or something worse?* She started to pinch herself to ensure she was still awake. Then she thought, *Okay, let's get a grip.* She took a deep breath and settled down.

She looked onto the path and saw there was a group of others on the trail. They seemed to be conversing, smiling, and laughing. She even recognized one boy from high school talking with her old friend Jonah. That told her that all was fine. That visual distraction seemed to settle the doubting voice in her head, thank goodness!

Lark took a mental picture of this place and returned home as it was turning dark, and Mom would start to wonder and worry where she was. Lark expressed gratitude for her experience and started her journey home in silence, wonder, and with a grand sense of curiosity.

She returned home and was greeted by her mom. Mom was happy that she took some time to enjoy the beautiful day. She inquired about her walk, but Lark did not want to engage just yet. She was also rather quiet and reflective during dinner. Her sisters attempted to cajole her, but she simply smiled as if she did not hear them. After a bit, they simply ceased to engage with her and turned their attention to Dad and Hope.

Lark was reflective the whole evening and waited with great anticipation for bedtime, when she was free to close her eyes and let go of the expectations of the day and let her mind and body relax and drift off naturally into a sound state of slumber. Lark wanted to recreate her experience from last night and meet the elder woman again and know more. She wondered how she could do that or if it was at all possible. Since it was after 8 p.m., she was not allowed to use her electronic devices. But if she could, she would do an internet search, "How to repeat a dream from the night before." She wondered how anyone could truly know how to do this with certainty. With that notion, she decided to get into bed and remember as many details as possible and let those thoughts carry her off to sleep.

She was comfortably in her bed with the covers almost covering her head. Lark started with today's stroll in the woods and all the peace it afforded. She thought about the trees and all the colorful leaves. Lark remembered giggling silently about the two words "gift" and "present." She then turned her attention to the dream from last night. She thought about the magical, beautiful woman, especially her hair, eyes, hands, lips, and even the pendant around her neck. Before she knew it, Lark was sound asleep. She slept soundly and oh so peacefully.

The night hours turned to dawn, and her body started to sense and anticipate wake-up time. However, she was still in a state of deep sleep, and it was then that *she* appeared to her quietly and solemnly, and all she said was, "I live among the trees in nature."

Lark wanted to ask more, but the mystical woman turned, walked slowly away, and faded into a thin blue mist. She remained perfectly still in bed, hoping to catch another glimmer of this mystical woman or hear a few more magical words.

Chapter 4:

A Tree Named Goldy

Beep, beep, beep, the sound of Lark's alarm. It was time to rise and shine, wash her hands and face, and get ready for the busy school day ahead. Lark was distracted at school that day. Her teachers noticed the usually talkative and inquisitive Lark was quiet and even introspective. Mr. Nalley, her social studies teacher, called on her in class and was surprised to find his most curious student so enthralled by the blue sky outside the window. He gave her a pass, as Lark is usually engaged and attentive in class. And she rarely attempted to peek at her cell phone during class to check social media, as the other students felt compelled to do frequently.

Finally, the last period bell rang, and the school day ended. She rode the school bus home with her friends, though more quietly than normal. She yearned again for the quiet, solitude, and wonder of the woods. Luckily, she did not have any homework or tests the following day, so when she arrived home, she was able to dodge her sisters and sneak out of the house. Lark sent a text to Mom to let her know her whereabouts and promised to be home before sunset.

Lark walked down the same path as yesterday until she came upon that same thin tree with golden oval leaves. As she approached the tree, she became very quiet and decided this exquisite tree needed a name. She called the tree "Goldy." It seemed fitting as the leaves sparkled with a golden color. Lark loved giving objects names, as she knew everything had energy and purpose.

Lark remembered the stillness from yesterday, and when her mind was quiet, she could feel the mystery of the sanctuary within the woods. Lark focused and steadied her breathing as she looked with fresh eyes and a curious mind, as if seeing this tree for the very first time. She had a sense of wonder and pure joy today.

She enjoyed the aroma of the trees and the breeze on her face. She was also delighted by the noise from her sneakers as she crunched the leaves with her steps. It was all magnificent, and Lark felt at home. As she continued to enjoy this experience, she felt as if Goldy was speaking to her. It was not like hearing words or anything like that; it was a knowing she felt in her mind and body. She believed Goldy was saying a friendly *"Hello. I am so glad you are here. Welcome to the Sanctuary of Life. I hope you have a grand time and make lots of new friends."*

Lark looked at Goldy's golden leaves, and it was as if they began to flutter and sparkle even brighter. Lark giggled to herself. If only trees could talk… Or could they?

In that moment, the mystical, elder woman appeared. As Lark saw the figure, she held her breath so the figure would not be startled, run away, or disappear. She acknowledged Lark's presence with a gracious bow, a soft smile, and welcoming eyes.

Chapter 5:

Wisdom Finally Appears

She smiled gently at Lark and, in a very soft, soothing voice, said, "Hello, I am so glad you are here today." She motioned for Lark to enter what Goldy referred to as the "Sanctuary of Life."

Lark was a bit nervous and held her breath as she took her first steps into the Sanctuary of Life. Upon entering, Lark's eyes widened with joy, eagerness, and excitement. It was the most exquisite, colorful place she'd ever seen or imagined. The trees were full of life, and the leaves were bright and vivid. There were even more colors than she had seen the previous day. Lark was like a kid in a candy store.

The elder woman got closer and closer to Lark. Her mere presence was like a warm, embracing hug. Lark felt so adored, loved, and accepted.

She finally spoke and said to Lark, "I have been expecting you today, and I'm so glad you have arrived. It's okay to breathe deeply and softly, for the more you do so, the more you will experience." She let Lark settle down and simply breathe in all the sanctuary could offer in the moment.

Lark relaxed and started to admire the tall, majestic trees with all their colorful leaves. She followed her deeper into the sanctuary and noticed even more trees. Some even seemed to wink at her, and she saw they all had unusual knotholes and special markings that looked like human eyes.

Lark reveled in noticing the eye markings on the trees and all she took in with her senses. She adored the colors and the shapes of the trees. She loved the sound of the crunching leaves beneath her feet and the coolness of the fresh air, as well as the fragrant aromas of the sanctuary.

The mystical woman motioned for Lark to rest and sit on a tree trunk that had fallen hundreds of years before during a particularly cold and harsh winter. Over the years, it had settled and flattened smoothly for people to enjoy a break from their day and to enjoy the peace and solitude of the Sanctuary of Life.

Lark sat beside her, and it was quiet for a while before she spoke. Lark was a bit nervous, if truth be told. She did not understand how this was all possible, how everything in this magical place had come to life. There was a bustling energy that was like nothing or nowhere she had ever experienced. Everything felt so alive.

Lark was enthralled. Her dream was coming to life. *But how can this be? Who is this person, and what shall I call her? What does she want of me? Why is she appearing to me?* Lark's mind was full of questions. She also wanted to be polite and reverent, as she was taught to be respectful of her elders. Lark was flooded with mixed feelings ranging from joy and excitement to fear and trepidation. *Okay, contain my composure and be as still as possible.*

Very faintly, she whispered, "Hello, Lark, my name is Wisdom. I am ever so glad you are here." She took Lark's hand gently into her own. "I know you have many questions and are very curious today. Do be patient, please, as all will be revealed in good time."

Lark had no words. She could not believe Wisdom was able to read her mind. *How can this be?*

Wisdom answered Lark's unspoken question directly. "I can read your mind, as thoughts contain energy, which are vibrations. I simply used multiple senses together to interpret your energy field. I used my eyes to see the look on your face and the posture of your body, my ears to hear your beating heart, and my hands to subtly feel the circulation and warmth in your hands. I also know our meeting is quite unusual and out of the ordinary."

Lark's eyes widened and sparkled. She was mesmerized by Wisdom. "What are vibrations?" she sheepishly asked.

Wisdom smiled and said, "Simply put, energy vibrations are units of measurement, like body temperature. You know when you are experiencing illness, you don't feel your best, and your mom says you're running a high temperature?"

"Of course! Last week, Hope had a high temperature and was miserable."

"That's very good, Lark. You see, I was able to tap into your vibrational field and interpret what you were thinking by observing your body language and by trusting my instincts. It takes practice, patience, and persistence.

"Here's a question for you: Did you ever walk into a room where people were arguing? You inquired if things were okay, and they assured you all was well, when that was not the truth?"

Lark nodded her head in agreement.

"Well, that is an example of being able to interpret energy. Your gut was able to give you signals to the contrary. The others were attempting to perhaps protect you or simply not bother you with their concern. But this dismissal of truth causes what we would call a mismatch of energy or signals. What do you think of that, Lark?"

Lark's face beamed with excitement. "Can I learn to read energy, too?"

Wisdom smiled and said, "Yes, I will first help you to tune into your own energy field to help you calm your mind. How does that sound?"

"Great," proclaimed Lark. She also shared how her mind is sometimes plagued with many thoughts that are confusing and cause her stomach to hurt.

Once again, Wisdom became very quiet and still. She refrained from speaking for several moments, which felt like an eternity to Lark. She was starting to teach Lark how to tune into her own energy field by showing and demonstrating, rather than by speaking.

Wisdom sat with perfect posture on the bench and breathed deeply and slowly. After a few moments, Lark naturally mimicked Wisdom's posture and breathing pattern. The two were in sync with one another. Lark started to relax and feel a sense of inner calm, a wonderful relief, and a welcomed state of mind. Wisdom praised Lark for the simple effort of following her lead and slowing down. She said, "You will be a very good student."

And Lark smiled.

Wisdom asked Lark if she could share a simple truth with her, a truth that could help her calm her mind and feel better in an instant.

Lark scooched closer to Wisdom, looked at her almost in desperation and said, "Yes, please do."

"Life is to be enjoyed. Life is a gift. A GIFT is a Grace-Infused Forever Treat. When you keep this truth at the forefront of your mind, it puts the obstacles of daily life into perspective. Like anything you wish to master, this will take patience and practice so that it becomes natural for you to remember and use."

Lark smiled and thanked her for sharing. She did not quite understand this message yet but had an inclination she would understand very soon.

Lark was now bursting with curiosity. She finally mustered the courage to ask Wisdom if others knew of her and the Sanctuary of Life.

Wisdom bowed her head and replied carefully. She explained the answer was both yes and no. Wisdom continued with a rather cryptic explanation. "You see, everyone is born with the potential to see and know about this sanctuary, a place beyond one's reality. For the sanctuary is inside your imagination and not in this physical place. This place is a magnificent manifestation of your true inner world, and you can visit this place as it exists deep within your heart and your mind. That is why you dreamt about it first and then followed your natural instincts that led you to experience this outer manifestation, which you are now seeing and experiencing. You are using more than your five human senses."

Lark squinted her eyes and furrowed her brow in confusion, with an inkling of understanding. Wisdom could see the wheels of thought spinning in Lark's head.

Wisdom explained it again to Lark by showing her a scene on a projection screen that magically appeared between two trees. It was like an outdoor theater. Lark was fascinated with Wisdom's magical abilities to make things appear out of thin air. She showed her a group of friends partaking in the delight of eating ice cream.

She pointed out that some of the friends just ate the ice cream with little joy or emotion, while others rushed to quickly devour it to avoid the confectionery from melting or dripping down the side of the sugar cone. And there was one young person who enjoyed every lick of the delicious, flavorful treat. This young girl noticed the sweet flavors hitting the various parts of her mouth and tongue and how every mouthful was an indulgence to be savored. She enjoyed the experience more than the others, as she allowed herself to simply enjoy and be present in the experience.

Lark was beginning to understand. She became curious about how her spirit was alive within, like a beautiful flame of a candle flickering, illuminating the darkness and melting the wick and the surrounding wax. Lark trusted her inner self to guide her on this day, to have this experience, because she was eager and ready for growth and expansion.

Lark had so many questions and could not contain her enthusiasm. Wisdom smiled with delight, knowing one day, as Lark matured, she would use this understanding and knowledge to illuminate others. She had a hunch her flame would light the flames of others to spread compassion, joy, kindness, and above all, love.

Wisdom knew the biggest obstacle Lark would face was patience, for humans lack patience and rely heavily on thought and the act of mental thinking. Wisdom continued to explain that all of life is a gift. And if she is willing to see the gifts all around her, whether they are people, places, situations, or things, she would be able to handle life's challenges more easily.

The two then rose from the bench and ventured through the Sanctuary of Life.

Wisdom noticed Lark's quiet fascination with the variety of colors of the leaves. The way her eyes followed the golden, amber, and crimson hues brought a smile to Wisdom's face. Wisdom complimented her for focusing on nature's beauty with wonder and curiosity. Wisdom encouraged Lark to be present, breathe, and look even closer at the trees and their colorful leaves and to stay open to receiving more wisdom and knowledge. She promised the trees would continue to be a source of knowledge for all time.

Lark continued to look, wonder, and embrace the beauty of this place. Wisdom followed Lark around like a protective parent. Lark noticed some of the trees were tall and wide, others tall and thin, while still others were short and thin, and that they lived together in a state of homeostasis. She then eyed knotholes again in so many of the trees. She told Wisdom they looked like little human eyes with which to see.

Wisdom admired Lark's perceptiveness and explained that knotholes are formed after a branch has broken away from its trunk to repair itself. The trees have a way of naturally adapting to changes in their structure and easily shed what is no longer strong or healthy. Lark was fascinated with this information about trees.

Just then Lark noticed the sun was beginning to set in the evening sky and decided it was time to return home. Wisdom thought that was a wise idea. She promised Wisdom she would return soon for another visit and lesson. Lark thanked her by bowing in respect, and with that, Lark turned around and was on the paved path heading toward home.

Chapter 6:

Mean Girls

The next day at school seemed emotionally challenging for Lark. Her friends were suddenly being cliquish and judgmental, and to several other girls in the school as well. This stunned Lark, as her friends Gwen, Ashley, and Nikki were always so friendly and kind. However, Gwen was known to have her moments of sarcasm. She thought of these friends as her sisters. Gwen chided Lark about her clothing selection for the day and seemed to distance herself from her in the hallway. Lark was taken off guard by this subtle behavior, and even more so when Gwen smirked at their other friend, Carly, in English class for no apparent reason. A knot in Lark's stomach caused her to wince and feel a strong sense of discomfort.

Later, during lunchtime, Ashley openly excluded Lark from a conversation the group was having about their favorite TV show. She rudely interrupted Lark as she was about to chime in on the conversation. Lark thought it was so strange, as that was their usual topic of conversation on Fridays after a new episode aired on the streaming TV service.

Then Nikki hip-bumped Lark as if to push her out of the conversation. The three friends laughed loudly as Lark's obvious disapproval and humiliation became obvious. Lark attempted to ignore her friends and gave a subtle laugh as the three of them continued to chat about their show.

Lark was not happy; she was bordering on miserable and very close to tears.

The next period bell could not ring fast enough for Lark. She was confused and stunned about what had just happened during lunch. What was up with her friends? *What's going on?* she thought silently to herself. She became distracted, and all she could think about was what had just happened at lunch. Her mind was spiraling down the rabbit hole of worry. She was not paying attention in class and wanted to cry. She tried to think of anything she did wrong or could have said to possibly offend her friends. Nothing really came to mind.

Lark did not like these familiar feelings one bit. She kept quiet, ignored her so-called friends and attempted to go about the rest of her day as if nothing unusual had happened. As the last period bell rang for school dismissal, Gwen gave Lark another dig about her messy hair. Lark wanted to explode with anger, but kept quiet while giving Gwen a half smile.

When Lark arrived home, she burst into tears, utterly confused with Gwen's, Ashley's, and Nikki's strange behavior. She wondered what she had done wrong to attract such criticism and condemnation from her good friends. Her mind began to spiral again, and she repeated the events of the day over and over in her mind. *What did I do? What did I say? What is wrong with me? What if they don't like me anymore?*

Lark wandered down to the kitchen for a snack. She was met by her twin sisters, who also seemed to sneer at her for no apparent reason. Lark even sniffed her armpits to see if she smelled or something. And then a huge burst of emotion sprang within her. She ran from the kitchen up to her bedroom. She was in tears and dumbfounded by the day's events. She wondered what was wrong with people. After a long cry, she dried her eyes and thought about her experience with Wisdom in the Sanctuary of Life the previous day.

She thought about the beautiful trees along the path. The colorful leaves and the knotholes. Then she thought about Gwen, Ashley, and Nikki. They were her friends and not old, tired branches to break away. She was not going to let her friendships fall away. And there were those worrisome, doubtful thoughts. They plagued her mind and made her feel so uncomfortable. *What am I going to do? What if the girls are mean to me again tomorrow? What should I say? How should I act? What if they humiliate me worse than today?*

Lark decided to stop the worrisome thinking and focus on having met Wisdom the previous day, her experience in the Sanctuary of Life and, most importantly, Wisdom's words and guidance. She now attempted to let the events of the day simply fall away like old, dried-out leaves. And as she had that epiphany, she heard a whisper in her ear, *"Tomorrow is a new day for a better day."*

With that slightly better feeling and thought, she went downstairs to have dinner with her family. And with that simple, better thought in her mind, dinner with the family was a pleasant meal and a better experience.

A few days later, Lark returned to the Sanctuary of Life. She attempted to enter, but there appeared to be a heavy steel gate blocking her entrance. Lark did not even notice the gate before, and she was quite confused, to say the least. She could not find a door or a latch, or anything to allow herself entry. Wisdom noticed Lark on the other side of the gate. She approached her and explained about the reason for the gate and how to open it for entry.

"Lark, darling, you must learn to quiet your mind. Pay attention to your breathing and the content of your thoughts. I understand this is not always easy to do. I will teach you and help you to master your mind and the quality of your thoughts and thinking. With practice, it will get easier. Life will continue to give you challenges to overcome. In those times, this will be a great skill to rely upon.

"Some days will be easier and more enjoyable, like a bright sunny day. There will also be stormy days where your efforts will be shaken, and you will find the cold of a winter's day will freeze your heart, and everything will feel like an uphill climb. But I promise you, dear child, the rewards will be worth your efforts. You are the creator of your own life. You get to choose how you want to show up in life, day by day. There will be days when you choose compassion, kindness, and patience. There will be other days when you choose to be strong and courageous. And there will be still other days when getting through the day will simply be enough, and a stream of tears will be your best friend.

"Now, sweet Lark, let's show you how to open the gate with your heart and mind working together."

Lark was honored and felt so special to receive Wisdom's advice and guidance. At the same time, she was scared and overwhelmed. What challenges would life bring? What was her path? Could she learn to control her thoughts and direct her emotions? Her daily worries seemed to be so real and persistent.

Wisdom looked at Lark. "Enough of all this worry. I know it feels so real, true, and justified. However, all it does is create more worry and make unwanted feelings worse."

Lark agreed and shook her head. And as if by magic, Wisdom popped around to the other side of the gate. She stood with Lark, and they both stared at the large steel gate. The gate itself was large and felt so cold, heavy, and overwhelming.

Wisdom took Lark's hand in her own. They sat down gently on the cool ground. Then Wisdom had Lark close her eyes and breathe deeply. She said, "First, imagine you can drop your mind into the center of your heart."

Lark gave Wisdom a funny look. "How can I possibly do that?"

"Simply imagine or even pretend that your thinking mind and all those thoughts are contained in some kind of a box. Can you picture this in your mind in some way?"

Lark nodded.

"Good! Now, imagine that box is slowly descending downward, like going down an elevator, into your heart. All there is to do is imagine."

Lark closed her eyes, steadied her thoughts, and then imagined them sinking down, down, down... right into her heart. She imagined her heart was like a beautiful pink rose that was blooming wider with each breath.

"That's very good, Lark! Now imagine you can breathe in and out of your heart. Take your time and have fun with this. You are just breathing in and out of your heart, and as you do, imagine your heart fills with more and more love and calm." Wisdom gave Lark a few moments of silence to do this exercise.

"You are doing so well, dear child. Slowly and steadily let the chatter in your mind and the thoughts of the day float and fade away, the same way clouds float and fade away on a beautiful, warm, breezy day. Take your time."

After a few moments of silence, Wisdom continued with words of praise. "You are doing great."

Wisdom let Lark enjoy this for a few more moments and then said, "Enjoy this inner calm. Give yourself this gift of time and patience to settle your mind and body. There is no rush; just embrace your inner calm."

Wisdom was patient and quiet while Lark merged her thinking mind with her heart. Wisdom started to notice the calm expression on Lark's face and the physical relaxation in her body. She let her enjoy this experience in quiet serenity.

When Lark gently and naturally opened her eyes, Wisdom softly smiled and inquired about her experience.

Lark said, "It was weird at first, and I really did not want to do this exercise, but then I noticed my heart stopped racing, my mind became quiet, and my body relaxed. I decided it was best to trust you and be a good student."

Wisdom smiled and said, "You are a good student and learning quite nicely!"

As the two rose from the ground, Wisdom encouraged Lark to walk around and appreciate the elements of nature, the same way she did when she first discovered the Sanctuary of Life. She reminded Lark how her mind and spirit were incredibly joyful the other day when she met Goldy and how good she felt.

Lark did remember that magical feeling; it was the best feeling in the world to be so completely immersed in nature. Lark continued to relax and felt her own breath going in and out of her lungs, expanding her abdomen, and, to her delight and surprise, the more she breathed, the calmer she felt and the more grounded she was in the present moment.

Wisdom explained that these good feelings were her inner compass guiding her in the right direction. She went on to encourage her to always follow her inner compass, as it's reliable and will point her in the right direction.

It was in that very moment that the large steel gate vanished into thin air. She looked at Wisdom with sheer delight, amazement, and so much pride in herself. Her heart opened the gate, and she was able to enter the Sanctuary of Life. Lark again appreciated the beauty and abundance all around.

Wisdom, too, felt pride for her student. They walked together in silence. Wisdom wanted Lark to appreciate the gift of solitude and her own inner calm. After a while, they made their way back to the outdoor classroom with the long log bench.

Then Wisdom said, "Tell me, Lark, what was so upsetting for you today?"

Lark told her about Gwen's unusual treatment of her and how it took her by surprise. Gwen, Ashley, and Nikki were childhood friends, and as if out of the blue, Gwen turned on her, and the other girls followed Gwen's lead. She did not understand why they were suddenly mean and catty to her, and frankly, the treatment felt like a betrayal, and it truly hurt her feelings and caused her mind to race with worry.

Wisdom looked at Lark compassionately, nodded her head, and gave her a smirk. "No wonder the gate was closed today. You shut down your heart, and the sanctuary responded to your energy."

Lark stood up, put her hands on her hips, and defensively said, "Well, it was their words and actions that caused my hurt feelings. I did not do anything wrong. I did not shut my heart down on purpose." Then she broke down with tears streaming down her face. In the privacy of her mind, Lark began to think that even Wisdom did not understand. She began to feel defeated and hopeless.

In that moment, Wisdom took Lark into her soft, comforting arms and acknowledged Lark's pain, hurt, and confusion. She let Lark cry it out to release the stress and tension. She told her that crying is very cathartic and cleansing and helps the body get back in balance.

Wisdom then took Lark on a walk deeper into the Sanctuary of Life and told her to look at the elements of nature even closer. Lark noticed little critters such as spiders and ants running up and down the tree trunks, wild mushrooms growing through the earth, and the beautiful flowers at the foot of the tree trunks. Lark did not understand how spiders and mushrooms related to her hurt feelings. Wisdom explained that in any environment, there are many elements needed for the natural cycle of life. Even in the dark and hidden places, life is working.

For example...

"Mushrooms break down dead plants, animals, and organic matter. This decomposition returns nutrients to the soil, making it rich and fertile... so new life can grow.

"Spiders help protect the trees by catching tiny bugs that could hurt the leaves or bark," Wisdom said softly. "Their webs may look delicate, but they're strong... just like you.

"Ants may be small, but they're helping the trees in ways most eyes don't see. They protect trees from harmful insects, as they clean up what's fallen. Some of them even carry seeds to new places so the forest can keep growing. They also eat the pests, like caterpillars that would otherwise damage the trees' leaves or bark."

Lark furrowed her brow. "I think I get it… a little. But mostly, I'm still confused. What do wild mushrooms, spiders, and ants have to do with my friends being mean to me today?"

Wisdom nodded kindly. "That's okay. Understanding comes in waves. You see, Lark, nature follows a natural rhythm, like sunrise and sunset. There are times of the year to plant seeds and other times of the year to reap the rewards of planting and enjoy fruits and vegetables. You're at a time in life when your body is in a constant process of change and maturity, which you refer to as puberty. It's how girls grow into women and boys into men. It's a process that does not happen overnight."

She paused, giving space for the words to land and for Lark to comprehend this information in her mind.

"These changes can feel strange, uncomfortable, and even painful sometimes. And what makes it harder is that we don't always realize what's happening. The body reacts, even if the mind hasn't caught up yet. This is happening for you and your friends."

Lark looked down at both sides of her hands, then back up.

Wisdom continued. "That inner friction, what feels like tension or discomfort, it's not just happening in you. It affects the energy around you, including your friends, who are also in the same stage of life. But that's not a bad thing. It's how transformation begins. In order for things to change, there must be change. Let me clue you in on a little secret: Change of any kind tends to cause people lots of stress and anxiety. It can be something as minor as the grocery store stops selling your favorite breakfast cereal, which is part of your daily routine. People tend to resist change and don't like it when things must change. However, when people embrace change and go with the flow, things tend to work out for the best.

"Creation is always in motion and happening, Lark," Wisdom said gently. "If things never changed, we'd never grow. We'd just stay stuck. And life isn't meant to be stuck: it's meant to keep moving, like a river that's always flowing forward."

Lark looked at Wisdom with desperation and confusion on her face. "I still don't understand how all this relates to me and Gwen. She was rude and mean to me, and some of the other kids were too. It was not nice and made me very, very upset." Lark stood firmly with her hands at her waist and stomped her feet.

Wisdom asked, "Are you closing your heart?"

Lark said an emphatic "No!"

"Okay then. So, how do you feel in the very moment?"

Lark retorted, "Not happy!"

"Now check in with your heart center. How does it feel?"

Lark gave Wisdom a look with a tear rolling down her cheek and replied, "Very tight and uncomfortable."

Wisdom said, "You now have your answer." Wisdom instructed Lark to repeat the mind-heart connection exercise.

"Again?"

Wisdom smiled. "Yes, again. This is a strategy that takes practice, dear child. This practice should become a good habit for you to establish. And just like any muscle, to grow in strength, repetition and practice are necessary."

Lark conceded and repeated the exercise. It took her a few minutes, but she successfully got her mind quiet in her heart center.

Wisdom looked at Lark. "I am very proud of you, as this is not easy to understand or do. Most grown-ups are clueless about how to quiet their own minds. Okay, let's chat about your day again. I understand why you are so upset, and it is upsetting when other people's words or actions disrupt your day. Can I share with you how to begin to learn to master this game of life so that you are not so negatively affected?"

Lark finally began to relax a bit and let go of the unwanted energy from the day's events and even the drama with Gwen, Ashley, and Nikki. "Yes, please," she replied to Wisdom.

Wisdom took her own deep breath. She wanted to help Lark understand but knew it would take time for the young girl to truly understand and put it to practical use. "Lark, do you remember how we were talking just a little while ago about the mushrooms, ants, and spiders?"

"Yes," Lark proudly replied. "They all help the trees to grow and survive."

"That's right," Wisdom said. "You also know that the earth and its inhabitants need the rainwater from a rainstorm to survive?"

"Yes," she replied again.

"Well, sometimes people need to be shaken up to grow, mature, and become resilient."

Lark pondered this for quite a while in silence.

She paced around the Sanctuary of Life for a bit and went back to Wisdom and said, "So, Gwen was mean to me today so that I could get emotionally stronger and not take her bad mood personally?"

Wisdom's eyes sparkled with delight. "Yes, indeed. That is a very good interpretation and learning for the day's events. So, Lark, how does that insight feel in your body?"

"Stronger. BUT... I really don't think it was Gwen's intention for me to toughen up and get emotionally stronger. That was probably the last thing she was thinking. I think she wanted to have a laugh at my expense."

Wisdom smiled again. "You are doing very well, my student. You see, life is always preparing us for change, to be strong and capable of handling new things. Sometimes these preparations are not always fun, but they are necessary. Here is an inside secret: People we love the most can also trigger us the most, as they mirror our emotional wounds and limitations. And when our loved ones mirror our hurts, we get angry at them for causing unwanted pain. We get so mad at them for not being kind and not helping us to feel safe, when they should know better."

Lark's eyes widened and brightened, and she said, "Exactly. Gwen should know I am sensitive after all these years, and Nikki and Ashley should have stood up for me."

Wisdom became very quiet and nonreactive to Lark's outburst, so quiet you could hear the birds chirping playfully in the background. After a moment or so, she looked at Lark with her big, beautiful eyes and said, "If I understand you accurately, your wish is to remain sensitive and fragile?"

Lark retorted almost immediately, "NO, not at all, and I did not say I did!"

Wisdom gazed at her again and said, "But you did with your desire. You wanted Nikki and Ashley to stand up for you because you are sensitive. Is that correct?"

Lark lowered her head and said, "Yes."

"With those words, you are claiming to the universe that you are sensitive. And it's not a bad thing to be sensitive; it's actually a commendable trait. But too much of anything is not always ideal. So, when you allow yourself to be too sensitive, you are limiting yourself from more challenging experiences. The idea is to seek balance, perhaps a balance of being sensitive and strong."

This time, it was Lark who became very quiet and introspective. She needed time to ponder this and let it all settle in her mind so she could comprehend this truth."

"So, you think maybe Gwen just wants me to toughen up?" Lark asked.

Wisdom smiled and asked, "What do you think?"

"Maybe. Can I think about this for a while?"

Wisdom took her by the hand and said, "Take all the time you need. Learning and growing do not happen in an instant. Be patient with yourself."

Wisdom changed the subject so Lark could absorb what would be most helpful. "Do you remember when you were in kindergarten, and you had to learn how to take turns on the swings?"

"Yes. Jonah would always take so long and make me wait extra-long for my turn."

Wisdom giggled and said, "Children can struggle taking turns and being fair with their friends. But you see, this struggle and tension help to prepare the child for grander experiences and harder conflicts. So, first, people must learn to deal with the small stuff before learning how to handle the bigger stuff. 'Little people, little problems; bigger people, bigger problems.' Life is purposely designed to help you grow by giving you a variety of opportunities and experiences. Life's struggles and quests come with great rewards. Let's face it, you would not want to stay in kindergarten forever, would you?"

Lark smiled and giggled at Wisdom.

"Would you like to learn a little bit more for today, or have you had enough?"

Lark was actually quite eager to hear and learn more.

Wisdom continued and described that everything has energy, and humans have a habit of judging energy, people, places, or experiences as good or bad, and that very judgment creates inner conflict. She said that when Lark has these hurt feelings, it would be wise to get into the habit of dropping her thinking mind into her heart space. Wisdom promised that is where one's true source of energy resides.

Once again, Wisdom had Lark close her eyes and imagine just that, a journey into her own heart. Wisdom encouraged Lark to get quiet and listen to her breathing.

Lark said this time her heart was many shades of pink and purple with feelings of warmth and soothing sounds. Lark loved the swirls of colors and the calmness of the experience. She was pleasantly surprised that all this inner calm was within her own heart.

Wisdom explained to Lark to always first look within rather than outside herself for feelings of peace and calm. When someone stays true to their own heart's desire and guidance, their life tends to be better. It will not be without conflict or hardship. It just helps people get through rough times a bit faster and with more resilience.

Wisdom had Lark continue with the experience of heart expansion. Lark's sense of peace was holding steady and still. She loved the experience and its profound sense of ease. Wisdom suggested she take all the good feelings and send them to all the parts of herself, from the top of her head all the way down through her whole body, fingertip to fingertip, head to toe, and let that colorful aura spread all around her for the world to see.

Lark rested in the experience, and her mind and body settled down. It was as if she became a clean slate, and the worries of the day melted away. She appreciated the stillness in her mind and the comfort in her body.

When Lark was ready to open her eyes, Wisdom was there waiting for her with a warm beverage. Lark took small sips of the tea and commented on how soothing it felt going down her throat. Wisdom explained that everything we need can be found in nature. Wisdom let Lark smell the chamomile and lavender flowers used to create the tea. Lark was surprised because she did not usually care for the scent of chamomile, but when brewed delicately, the aroma and taste were pleasant.

"Now that you have been nourished, let me show you how to design your day."

Chapter 7:

Scripting Desired Outcomes

The two journeyed back to the outside theater, which was more like an outdoor classroom. They sat on the long log bench once again. Wisdom told Lark to imagine that between the two large trees in front of her, there was the same giant movie screen from the other day. And as Lark used her imagination with intention, the movie screen appeared!

Wisdom said she could project playing out different scenarios onto the screen. Wisdom told Lark she was the director of her own life and that her family, friends, teachers, and other students at her school were all actors she hired to play the game of life with her.

Since Lark was the writer, director, and even producer and editor, she could cast the movie and play out scenes any way she wished. She could even cast scenes in a variety of ways or have different outcomes or endings.

Lark smiled with delight at this concept. But then she looked at Wisdom with her wide, this time doubting, eyes and looked skeptical. *How can this be true?* Wisdom had Lark sip on her tea and told her to have fun with this exercise.

Wisdom encouraged Lark to write a script for tomorrow at school with Gwen, Nikki, and Ashley any way she desired. She suggested considering the events and circumstances of the day, plus the peaceful feeling she experienced with the heart expansion process.

Lark thought this was going to be very difficult because she knew she couldn't control the actions or dictate the moods of her teenage, hormonally imbalanced friends.

Wisdom winked and said to give it a go and have fun with the scripting exercise.

Lark took a deep breath, sank back into her heart, and started to be the director of her life. She yelled "ACTION," and the new scene began…

Lark saw herself awakening from a good night's sleep, popping out of her bed, washing her hands and face, and brushing her teeth. She went to her closet and selected her favorite outfit: a warm, fuzzy pink sweater, skinny jeans, and warm, comfortable boots. She embellished her outfit with a suede belt. And, of course, she packed her school backpack.

She went into the kitchen, smiled at her mom and sisters, and gave her dad a big morning hug. Her family was thrilled with her morning demeanor. The energy in the kitchen felt like a warm, bright, sunny day, just like Lark's smile and optimism. Her whole family noticed her good mood with delight, and her enthusiasm was certainly contagious.

She then saw herself entering the wide double doors of the school. She was smiling, very chatty, and enthusiastically greeted her friends. She felt comfortable in her own skin and loved the way it felt to set the tone for the day. She wanted this to be a good day, to flow calmly and confidently, and to enjoy her classes. She wanted to learn the class material easily from teachers who truly enjoyed teaching and sharing with the students.

Lark first saw Nikki in the hallway. She always admired Nikki's long, dark hair that always had a shine and sparkle. Lark felt it quite natural to engage in conversation as usual. It was as if the events of yesterday in school were long ago—yesterday's news.

Ashley soon joined them and gave Lark a warm smile. A few moments later, Gwen approached with a humble demeanor, almost apologetic for her behavior the previous day. The girls all chatted as usual. Their group conversation flowed comfortably. All went well, and Lark found it easy to breathe and be herself.

"BRAVO," exclaimed Wisdom. "You are a wonderful life director, editor, and producer."

She inquired how it felt, and Lark declared, "Natural and normal." She found it fun to be the boss of her own brain and the director of her life.

Wisdom winked at Lark and said, "This is a good time and space to offer gratitude for the experience and then finish your beverage before the journey back home."

Wisdom poured Lark some more of the chamomile and lavender tea, and the two of them sipped their tea in silence and peace.

Chapter 8:

Déjà Vu

The next day felt like déjà vu for Lark. Everything happened almost identically to the way she scripted everything in her mind the day before on the magic screen. On further reflection, it was even a bit better.

As she had scripted, Lark first ran into Nikki in the hallway by the lockers. She smiled affectionately at Lark and chatted away about their upcoming history test. It was as if the events of the day before ceased to be a memory for Nikki. Lark was pleasantly surprised at how calm and natural she was acting and was proud of herself for allowing Wisdom's teaching to work for her so well.

When Ashley came up from behind Lark to startle her for a reaction, Lark simply turned in her direction and offered her a big, confident smile and a "Hi." Lark's confident nature instantly shifted the energy with Ashley. It was as if by magic their friendship dynamic was back on track. Lark smiled to herself, pleased with her inner confidence. Lark then had another thought, a thought that was so quiet it was almost a whisper. The simple, profound thought, *Was our friendship really off-track yesterday, or was I catastrophizing?*

Ashley quickly grabbed her arm and said, "Come on, we can't be late for Mrs. Harper's math class; you know how she gets. I am not in the mood for one of her lectures about punctuality."

The girls laughed simultaneously and made their way to the classroom.

After math class, Lark and Ashley met up with Gwen for lunch. Gwen sheepishly looked at Lark and inquired what she had packed for lunch.

"The usual, PBJ on organic bread."

Gwen laughed and said, "Lark, you are so predictable!"

At that moment, Lark felt a huge sense of relief. All seemed to be okay with her friends, especially with Gwen. The incident from yesterday reminded her of when they were in sixth grade and on the same soccer team. Lark was having an off day, making fouls and missing shots. Gwen took it upon herself to reprimand Lark in front of the entire team and the parents watching the game on the sidelines. Lark was mortified not only with the way she was playing but also with the way her friend found it so easy to exacerbate the situation and taunt her. She was mad at Gwen for the rest of the season and at herself for not standing up for herself. Several weeks later, things did settle down and returned to normal.

This time, after Gwen engaged in a friendly conversation, Lark could relax and be herself. She thought, *All is well in the world.* She was so happy she had spent time with Wisdom yesterday, and for all she was learning.

The school day seemed to fly by! Her classes were good, and she got an A+ on her science lab project. Lark was amazed that a simple shift in thinking could help her feel better quickly and easily.

On the bus ride home, Lark was very, very quiet and started to reflect. *Why me?* She had never heard of her friends, sisters, or parents meeting a mystical teacher in the woods by the path. Maybe she was eating too much PBJ! She started to wonder if she was hallucinating, maybe she had a brain tumor, or was somehow possessed. Now she was starting to worry, felt knots in her stomach, and started to sweat.

But everything she encountered in the Sanctuary of Life Garden and with Wisdom felt so good, comforting, and even practical. So, if she didn't have a brain tumor or any other problem, why did she meet Wisdom? How exactly did she meet Wisdom? Was she chosen for something?

"Uh oh." The whole thing was so much to wrap her head around. What was this? Why was this? What was she to do with all this information? Was she supposed to share this information or not tell anyone? But if she did share… share with whom? *OMG!* thought Lark. *Everyone will think I am crazy and take me away. Okay, I need to keep quiet and not tell a soul for fear of utter embarrassment and ridicule. Yup, say nothing, keep my composure, and be super cool!*

Lark went home for a quiet afternoon. She needed to take in and contemplate all she experienced over the last few days. It was like a dream and way too good to be true. But this was not a dream; this was happening. But how? Why? *Oh no, there goes my racing, overactive, controlling mind again.*

Lark pondered. Was she worthy to experience this meeting with Wisdom and all the amazing guidance and wisdom she had shared over the last few days in the Sanctuary of Life Garden? *Who am I? What does this all mean? What am I to do with all this?*

She decided to let it all settle down for a while and that it was perfectly okay to keep this experience to herself, at least for a little while longer, until she received clarification and even permission to share what was being shared with her.

Lark closed the door to her bedroom, narrowly eluding her sisters. She sat down on the purple carpet and practiced dropping her thinking mind into her heart. She began with a few slow, deep breaths and immediately felt calmer. She then imagined all her thoughts contained nicely in the shape of a teardrop. Then ever so slowly and with the rhythm of her breath, she allowed her thoughts to sink into the expansiveness of her heart. She imagined her heart blooming like a beautiful pink rose. It felt so good to practice Wisdom's teachings. She loved her inner calm and serenity.

A few moments passed, and then she remembered Grandma giving her a beautiful red, leather-bound journal with a gold ribbon for her twelfth birthday. She did not like it so much when she opened the gift wrapping and had forgotten all about the present until now. It somehow got buried under a pile of old clothes. She held it in her hands and thumbed through the blank, lined pages and felt the thick paper with her fingers. *This is the perfect place to write down the lessons from Wisdom so that I will never forget.* This felt like a great idea! She then tucked it into her backpack for safekeeping. As she zipped her backpack, she had another thought that jolted her out of her peaceful mood. What if someone finds the private journal? Lark was petrified about what others might think if they read her journal and knew about her secret adventures with this mystical woman. The public humiliation would be awful, especially by Gwen. These thoughts exhausted her mind.

She crawled into her bed for a nice, refreshing nap. The nap did her the world of good and allowed her to clear her mind of the run-on thoughts and worries. As Lark stretched from her rest, she realized something important. Wisdom had taught her how to recognize and become aware of the content and quality of her thoughts and how her own thinking made her feel in her body.

She took a nice breath and realized she had a choice about where to focus and place her attention. Lark could choose to change her thoughts to another subject. To change her state now, she walked around her room for a few minutes, and moving the energy felt great. Lark then retrieved the journal from her backpack and wrote down Wisdom's first teaching: *Become aware of thoughts and feelings in the body!* It was a nice first entry for her journal. She also took time to detail the heart-mind connection. Lark was pleased with herself, and rightly so.

Almost two hours had passed, and she chuckled to herself and remembered she had science homework to do. Well, that certainly is another subject! With that amazing epiphany, Lark opened her science textbook and got to work. She liked getting good grades, which helped her to naturally feel a sense of earned confidence.

The next day at school was rather pleasant for Lark. She wanted to try out an experiment. She decided to simply be mindful of her thoughts and how they affected her interactions with friends and teachers.

This is a pretty mature experiment for a teenager, she thought proudly to herself. She went about the day with an attitude of gratitude that she had a nice school environment and the opportunity and privilege of a good education. She knew there were girls around the world who were not offered the opportunity of a formal education to advance their minds.

She smiled whenever possible and mindfully paid attention to her teachers during class. She was amazed at how much easier it was to retain the information when she was consciously paying attention and not attempting to check her cell phone. What a concept!

Chapter 9:

Be the Boss of Your Brain

Lark was so pleased and proud of her school experiment; she was grinning from ear to ear. She felt like she knew the world's greatest kept secret and was bursting to share her joy and the events of the day with someone. Lark was also delighted she had decided to make good use of her grandma's gift and made a mental note to write her school experiment down in the journal for future reference.

Lark took the bus home and greeted her sisters. Grace was especially excited to see her big sister and wanted her to help her with her math homework. Lark had an exceptional way of explaining things to Grace. She was very soft-spoken and patient. Academics came naturally to Becca, Grace's twin sister, and that made Grace feel self-conscious and inadequate. It seemed almost unfair that her twin got all the academic genius, almost an unfair distribution of gifts in the womb.

Lark promised to spend time with Grace in the evening after dinner. She gently explained she needed to complete her homework and wanted to go for a walk outside on this beautiful day, as she loved fresh air after being cooped up in school all day. Grace, enamored by her older sister, smiled and said, "Okay, it's a date."

Lark walked into her room and gently closed the door. She set the intention to focus on her homework assignments diligently for one hour and then write in her journal. At that point, she would finish up and give herself a well-deserved break.

Lark was utterly amazed at how quickly the time flew by. She was able to focus intently on the various subjects, remembering all the lessons from the day, and recalling all the information easily to answer the homework questions and do the essays. She did not struggle or even allow herself the distraction of her cell phone. In fact, she intentionally turned off her phone and slipped it into her top drawer. Lark felt a sense of freedom, disconnecting from the random distractions of social media, and then an empowering sensation flowed around and through her. This was something else to also include in her journal, the freedom of disconnecting from her phone. She noticed the content of her thoughts and was proud of her efforts and her open-minded attitude. She also felt a sense of pride that Wisdom was taking her under her wing to share her wisdom and knowledge.

And there popped that nagging question in her mind: *Why was this all happening?* Lark had conflicting thoughts. On the one hand, her adventures with Wisdom were magical. On the other hand, she thought she was going crazy because Wisdom was not a real person; Wisdom was someone in her dreams who came to life.

How can this be? Lark thought to herself. She shrugged off the inner dialogue and got ready to leave the house.

It was finally time for Lark to head outside to the Sanctuary of Life. She waved goodbye to her sisters and promised Grace she would help her with her math homework after dinner. Mom was in the study room working, and Lark said she would be home before dinner. Her mom said, "Don't forget your phone," followed quickly by "I love you."

Finally, Lark was out the door and on her way to the Sanctuary of Life.

When Lark arrived, she noticed the large steel gate was up, blocking her entry. She was perplexed because she was in such a proud, victorious mood. She walked aimlessly around for a few moments while looking for Wisdom. *Hmm, I wonder where she is today.* Lark's mind started to spiral again, and she thought, *Maybe I have been hallucinating, and all this has been a crazy, strange dream. Hmm.* Those thoughts in her mind just did not feel right; they felt anxious, and an uncomfortable feeling began to fill her mind and stomach.

Okay, okay. What shall I do? Lark stopped and stilled her body. She took a nice, long, deep breath into her abdomen, and she paused. She allowed her mind to settle, and then her body calmed down even more. Lark began to remember how Wisdom taught her how to drop her thinking mind into the expansive space of her heart. She remembered how delightful it felt to feel inner peace in contrast to the rush of worrisome thoughts. She was so happy and quickly retrieved her red, leather-bound journal and made a note of this important teaching.

Lark began to focus more on her breathing. She observed how naturally her belly rose when she inhaled and how it sank toward her spine on the exhale. She also noticed there was peace and quiet in between her breaths while she breathed intentionally and deeply. She marveled at her body's ability to become calm and steady with something as normal and natural as the breath.

Next, she imagined her mind was dropping slowly down, down into her heart, which felt eternal, mystical, and magical. She continued to draw her mind into her heart, like two best friends coming together for a fantastic adventure in unison.

She imagined swirls of pink and purple all around her body. It was a glorious aura, and Lark was at peace without a care in the world. At that very moment, the steel gate magically disappeared into thin air. Lark smiled with delight, felt proud of her accomplishment, and started to jump up and down with joy.

Wisdom was patiently and quietly waiting for Lark. She did not clap or offer any words of recognition or praise, because that was not necessary. Wisdom just smiled, and Lark gave herself credit and validation. Lark knew just how capable she was all by herself. Lark also realized self-validation felt better and more satisfying and was more important than validation from her teacher, friends, parents, or anyone else.

She made a note to write this observation in her journal: *Self-validation is best!*

Wisdom began to walk into the depths of the Sanctuary of Life. Lark proceeded to follow her a few paces behind. Lark marveled at the changing colors of the leaves, the little critters, and all the magnificent tall trees. It was as if the trees were alive with souls and talking heart-to-heart with Lark. There was one rather large oak tree that looked regal and majestic. Lark noticed how this tree's branches were shaped in a semicircle. The roots appeared strong, and right in the middle of its wide trunk, there was a distinctive knothole. Wisdom told Lark this elder tree was sometimes called Henry, as the tree has been thought to have been around since the days of King Henry VIII. Lark looked astonished and curtsied in respect. Wisdom smiled, then motioned for Lark to follow toward the outdoor classroom.

Finally, Wisdom sat on the bench, and Lark was eager to share all the events of the day. With pure enthusiasm and delight, Lark told Wisdom all about her night and the day at school and how she felt naturally confident and extremely focused in her classes. Lark went on and on chatting at the speed of light. Wisdom simply looked at Lark with a kind smile, for no words were necessary. She just let Lark have her moment, her very own epiphanies and her realization that she can be the director of her mind. Lark also started to realize she could control her experiences and reactions. Wisdom was so pleased that Lark was becoming the "boss of her brain."

Wisdom took a deep breath and continued to smile at Lark. This went on for a few more moments until Lark began to settle down from her joy and excitement. Then Lark began to mirror Wisdom's breathing. She felt her mind begin to settle, and her body was washed with a sense of peace.

Then Wisdom said these two simple words, "That's right." Over and over. "That's right."

After several more moments, Lark was in such a relaxed, peaceful state. She looked at Wisdom and sheepishly inquired, "How did you do that?"

"Quite naturally and with lots of deliberate practice."

Lark repeated with a questioning tone, "With practice?"

Wisdom confirmed. "Yes, loved one, with practice."

"Is that why the gate was closed when I arrived today?"

Wisdom gently nodded her head and said, "Yes. You are to practice all that you have learned again and again and again. Just like homework assignments from school help you absorb the material and knowledge. You are to practice until your mind and heart are at one, like best friends. And I am pleased you are using your grandmother's gift to reinforce your learning!"

Lark looked at Wisdom with sheer astonishment! "How did you know I found the journal?"

Wisdom just smiled and said nothing at all.

Wisdom continued with her lesson for the day. "I would like you to keep this bit of knowledge at the forefront of your mind, for it is important. There will be days when you and your friends will disagree or conflict with one another. But remember the love, joy, and fun you all share. Practice focusing your thoughts to create your experience and watch the words you say to yourself and the thoughts you believe about yourself."

Lark looked at Wisdom and said, "I don't like conflict one bit, but the last few days really showed me that I can be the boss of my brain and design my day. I will do my very best and keep this in mind, especially when Gwen is in one of her moods."

Wisdom responded kindly. "Let's be a little easier on Gwen, please, for you do not know what she may be experiencing at home."

Lark gently bowed her head like a good student and agreed to be more compassionate and understanding. But she looked confused and asked if anything was going on in Gwen's home. Wisdom just gave one of her gentle nods, as if she were the keeper of all secrets and knowledge, and said, "That is not the point. What I want you to remember now and always is that you never know what a person is experiencing in their own life away from the view of the public. It will serve you well to remember this fact."

Lark promised she would be more patient and not be so quick to jump to conclusions.

With a warm smile, Wisdom nodded her head and said she had complete faith in her abilities. She also gently cautioned that this is something that takes patience, practice, and persistence.

Lark nodded her head in agreement and promised to start being more aware of when she was jumping to conclusions too fast. She then turned around and realized the sun was beginning to set, and she ought to head home. Wisdom agreed it was a good time to end the sanctuary session for the day.

As she walked toward the path to home, Lark said, "I have a couple of questions." Wisdom smiled as she asked, "Why can I see and experience the Sanctuary of Life? And where do you come from, and where do you live?"

Wisdom looked lovingly at Lark and said, "Those questions and answers are for another day. Go home to your family, enjoy your evening meal with them, and then help Grace with her math homework."

"How do you know I promised to help Grace?"

Wisdom just smiled once again and vanished into the Sanctuary of Life as Lark made her journey home. All that was left was a blue mist.

Chapter 10:

The Math Lesson

Lark arrived home in a rather content mood. Mom even noticed her jovial spirit and commented on how her smile brightened the room, especially after her long day at work. Dad arrived shortly after from his day at the shop. He greeted his wife and daughters quickly, then went upstairs to shower before the girls ran away from him because he smelled so bad from the day. Dad knew the drill and appreciated a warm shower before his evening meal with his family.

Lark helped Mom prepare dinner and set the table. The twins were occupying their little sister, Hope, who was learning to get into everything and could be mischievous. Lark winked at Grace and said, "Math tutoring begins straight after dinner."

Grace looked relieved and continued to play with Hope. Becca engaged in some of the playtime, which was unusual, as she was such a dedicated student and there was always something to read or homework to complete. Grace felt intimidated by Becca's natural ease with schoolwork, but she was the more fun sister and enjoyed the free time to play with her sisters and friends.

During dinner, Mom and Dad inquired about Lark's recent outings in the woods. They were a bit concerned about her walking alone and insisted she tell them where she was going, and her phone was always to be charged. Casper was a beautiful and safe town, and there was never a need for concern. But moms will be moms and tend to worry. Lark promised to always let Mom and Dad know where she would be, and Lark knew that was for the best.

Then Mom inquired about her journey and what she enjoyed the most. Mom looked at Lark with great wonder and anticipation as Lark began to tell her family about her adventures and how much she enjoyed being surrounded by nature. She told them of her fascination with the trees, their beauty, their strength, and how they seemed to all have personalities and souls and be alive the same way people existed.

The twins chuckled, but Mom was quite curious. She hushed the girls and encouraged Lark to continue about her experience.

Lark described the peace and serenity she felt when walking along the path in nature. She said, "Every day is a new adventure as nature is changing every day. No two days or walks are ever the same. Everything impacts everything else, and all the elements in nature are necessary for life in nature to thrive."

She told her how her walks were helping her to go with the flow in school and not be so affected by other people's reactions, actions, or behaviors. Being a sensitive child, Lark was always worrying about what others were thinking about her. And she had a habit of putting the needs of others before her own. In the back of her mind, she silently thought that if she were always a great and helpful friend, she had lots of practice being the oldest sister, she would always be liked and accepted in her friend group. Putting others' needs first was a sure-fire way to ensure social standing.

Lark looked at her twin sisters and said, "Everything about the woods is just so peaceful. Nature, especially trees, can teach us useful lessons. Things in nature are always changing, and nothing stays the same. Some days are bright and sunny, and other days are wet and cold." Lark continued to explain that the trees are in unity and harmony, all working together.

The twins chuckled again and thought the whole thing was weird, and Lark frowned. She glanced over at Mom and Dad, who were speechless. Dad looked a bit nervous and wondered if his eldest daughter was okay. Mom gave him a kick under the table and a dirty look that said to stop that nonsense. She smiled peacefully at Lark but had no words.

After a while, she took a deep breath and said, "Lark, my sweet, you are very wise." She asked if she could join her on her walk over the weekend.

Silently, Lark did not want to share the experience with her mother but replied, "Of course, Mom, we can walk together over the weekend."

By then, the family had finished their dinner. The three oldest girls helped Mom clear away the dishes and tidy the kitchen. Hope was too young to be useful, but she did bring her plate into the kitchen. Becca smiled, took her dish, and put it in the sink.

Lark looked at Grace and said, "Ready?"

Grace took a deep breath and said, "Yes!"

Lark invited Grace into her bedroom rather than the family study room. Grace loved being invited into her big sister's bedroom. She studied the posters on the walls and, of course, her sister's cool clothes, which were all over her room. Lark had a habit of being messy, which drove Mom crazy.

Together, they made space on her bed to be comfortable. Grace opened the chapter in her math book about linear equations. The whole subject matter brought her to tears. Lark saw the look of defeat in Grace's eyes as the tears started to trickle down her face.

Lark had Grace close the book. She handed her a tissue and said, "I get it. Math can be scary with all those numbers and formulas to consider."

Grace sighed and said, "I am just so confused, and Becca and the other kids just seem to get it so easily; it's not fair!"

Lark smiled gently and said, "Okay. Let's just take a deep breath and figure this out together."

They breathed in unison until Grace was calmer. Lark first had Grace change what she was saying to herself about math in her mind. She said, "Grace, what do you believe about math?"

"Math is hard, and it's not fun."

"I've got a secret to share with you."

Grace looked at her wide-eyed and inquired, "What's the secret?"

"Your word is like a magic wand," Lark said. "If you say something will be hard, it will be hard."

Grace grimaced. "That's not a secret at all, and it does not make sense! Math is hard for me and easy for Becca." Now she was pouting.

"Okay then, if you want math to be hard for you, it will be."

Grace took another tissue, cried some more, and said, "Math is hard, and I don't like it at all, and I don't see why I have to learn such things or even do this stupid homework!"

Lark was silent as she waited for Grace to settle down a bit.

Finally, Grace conceded and said, "Fine, let's try it your way."

Lark said to Grace, "Let's start with a few more deep breaths, just like before."

The sisters breathed quietly together, as Grace followed Lark's lead. Grace started to settle down and said, "Okay, I am ready to learn how to do this math," and at the same time another tear rolled down her face.

Lark giggled and promised to make it easier. She said, "Let's set a simple intention for the next forty-five minutes." Lark thought silently to herself that she was acting just like Wisdom earlier today.

Grace made a face and said, "What is an intention?"

"It's a statement of your desired focus and desired outcome, what you want to achieve in the next forty-five minutes."

"Oh, that's easy; I want to be as good in algebra as Becca."

Lark smiled and said, "Okay, well, I cannot exactly promise you that, but we can start to make things easier for you. Let's get to work."

"For the next forty-five minutes, I will focus all my attention on learning and understanding linear equations easily." Grace then smiled with enthusiasm.

"Think of math problems as mini puzzles to solve. Math has answers, and puzzles are fun," Lark said.

"I love doing jigsaw puzzles."

"That's great," Lark replied. She started teaching Grace the basics. "X and Y are variables, meaning those letters represent a number to be solved, like putting jigsaw puzzle pieces together, and with a bit of practice and patience, you will get the answer."

"Are practice and patience like twin sisters?"

Lark laughed, smiled, and replied, "Absolutely!" She went on to explain that the job is to find out what number is represented by the letter, and there are simple formulas to follow to help solve the puzzle.

Lark wanted Grace to remember the simple math rules.

Grace asked, "More rules?"

Lark went on to explain some math rules, otherwise known as the "order of operations," which make math easy to learn and master. "First, work on parentheses, exponentiation, multiplication, division, addition, and subtraction," she said. "The acronym PEMDAS makes this super easy to remember, especially in school during tests."

She showed Grace a simple example, then created one for her to complete. She reminded Grace of her intention, and just like that, Grace solved the first equation. Lark applauded her work and gave her a few more problems to solve for practice and to build her confidence. Each time, Grace got faster and faster, and Lark praised her efforts.

Then Grace brought out her homework. Lark reviewed it and said, "I think you are up to the challenge. If you look closely, Grace, you'll see it's the same repeating type of equation to solve. Not too bad, huh?"

Grace smiled.

"Now, since we set the intention to be done in forty-five minutes, let's see if you can stay focused and complete this in the remaining twenty minutes while I sit with you."

Grace smiled and started her homework. She liked that Lark was sitting patiently as she started her homework. Lark helped her to feel safe so she could learn. Grace took another deep breath and began the assignment. In about fifteen minutes, she was finished. Lark checked her work, and every answer was correct. Grace cheered and felt a sense of relief and a surge of energy.

Grace then declared loudly, so the whole house could hear her, "I don't have a math problem; I have a mindset problem."

Lark looked at Grace proudly and said, "You are right! You are more than capable of doing well in math. You've got this. Math is easy. Now you know how to focus your mind. And remember, it will take 'practice and patience,' the other set of twins to help you! Can you do that?"

Grace hugged Lark and said, "Yes, I will begin right away." With that feeling of victory, she leaped off Lark's bed, thanked her big sister, went downstairs to the family room, and declared, "I am all done with my homework."

Mom smiled at her and quickly went upstairs to inquire what Lark did during their time together. Lark sheepishly replied, "I just had Grace relax and focus her mind differently. It was easy."

Mom gave Lark a big hug and said, "Thank you!" She then left the room and closed the door. But then she opened the door a little, peeked back into Lark's room, and inquired, "How did you get so smart?"

Lark simply shrugged her shoulders, turned off her cell phone, and read a book for a while before bedtime to decompress from the day and relax.

Chapter 11:

I've Got This

The next day, Grace arrived at math class a bit nervous as well as enthusiastic. The mix of emotions surprised her. She paused and noticed how she felt two emotions at the same time. She acknowledged her nerves without judging those feelings as bad and then decided to focus on how Lark helped her change her mindset. Grace decided to think of math as simply puzzles to complete. Her only mission was to use the formulas to solve the equations. She kept this to herself, for there was no need to sound weird to her friends.

Mrs. Clements started class in her usual way by posting the math problems on the front board. The class broke up into three groups, and the students lined up to solve the equations. The team with the most correct answers got points to add to their grade bank.

Grace was first up for her team and was easily able to solve the equation. She took a breath, remembered the order of operations, and just like that, she solved the equation quickly.

Mrs. Clements smiled at Grace and whispered, "I knew you could do it."

Grace proudly responded to her teacher, "Now I know that too." She went back and sat at her desk, completely relaxed. She heard Lark's words echo in her mind, "You've got this. Math is easy."

Grace really started to believe the simple truth: She is smart and capable, and it's safe to let it show. Math class seemed to fly by, and she was so excited to go home and share her success with Lark.

Chapter 12:

The Sacred Stream

Meanwhile, Lark too was eager to get home from her school day and head back to the sanctuary and enjoy the rest of the beautiful day.

As she arrived, Wisdom was joyfully waiting for her, not as serious as over the last few days. Today, Wisdom asked Lark if she would like to take a walk to the sacred stream. Lark was delighted and a bit surprised because in all her years strolling through these woods with her family and friends, she had never seen a stream, let alone a sacred stream.

Lark thought about all the times she explored the woods with her family and her friend Jonah and his family. Jonah had attended school with Lark since kindergarten. Their parents were close friends, and she and Jonah spent many good times together, even though Jonah tends to get on Lark's nerves. Jonah has an older brother, Brian, and a younger sister, Ellie, who is the twins' age. Their families would spend many good times together and sometimes went fishing at a stream in the next town, which was about a twenty-minute drive from their homes. It would have been so much more convenient if there were a local stream to enjoy. Lark racked her brain and just could not remember any rivers or streams of water by the woods or the local walking trails.

As they started their afternoon stroll, Wisdom reminded Lark to drop her thinking mind into her heart and breathe deeply and completely. She said, "The human body loves and appreciates deep breathing, and it helps to purify and rejuvenate the cells with oxygen to function at their best."

So, they both stood in front of a beautiful tree and purposefully took some nice belly breaths. Lark imagined her thoughts of the day and the dramas of her friends dropping into the expansiveness of her heart. And suddenly nothing seemed to matter or be significant. Slowly, the two began to journey into the woods. Lark noticed different species of flowers from the day before. Wisdom praised her for noticing and being aware of her surroundings.

They continued their walk in respectful silence. A while later, Wisdom pointed down below to a gorgeous and spectacular stream of water originating from a waterfall that seemed to spout directly from the earth. Lark marveled at the beautiful sight. The water looked so luxurious as it spread its water over the rocks that glistened in the sunshine. The greenery and the foliage surrounding the stream of water were lush and vibrant.

Wisdom explained. "The natural element of water can both heal and destroy, so we must respect elements of nature. That is why I wear this pendant as a sign of respect to the elements of nature. The top white stone represents air, the blue stone represents water, the red stone represents fire, and the green stone represents the earth or the ground on which you stand."

Lark looked closely at the pendant and thought it was very special.

The two made their way down closer to the stream. Still standing on the ground, Lark saw salmon swimming upstream, which amazed and surprised her. Wisdom chuckled and said, "Easy for them, as salmon have strong tailfins to propel themselves through strong currents. Which way would be easier for you to swim?"

Lark said a resounding "Downstream."

Wisdom smiled. "Yes, it is easier to go with the flow of water. And it's easier to go with the flow of your inner spirit and what is meant for you, dear child." Wisdom bent down to the ground and found a small branch with some leaves still attached to it. She handed it to Lark and motioned for her to toss it into the stream and watch it until it was no longer in sight.

Lark followed the instructions, and within a few seconds, she could no longer see the branch. She said, "That was fun!" She was curious why Wisdom had her toss the branch into the stream in the first place. Wisdom encouraged Lark to answer for herself.

Lark pondered thoughtfully for a few minutes. She finally replied, "To show me how strong water currents can be and to be careful."

Wisdom smiled and acknowledged the truth in her words and said, "Yes, child, you are correct to take good care about being in water, and it is wise to be supervised by your parents or other responsible adults who can handle dangerous situations. So why else might I have had you do that exercise?"

Lark thoughtfully pondered this question. Then she said, "Oh, that's easy. To show me how to easily let things go that bother me."

"Exactly, water naturally heals, cleans, and cleanses in just the right way." Wisdom also shared the fact that water makes up more than 50 percent of the human body, and therefore, it is important to stay well hydrated so the body can function optimally.

Wisdom shared the ability to let go and to go with the flow is an important life lesson and a helpful life skill. She said, "Lark, in life you will encounter all types of people. Many you will admire and respect, and others you will not like or want in your circle of friends. People have different opinions and beliefs. Just like there are many types of trees, leaves, flowers, animals, and birds. All have their purpose in the cycle of life."

Wisdom went on to remind Lark that when she first entered the Sanctuary of Life and admired the trees, she was looking at everything and had certain preferences for the ones that appealed to her eye. She reminded Lark how much she loved Goldy the tree. Wisdom said in a way that could be considered judgment or simply a preference.

Wisdom took a deep breath and said, "Humans frequently dislike the feeling of being judged by other people. This causes a lot of inner discomfort."

Lark quickly interjected. "Oh yes. I did not like it one bit when Gwen judged my clothes last week. I was so mad at her for saying that in front of Ashley and Nikki, who had smirked in agreement."

"Exactly, that's a feeling of being judged." Wisdom went on to say, "I have a secret to share with you."

Lark's eyes widened, and she asked, "What's the secret?"

Wisdom lowered her voice. "People tend to worry about what others think of them. They also worry they are being judged by others all day long. This is called the 'spotlight effect.' It causes people a lot of unnecessary emotional pain, and it's a real burden.

"But here is the truth: the human mind is always thinking, thinking, thinking. So many thoughts humans have in an ordinary day. The reality is people are so busy thinking about themselves and really do spend way less time thinking or judging others.

"So, this is where the releasing process is helpful and easy to do! All there is to do is imagine you can release the worries or judgments of others away into a stream of water, the same way I had you cast the stick out into the sacred stream a few moments ago. The current of the water carried the old stick away. Eventually, the stick will decompose and return to nourish the earth."

Lark smiled with delight and said, "I should pretend Gwen's nasty comments about my outfit are like thorny branches that can easily be released by my intention to be free of the hurt into the wondrous waters, to be transformed back to love so that I don't have to carry the memory of her hurtful words around in my mind and body."

Wisdom smiled softly and said, "Yes, dear child, you do understand. Now give yourself patience to practice this skill. Life and people will be your biggest challenges and triggers. They can also be your best teachers for emotional growth, that is, if you let them without getting sucked into inner drama and turmoil."

Wisdom and Lark sat in silence for quite a while, admiring the beautiful stream and how the gentle currents washed over the rocks, smoothing and polishing their surfaces to perfection, providing soothing sounds, and creating an atmosphere of peace.

Finally, Wisdom escorted Lark carefully back to the entrance and back on the path. Before Lark departed, Wisdom asked what she had learned today.

Lark replied thoughtfully. "All the elements of nature are a blessing. They can be both healing and destructive, so one must respect nature."

"Yes, indeed," replied Wisdom. "What else have you learned?"

"That water can wash away wounds that are mental, emotional, and physical. We should use water wisely and let it do its job. And our job is to set the intention on how we want to feel and what we choose to focus on and believe. We can also release the judgments and words of others so that we can be unburdened."

Wisdom smiled at her astute student and said it was time for Lark to return home to her family. As Lark turned to wave goodbye, Wisdom magically vanished into the dusk of the evening. All that remained was her usual blue mist.

Lark strolled home with a deep sense of gratitude and appreciation for all she had learned and would continue to learn. She had trust and joy in her mind and body. As she walked, she felt a mental state of calm. It was a serenity that was a welcome gift from the ordinary worries of the school day and the dramas from her friends. It was then she noticed she had missed a multitude of texts from her friends and a rather long text chain from her friend group chat. But Lark was unfazed and not in a hurry to catch up with the messages. She liked the feeling of being connected to her spirit and the guidance from Wisdom.

She also appreciated simply being outside, surrounded by nature's beauty. *Why look down at a screen when you can choose to look up and all around?*

The evening air was delightful, and all that mattered to Lark was this moment and her walk home. As she continued her stroll home in a leisurely fashion, she pondered once again on how and why Wisdom does not seem human but appears to be human. She wondered if others in town knew about Wisdom. Surely some of the grown-ups who lived in Casper must know who she is and have also experienced the miracles and lessons in the Sanctuary of Life? In any case, Lark felt a deep sense of peace and wondered what her next encounter would reveal.

When Lark arrived home, everything was in full motion. Mom was preparing dinner for the family, Dad was taking his evening shower, and her sisters were playing in the family room. It was Grace who heard Lark's arrival and ran to the door. She was so excited to see her big sister. She barely let Lark remove her sweatshirt as she was eager to tell her about her school day. "Mrs. Clements is thrilled with my improvements in math," she said. And she was so proud to show Lark her A+ grade from today's math pop quiz.

Lark felt a sense of pride and was thrilled she could help her sister feel more capable. Then Grace shared she was beginning to feel more confident in other classes. She was hopeful things would only get easier and would make more steady improvements. She thanked her sister once again for her help by giving her a great big hug. Lark was thrilled to be of service and offered more tutoring any time some extra encouragement would be appreciated.

Just then, Mom popped her head into the family room and winked at Lark. It was finally time for dinner, and Lark was famished. Dad joined them all and was eager to hear about his family's day. As everyone shared something from their day, Lark was completely at ease, enjoying the meal and the time spent in conversation with her family. She secretly thought this was true happiness and what life was all about. She soaked up all her blessings along with the delicious meal.

After the relaxing dinner with her family, Lark ventured outside to the backyard. It was a beautiful evening with a full moon, and the stars were twinkling. She recalled Wisdom's beautiful necklace and pondered her lessons from the day about releasing worries into a metaphorical stream. As she looked up into the sky again, she wondered just how much conflict she would endure over her life. Noticing that thought did not feel so good, she let it go into the mist of the evening sky and embraced just how quickly her mind went calm again.

Chapter 13:

Holding Friends Accountable

Lark arrived the next day at school and noticed Gwen was in rare form. She seemed to have an air about her. Lark suddenly realized she had not read her text messages from the day before. She quickly opened and read the text thread to see that it was about something that happened in Gwen's ELA class the previous day. The teacher had the students read passages out loud from a book, and Molly fumbled over a couple of the names and words in the passage she read out loud in class. Gwen thought it was hilarious and seized the moment to torment Molly verbally, but ever so quietly so the teacher could not overhear her comments. Gwen thought it was ridiculous that anyone could fumble over such easy words and names. Gwen chuckled to herself, thinking Molly's error was funny. She observed how Molly recoiled with utter embarrassment, knowing she had trouble pronouncing those names in front of the entire class. She could feel Molly's discomfort and inner turmoil as the girls were seated at desks next to each other.

That discomfort Molly felt was a familiar, despised feeling for Gwen. Gwen's father would frequently berate her at the dinner table when her grades were less than stellar. In those moments, she wanted to shout at her father but knew it would make matters worse. He thought scolding her would make her try harder. Gwen kept her rage inside, all neat and tidy, so her father would not see her displeasure. She would agree with him and promise to improve her grades so that he would change the subject. Gwen's anger was always close to the surface and ready to explode.

Poor Molly was about to be on the receiving end of Gwen's pain in an unfair manner. Gwen seized the opportunity to feel superior. She fired off a text message with a play-by-play of what happened in class, hoping the group chat would burst with laughing emojis. Making Molly the punchline made Gwen feel powerful. Or at least, that's what she told herself. Nothing felt better than reminding everyone who was in charge, at least at school.

Lark read and reread the text message. She was embarrassed that her friend could send such a message. She considered how to reply and what to say privately to Gwen. If she laughed to join in on the fun and games, she would be dishonoring her personal value of kindness. On the other hand, confrontation was one of her biggest fears. She took a deep breath and knew what had to be done. She chose not to respond and speak directly and bravely to Gwen.

When Lark did not respond immediately to Gwen's message, she took it as a personal affront. Lark was not swayed by Gwen's obnoxious attitude. After class and in the hallway, she pulled Gwen aside. "I would like to share why I did not reply to your text. It was rude. Have some compassion for Molly. Everyone makes mistakes and fumbles in school. It's hard to be put on the spot and read out loud to twenty-five other students. She was embarrassed enough and did not need you to text the events in class to your friends. It was not kind, and I did not want to participate or respond."

Gwen gave her a sarcastic look and walked abruptly away.

Nikki overheard their conversation and, to Lark's relief, agreed with her position. She felt shame for participating and laughing at the text thread.

Lark smiled at Nikki and said, "I have messed up so many times in class. I feel bad for Molly and know how embarrassing those moments can be, and I did not want to cause her more pain."

Nikki nodded her head in agreement.

Lark then changed the subject and asked Nikki, "Is Gwen okay?"

Nikki lowered her head and said, "Gwen has been rather upset lately because her parents have been fighting more than usual, and it's been hard for her to handle. I think her dad has been mean to her as well, yelling at her for no apparent reason and getting on her case about her grades lately."

Lark nodded her head, a gesture of empathy for Gwen, and thanked Nikki for confiding this information. The class schedule bell rang, and the girls went their separate ways.

As Lark walked the school halls toward her next class, she felt sorry for Gwen. She knew her parents tended to argue, and even the slightest disagreement would cause Gwen to feel unsettled, shake, and even feel anxious. But Gwen would never let it show on the outside. Lark made it a point to let go of the situation regarding the text thread because she had made it very clear she did not approve of or condone her treatment of Molly. She also promised herself she would show kindness to Molly. After all, kindness and kind words and gestures can go a long way to brighten someone's day.

Finally, the bell rang, marking the end of the school week. The buses were waiting to take the students home for the weekend. Gwen was already on the bus, in her usual spot, peering out the window. Quietly, Lark sat down next to her.

Gwen gave her a smug look and said, "I'm surprised you want to sit by me after your big-shot comments this afternoon."

Lark replied, "One has nothing to do with the other. Yes, I did not like or condone your comments because they were uncalled for, rude, and hurtful toward Molly. I had to let you know where I stand." Then with a smile, she said, "And you are my friend, and friends can disagree. If a friend can't call you out on your bad behavior, who can?"

Gwen was silent, bowed her head, and then replied, "Okay, I guess you are right. It was kind of mean."

Lark noticed a tear rolling down her cheek. "What's the matter, Gwen? I'm here to listen or help if you wish."

Gwen confided that her parents were fighting more than usual and not speaking to each other. "There's an icy feeling in my house, and it's not fun going home and experiencing the interactions with my parents."

Gwen said her brother, Matt, uses headphones to block out the chaos. Gwen wished she too could drown them out, but not knowing what was going on seemed worse. She said, "They don't even ask me how things are going in school, about my grades, or about my friends. I would rather have Dad get on my case about my grades instead of his lack of interest. What can I say? It's been rough."

Lark wished she had words of comfort, but nothing came, so she moved closer to Gwen, put her arms around her, and gave her a hug. Gwen took a tissue from her pocket to wipe away the tears rolling down her face and said a gentle thanks to her friend.

The bus then arrived at Gwen's stop, and as she got up to get off the bus, she turned to Lark and said, "I'll focus on my homework tonight, and maybe I'll get an A on my ELA essay this week."

Lark said, "Goodbye," and encouraged Gwen to call if there was anything she could do. Lark felt so helpless and wanted to do more for her friend who was struggling.

As the bus continued to make its usual stops, Lark thought about Wisdom. What would she advise her to do? Lark went blank and thought this situation was very rough for Gwen. The bus arrived at her stop down the block from her home on Maple Drive.

Lark departed the bus and slowly walked home. She felt empathy for her friend in such a rough predicament. *Gwen is a kid and can't control the actions of her parents, yet she is badly affected by their behavior.* Lark wondered how she could be a friend and help. How could she support her? What words of wisdom could she share with Gwen to be helpful?

Chapter 14:

Who Is Doing the Thinking?

Lark arrived home and said a friendly hello to her mom and sisters. Grace was enamored with her big sister ever since she helped her with her math homework. Her grades were improving, and she felt more confident. Grace was starting to participate more in classes, and her friends were starting to notice she was more outgoing and social.

Mom was happy as well. She always felt a bit bad for Grace, as Becca was naturally confident and academically gifted. Being twins had benefits, but also had the added stress of unspoken competitiveness. Becca loved her twin and considered Grace her best friend, but also inwardly loved being overtly smarter and faster. Mom was relieved that Grace wholeheartedly embraced her big sister's guidance and was amazed at just how quickly things turned around for her at school.

Lark was in a hurry to take her walk to the Sanctuary of Life. She was excited to change out of her school clothes and go outside.

But Mom seemed a bit concerned that she was spending too much time alone and not with her friends.

Lark said, "I see my friends in school all day and chat with them in the evenings."

Mom reminded her that it's important to be social and that friendships, just like sisters, need love, time, and attention. Mom made it clear she was concerned Lark had been neglecting her friends. With that motherly advice, she reminded Lark to be home before dark.

"I know, Mom," Lark replied in a condescending tone and was finally able to make a mad dash out of her house and onto the path.

She arrived at the entrance gate, which seemed to be even bigger and tightly shut. Wisdom was nowhere to be found. Then Lark noticed a bunch of red cardinals singing their song and chirping away. Lark found a spot to sit down and closed her eyes to enjoy the warmth of the sun and feel the beauty all around. She had no expectations for the afternoon and seemed to be content even if Wisdom did not appear. She continued to breathe calmly and surrendered to the present moment, exactly as it was, with the big steel gate and all. The birds continued to chirp, and Lark surprised herself at how still she was in her mind and body by just being present in the moment and breathing.

Lark allowed herself the gift of being present in nature with no expectations or input from Wisdom. She truly enjoyed the experience of being and allowing her body to be, and it all felt so natural. Lark continued to explore her surroundings and found a place to sit and sit she did; it was as if she had been there for ages without a care in the world. She closed her eyes and enjoyed the feeling of the cool ground beneath her, though a bit uncomfortable, she enjoyed it and surrendered to it. She continued to breathe in the fresh air of the afternoon. The chirping birds were a natural acoustic for meditation and stillness. Even though her mind started to race, Lark was able to notice the thoughts without having to be involved in the meaning of them. Lark sat and enjoyed the pleasure of not doing and the simple pleasure of being.

In the stillness, she had her own epiphany that it was not her job to fix everyone and everything.

She suddenly felt a lightness in her neck and shoulders, like the weight of the world and her mental burdens were removed from her shoulders. Lark felt liberated. But then quickly her mind pinged with other thoughts. *You need to tell everyone about this experience and how to do it! Yes, let's tell all our friends and then the world!* At that very second, she felt the pressure come right back onto her shoulders.

Then there was the another thought that raced through her mind. That sharing about this place was not her task, job, or responsibility. She felt like Wisdom was there with her, but only in her mind. Then she wondered, *Which part of me is doing the thinking? Hmmm, are there multiples of me in my head? How can that possibly be? What's going on here?*

Lark was able to get a grip on herself and redirect her attention back to the sound of the chirping birds, the feeling of the cool ground beneath her bottom, and the rhythm of her breath. She stayed in her space for a little while longer until that inner peace returned. She loved that feeling, the feeling of inner bliss and solitude. Her mind felt clear and almost empty. The peace encapsulated her entire being. In that moment, she placed her hands over her heart and felt even more grounded and still. The air was cool and refreshing as it entered her nose. She felt a sense of rejuvenation. She said these simple words to herself: "I am okay, I am safe, I am loved." She repeated it again and again to let the mantra feel true in her entire body.

It became an instant mantra. The simple act of placing her hands on her heart, feeling the rhythm of her own heartbeat, and reciting those simple phrases, "I am okay, I am safe, I am loved." More peace and inner stillness washed over her from the top of her head and down and across her whole body. Her feet were also filled with this same stillness.

After several more moments, Lark rose from the ground and walked around the perimeter of the Sanctuary of Life. She admired the flowers at the foot of the gate and the tall trees all around. She looked avidly at the trees, and it was as if they were all smiling and applauding her presence. Lark was able to sense this all by herself without any prodding from Wisdom. She made a mental note of the experience.

She looked at the gate that was still closed. She was not distressed by this at all now. It did not matter at all. Though the gate was closed, it did not feel closed or shut tight, but rather a simple boundary that was temporary. She was not to enter today, for her experience was just where she was, at that place in nature. All was well and just as it should be. In that moment, she knew it was time to head home and be with her family and do her homework. She also had to study for her science test the following day.

As she was strolling home, Lark's mind was clear and fresh, and her heart was at peace. She then had another epiphany. The gate was locked for an important reason. Though it's fabulous to be in the Sanctuary of Life and experience its wonder and magic, life happens outside the mystical garden, with family, friends, neighbors, strangers, etc. The lessons and knowledge learned in the Sanctuary of Life need to be used outside this place in ordinary moments and regular situations. So, the real question Lark pondered next was, "Will I be able to remember what I learned and experienced today when I am back at home or in school?" She continued to think about this question. *Who is doing all this thinking? Ah, this is a good question for Wisdom.*

She thought about Gwen and sent her love from her heart. Then Lark's mind slowly but surely began to go down the usual path of thinking and thinking. And at that moment, Lark noticed how she was feeling in her body. She did not like those uncomfortable feelings, especially in her stomach. And then, suddenly, she realized answers are not contained in thoughts or the mere act of thinking. She also realized the thoughts about Gwen's family situation had caused her emotional disturbance. But what to do? How to fix it?

Lark began to get frustrated. *Did I not retain anything I learned today? It's not my job to fix this.* Once again, she placed her hand on her heart and said, "I am okay, I am safe, I am loved." She repeated that mantra all the way home. Then she thought, *I just want to help my friend feel better. This is a good thing and good thoughts.* But it was the flurry of worry that caused Lark to feel rattled and unsettled in her mind.

Just as Lark returned home and entered the doorway, she had another insight, her very own wisdom. *Helpful answers or solutions will become apparent in the space and quiet between thoughts, in ordinary moments.* What that actually meant left Lark perplexed, but it felt good in her mind and body.

Lark went inside and realized she was ravenous and looked forward to whatever Mom had cooked for dinner. She went right over to Hope and played blocks with her on the floor. It was fun just to play with her little sister. As she played with Hope, she watched the sheer delight she experienced just by playing. Hope then scooted over toward Lark and made her way onto her lap. Lark sniffed her hair and took delight in this little human she was blessed to call sister.

Shortly afterward, Mom called the family to the dinner table. It was lovely to eat together and share events of the day. That evening, Becca was extremely talkative about her day, her classes, and her upcoming soccer tournament with Grace. The twins were excited about the weekend games. Grace was extra confident she would score at least two goals. Becca was so happy to see Grace's confidence building and getting stronger.

Becca looked at Grace and said, "Together, let's be the dynamic duo and crush it!"

And they most certainly did!

Chapter 15:

All Is Revealed

It was finally the weekend. Mom and Dad were off to the twins' soccer tournament with plenty of activities and snacks for Hope. She needed to be kept entertained during the long outing. The twins were pumped about the tournament. They had several new players on their travel team who gave the team a competitive advantage. Becca had natural confidence when it came to sports. She took things in her stride and was always determined to play her best with the logical perspective that soccer is just a game.

Grace was not as athletically gifted as her twin but had stamina and could run very fast. She was more self-conscious, and though she too enjoyed the game, she felt internal pressure to perform well and feared fumbling. Lark knew this feeling all too well and had a lot of compassion for Grace. Before they left for the tournament, Lark reminded Grace to keep her mindset positive and to have a great time.

Lark was relieved she was not pressured by her parents to attend the all-day tournament. Although she did want to cheer on her sisters, the thought of attending soccer games all day in the hot sun was just too much. She was old enough to stay behind and relished the afternoon of freedom.

After sleeping late, she devoured the breakfast Mom left for her in the kitchen. She charged up her cell phone, brushed her pearly white teeth, and got ready for the long day. She was eager for some extended time in the Sanctuary of Life before heading over to Ashley's for a barbecue. She secretly hoped Wisdom would be there to greet her upon arrival.

She allowed herself the gift of time and a leisurely walk to the Sanctuary of Life. She wondered if her friends enjoyed the solace of alone time as much as she did. And on the other hand, she enjoyed the company of her family and the camaraderie of her friends. She felt grateful for having a full life and this secret adventure, something all for herself. This was her little secret. It still baffled her that Wisdom appeared to her in a place she had known all her life. Lark's mind continued to race with thoughts and questions about Wisdom and the Sanctuary of Life.

Then she took a breath and had an epiphany. *All this thinking is just a loop of asking and answering random questions in my head. It's an endless cycle of questions, considerations, and ideas. But which ones should I listen to, engage with, or take seriously? Which thoughts are real? Maybe Wisdom could help sort this out today.*

When she arrived at the Sanctuary of Life, Lark looked very closely at the steel gate. She remained very still. She did not move a muscle. What she originally perceived as strong, sturdy, and rigid seemed almost ethereal and misty. She looked carefully with an attitude of contentment. In her mind, she imagined the gate as energy that could be changed and transformed. She imagined the gate as a purple mist with form and structure. She wanted to believe the energy and love in her heart and the magic of the mind could make it evaporate, melt, and disappear into nothing! If she could achieve this, there would no longer be a barrier to entry. And just like that, to Lark's surprise and sheer delight, the gate disappeared, and Wisdom appeared.

Lark looked almost stunned and astonished. *How did she do that? Did Wisdom use her magical powers to melt away the gate? Or did I figure out a mystery in life and do this by myself?*

Wisdom smiled at Lark and said those wonderful two words, "Well done!"

Lark smiled and was pleased with herself.

Wisdom said, "Yes, you are learning, Grasshopper!"

Lark wondered why she called her a grasshopper.

Lark smiled again and, with all her joy and enthusiasm, entered the Sanctuary of Life and immersed herself in its beautiful surroundings. The trees were finally blooming after the cold winter, and the flowers were beautifully bright. Lark especially loved the pink orchard trees, the cherry blossoms. The whole place was a magical sight and a delight to her eyes.

Wisdom followed behind Lark. Wisdom felt so much pride for her young student, who was blossoming into a fine young woman, eager to learn the ways of nature and to create a life of harmony, adventure, and joy. She was proud of her youthful, budding student who was curious about the workings of her mind. She liked the fact that Lark was not too absorbed with technology, social media, and her cell phone. "Everything in balance," Wisdom would say.

Eventually, Lark and Wisdom made their way to the outdoor classroom, situated between the two large trees. They sat down on the long log bench with the smooth surface. Almost immediately, Lark wanted to ask questions of Wisdom.

Wisdom placed her index finger between her lips to indicate silence. She then placed a hand on Lark's back, in the middle of her shoulder blades. It was a simple suggestion for Lark to settle her mind into her heart, a simple but profound gesture. Once again, peace filled Lark's mind, heart, and body. They both enjoyed the solitude of their surroundings for several more moments. No words were needed.

After more time had elapsed, Wisdom welcomed Lark's question. "Child, what do you wish to ask?" Wisdom became quiet, yet very attentive.

Lark took a long, deep breath. She was shaking inside and could feel sweat beginning to pour down her back. Words became jumbled in her mind. She was questioning her own sanity and afraid her questions would offend Wisdom, and all this magic and mystery would disappear as quickly as it had all appeared. What if her questions broke the spell of this enchanted place?

Finally, Lark asked her long-awaited questions. "Who are you, and how come I can see you? You don't seem real, like other people or grown-ups I know, but you are so wise, loving, kind, and experienced." Doubt plagued Lark's mind as soon as the words left her lips. She was scared, not in a frightful way, that she was taking a risk and could lose her happy place.

Wisdom was ever so quiet and softly responded, "When the student is ready, the teacher will appear." She was then silent.

Lark furrowed her brow and was even more confused than ever. "I don't understand what that means," she said.

Wisdom continued her explanation. "We are all connected—nature, earth, animals, and people. It is the cycle of life. We all live in the same world, under the same sun and sky. However, we are not always in harmony or sync with one another. It saddens us to see people fighting and living in disharmony. There is abundance all around and enough for all. One of our finest elders, named Rachel, was famous for saying, 'We are here to love each other. The more we love, the more we get.' Our job is to focus on what we have, not what we lack. Gratitude and appreciation go a very long way. Appreciate what you do have, and what one appreciates tends to grow in value.

"Lark, we know who you are and the kindness in your heart and the intelligence in your mind. The day you walked by the Sanctuary of Life you started noticing the beauty of the trees and the individuality of the colorful leaves. That was the day you were ready to receive your wisdom. We saw you noticing and your natural curiosity. We saw you noticing beauty and awe. And on that day, you were ready, and I was able to appear to you. You were ready, and I appeared.

"So, you see, child, you were able to see me. You were able to perceive me. You were able to hear me. I have always been here for anyone ready and eager to use their eyes to see beyond the ordinary and obvious. To see is also to sense and perceive and to wonder and imagine. I have always been here for anyone ready and eager to use their ears to hear the truth. I have always been here for anyone ready and eager to use their nose to smell sweet fragrances. I have always been here for anyone ready and eager to trust and believe in themselves."

Wisdom became still and quiet. She gave Lark time to process her words. After some silence, she moved closer to Lark and inquired, "Do you understand?"

Lark was quiet, too. The truth was, she did understand. Lark had always been a seeker from a very young age. She had always been curious, and her thoughts always ran deep. She just did not have the language to articulate all she knew and perceived. Her original dream about Wisdom was her spirit's way of communicating to her that she was ready to grow and embrace her real self. Lark turned her body to face Wisdom and said a simple, "Yes, I do."

Wisdom went on to explain an important lesson. It is important to value and prioritize the relationship with yourself. When people are kind to themselves and appreciate their own inner spirit, it's easier to feel a sense of peace and inner calm. Peace and stillness reside in the pause between the inhale and the exhale. And within this peace and stillness resides intuition, which is an inner knowing. Sometimes, people call this truth a gut feeling or an ability to trust their inner guidance. People have many names for this way to inner peace, and all are good.

Lark placed her hand on her heart and felt the rhythm of her heart beating. She went quiet to also perceive the sound of her heart beating. She remained very still and quiet for a long time. Wisdom let Lark be, to take in what she just shared. She watched as her student absorbed this very deep information.

After a while, Lark turned to Wisdom and said, "So others can see you exactly as I see you?"

Wisdom smiled and paused, then replied, "Not exactly. You see me in this way, as this is a friendly form for your mind and your eyes. Others will perceive me differently in a variety of forms or likenesses: a person, an animal, and even an angel. This will depend on their beliefs, their family traditions, in their own time, in their own way, and, most importantly, when they are ready.

It's all good, and there is no one correct way to perceive ME. It is all about love."

Lark asked Wisdom, "How is it that I am alive, and my heart can beat all on its own day and night without being charged the way my cell phone needs charging?"

Wisdom giggled in her funny way and replied, "You are not a cell phone. You are a human being created from the union of your parents, the energy of love, and the source of everything. You get your energy and life force from the cycle of life that begins with your spirit, the life force that animates your body, as well as from rest, nourishment, water, sunshine, and so much more. You see, all things work in harmony. The plants and trees give humans oxygen to breathe, and humans produce carbon dioxide to nourish the plants and trees. There is a balance to life, including daytime and nighttime, land and sea, north and south, and hot and cold. The elements on our planet Earth include air, fire, water, and land. All elements are required and necessary to sustain life."

Lark pointed to Wisdom's amulet pendant and said, "Oh, that is why you always wear your necklace."

Wisdom nodded in agreement. She took a breath and then said, "Is this enough information for your young, beautiful mind today?"

Lark's wide eyes seemed to glisten even brighter. She said, "Oh no, I have more questions for you. Is that okay?"

Wisdom obliged her student and motioned for her to continue. At that point, Lark turned to inquire once again, "Who are you?"

Wisdom pensively thought and considered some more about how to reply to this young, inquisitive girl so she would understand. She replied, "I am a teacher, a teacher of consciousness, a teacher of love."

Lark's eyes opened wider, and her mouth dropped, almost speechless. Then she repeated, as if to really understand, "A teacher of consciousness? What is that? And do all kids have teachers of consciousness?"

Wisdom smiled and sincerely appreciated the question. She explained. "Remember earlier, I mentioned that when the student is ready, the teacher will appear? You were ready, and I appeared to you in this form, as in your dream. So, I am appearing to you in a way and form where you feel comfortable and receptive to learn. I represent you, Lark, and your highest potential. Teachers appear to people in forms they feel ready, open, receptive, and comfortable with. My form is not important, dear child. What's important is only the wisdom you learn and embrace in your own life.

"We learn best when comfortable and relaxed. Lark, think about teachers from school you liked, and when you enjoyed being in their classroom."

"Oh, I adored Mrs. Rivera."

"Did you learn a lot from Mrs. Rivera that year?"

"Oh, yes, I sure did, and my grades were great that year."

Wisdom replied, "Exactly. You liked your teacher, embraced the education, and your grades reflected your retention of knowledge in a tangible way, a good report card."

Lark once again became still and pensive. She asked, "If I were a boy, would you come to me in a male body?"

Wisdom said, "Yes, that's completely possible, but not necessarily an absolute. It depends on the person and what is friendly and receptive to the individual. That's enough for now. Let's enjoy this beautiful day."

Together, they admired the beautiful flowers and the various aromas they gave off into the air. Wisdom let Lark meander for a little longer while keeping a watchful eye on her. Lark also noticed a few butterflies fluttering around the trees. She saw monarch butterflies and a few blue butterflies with velvet black spots on their delicate wings. Lark loved looking at butterflies and told Wisdom that Hope liked to chase the ones on their front lawn. She said Hope would call them her friends.

Wisdom smiled and said, "Young children are often very receptive to energies and nature spirits because of their youth and innocence." She told Lark to encourage Hope to enjoy the butterflies and to ask Hope what she sees and experiences and why they are here at this time. "Let Hope freely express herself and respond to her with smiles and nods of the head. Children are sometimes our greatest teachers," Wisdom said.

Lark promised to spend more time with her baby sister and to listen very carefully. She said, "It would be good for both of us."

Wisdom urged Lark to head back toward home and spend time with her friends on this beautiful weekend day. She said friendships are necessary for fun, emotional growth, and do make life so much more fun. They also require time, care and attention.

Lark mentioned that Mom said something very similar this morning.

Wisdom replied, "Your mom is a great mom and loves passionately, so trust in her guidance always, even if she irritates you from time to time."

Lark laughed at Wisdom's sentiment and agreed wholeheartedly.

She turned around to hug Wisdom and offer her gratitude. She then waved goodbye to Wisdom, the trees, and especially to her favorite tree, Goldy. Then she was off on the path leading home and ready to spend time with her friends.

Chapter 16:

Nothing Like Old Friends

Lark was enthusiastically eager to catch up with her friends. The girls were at Ashley's house for an afternoon swim and evening barbecue. She texted Mom to remind her she was going to hang out with her friends for the rest of the day. Mom replied, "Thanks for checking in. Have fun!"

As Lark made her way toward her neighborhood, she ran into Jonah, who was heading in the same direction. Jonah was so happy to see Lark outside school. He said, "Hey, it's been a minute since we last had a chance to hang together."

Lark smiled and said, "Yes, you're right."

Jonah attempted to give Lark a hip bump, but she playfully and quickly moved away, and the pair laughed. Jonah asked, "Where are you coming from? I didn't see you on the trail when I was on my hike."

"Oh, sometimes I like to venture deeper in to enjoy the trees. It's so peaceful and quiet there. It helps settle my mind."

Jonah smiled and asked, "Just from walking in the woods? How can that be?"

"Well, you see, it's so quiet among all the trees, and there is so much to see. I love the different varieties of trees, all the beautiful colors, and fragrant scents. When I take it all in and focus on nature, all those worries and cares don't seem to matter too much. It's like a whole-body relaxation experience."

Jonah became wide-eyed and said, "Really?"

Lark blinked her eyes and proclaimed, "Yes, really!"

"So, what do you do once you are there with all the trees?"

"I simply notice them, appreciate their unique qualities, and sometimes I just admire the leaves or branches. Sometimes it's fun to notice their shape, size, or color. I admire the greenery wrapped around the base of their trunks. To me, it looks like those trees are wrapped in blankets. Sometimes I pretend they are speaking directly to me and greeting me with their outstretched branches. I don't really know, as every time it's a different experience. I just like being there.

"Other times, I use my ears and sense of hearing to listen to the birds chirping, who make their homes in the trees. Then sometimes it's nice to notice the fragrant scents, such as honeysuckle.

"You see, Jonah, when I notice all the elements in nature, I am not focusing my attention on other thoughts such as homework, what to wear to school, or who likes whom in school. All that stuff causes me to worry and ruminate. When I'm in the woods or even just walking on the trail, there is just this day, the present moment. I have also noticed that things tend to naturally work themselves out without my input or even trying to interfere with or control the outcome of a situation. I just started noticing nature, especially the trees. Hey, what can I say? This must sound weird."

Jonah looked bashful and said, "Not at all. That's really cool. I'd like to try that too! Thanks for sharing your experience with me. It gives me something to consider and to try for myself. I, too, tend to worry these days, and it's been a lot to handle by myself. I don't really want to tell anyone; they may think I am weak."

"Do your parents know you have been struggling?"

"No, I don't want to trouble them with *this silliness*. I am not sure they would understand something that is going on mostly in my head."

Lark resonated with her friend and nodded her head in agreement.

As the two continued to make their way back, Lark inquired about Jonah's worries. Jonah started to blush with a bit of embarrassment. He said, "Well, if you promise not to say anything to anyone?"

"Of course. We've been family friends since we were little kids, and I wouldn't do anything to break our trust bond," Lark stated emphatically.

"Okay then. Last year, I had a crush on a girl in class. I asked her to go to the movies, and she, well, she laughed. You know, one of those quiet, low-key laughs. She did not say yes or no; she just laughed, turned her back, and walked away. I assumed by her actions that it was a no about going to the movies. We used to chat in class all the time, but ever since that time, I have avoided her and now feel so self-conscious around her and girls in general. Well, except for you, of course. I wonder if she turned me down because I'm not cute enough, or maybe it's something else, or something is wrong with me! I'm also concerned that she told her friends because right after that, her friends giggled at me in the hallway. Do they all think I'm a weirdo? I regret ever asking Amanda to the movies in the first place."

"You asked Amanda out on a date?"

Jonah wanted to die in that very moment, as he had no intention of sharing her name with Lark. Amanda and Lark were on the same soccer team last year and were on-again, off-again friends. Lark always liked Amanda. She was kind and very levelheaded and seemed to be able to easily go with the flow. She was very good at avoiding Gwen's dramas; she just had no patience for Gwen's moods or attitude.

Jonah turned to Lark in sheer desperation. "Please don't share this with anyone. I would be mortified if anyone knew how embarrassed I am these days."

Lark smiled kindly at Jonah and promised not to utter a word. "Our circle of trust will never be broken," she continued with an empathetic demeanor toward her friend.

Jonah finally built up the courage to ask for Lark's advice. "What should I do? I can't stand these nervous feelings in my body one day longer. They're awful, and the thoughts consume my mind, and it's been hard to concentrate and focus on school. My teachers and parents have noticed my grades slipping. I really could use your advice. Seriously, anything would be helpful."

Lark became pensive and quiet. In her mind, she really wanted to get to Ashley's for the barbecue. She had been neglecting her friends and wanted some fun on this beautiful day. But she could not ignore the needs of one of her oldest friends, who looked so sad and lost. She was determined to help her friend feel a bit better. He is, after all, so nice, and she felt bad that he was struggling so much all alone.

"Okay, Jonah, let's put this into perspective. You said you asked her to the movies months ago. When exactly did you ask her?"

"At the beginning of the school year, sometime in September."

"Okay, that was a while ago!"

"Yeah, I know that, but to me it feels like yesterday."

Lark explained to Jonah that people think thousands of thoughts a day, about 60,000 thoughts per day, and most are repetitive thoughts.

"Wow, that's a lot. How do you know that, Lark?"

"Between you and me, I've been struggling with overthinking, too. One day, when I was bored, I Googled that subject and learned a bunch of stuff, and it made me feel better. So, I thought if I have all those thoughts, other people also have those thoughts, so they are probably more consumed with what they are thinking and feeling than with me! It helped me to put things in perspective."

"I like that a lot. It's kind of reassuring."

"Here's something else that has helped me as well. Just because we have a thought, it does not mean it is true or accurate. The brain is a thinking machine, generating thoughts to keep us safe and protect us. It's not concerned with our overall happiness; it just wants us to stay alive at all costs. Our minds are trying to protect us."

"But Lark, Amanda laughed at me and turned her back without even acknowledging my invitation to take her to the movies."

Lark agreed that it was not very nice or friendly. "But just because she was not polite does not mean there is something wrong with you. Who knows why she did that at the time? Why let one conversation rob you of your confidence and happiness? You see, Jonah, you created a negative meaning and belief from that brief interaction. Your brain does not want that to happen again and creates similar thoughts to keep you distracted and out of harm's way. Sounds crazy, huh? But the thoughts are the thing making you feel miserable."

Jonah took a deep breath and said, "You're absolutely right. I'm going to forget all about that day, or at least let it stay in the past, or try not to dwell on it any longer."

Lark inquired, "Do you feel a bit better now?"

Jonah smiled and said, "Sure do. I feel a whole lot better." Jonah felt happy to have bumped into Lark today.

"Great! You know, I feel bad we have not spoken for a while," Lark said compassionately.

They both acknowledged that life in middle school tends to get busy with school assignments, after-school activities, and recreational sports.

"Hey, let's make it a point to check in with each other. I think we could both use a good friend."

Jonah replied, "I would like that a lot. Maybe we could walk the trails together next Friday or over the weekend?"

Lark's eyes beamed, and she said, "I would like that too!"

At that point, Jonah reached the block where his home was, and Lark was eager to get home, wash up, and head over to Ashley's house.

"Thanks for our chat," Jonah said. "It really helped, and let's text at the end of the week to figure out a good time to go."

Lark smiled and headed home.

Chapter 17:

The Swiftie Sisters

It was around 4 p.m. when Lark finally arrived at Ashley's house. Ashley's mom greeted her with a big smile at the front door. She told her to go through the house and outside to the backyard. Ashley had a beautiful home. The rooms were large and spacious, decorated with light colors on the walls. Every room had a different color, and each room complemented the other.

There was always something fragrant and delicious cooking in the kitchen. She envied Ashley as her mom worked and loved cooking scrumptious meals, and her dad loved grilling on the barbecue. Truth be told, though Lark's mom always had a meal prepared, it was not always that flavorful or interesting. Lark never complained but secretly loved eating at Ashley's house.

Lark made her way through the kitchen and out the large sliding door leading to the backyard. Ashley's backyard was always well-manicured and had springtime flowers planted neatly and organized by color. Lark loved the way the pink and white flowers were illuminated above the dark mulch. There was a paved patio with outdoor furniture, an outdoor kitchen for barbecues, and, of course, an inground pool with reclining chairs surrounding the perimeter. There were enough lounge chairs for everyone. *This is the life*, Lark thought quietly.

Ashley, Nikki, and Gwen were in the pool having a grand time. It was a perfect early spring day. The sun was shining, and even the mountains in the background could be seen without the usual fog. Ashley noticed Lark first and motioned for her to join everyone in the pool. Lark went into the small cabana and changed into her swimsuit. She placed her bag on one of the chairs, removed her flip-flops, and walked over to the pool. She sat down along the edge of the pool to get her feet wet, then immediately jumped in. She was happy to hang out with her girlfriends away from the confines of the school.

Lark swam alone for a minute or so, dove beneath the surface to wet her hair, then swam over to the girls. The three were laughing and having a great time.

Ashley asked inquisitively, "How's it going?"

Lark said, "Great! My family is at the twins' soccer tournament today. Mom said both girls scored goals today!"

Ashley looked at Lark with judgmental eyes and inquired, "Then where were you all day?"

Uh oh, there it was, that dreaded feeling, that feeling of judgment, the feeling of exclusion. Lark sheepishly replied, "Well… well, I slept late, then decided to go for a run on the trails." It was only a small white lie, but a lie it was.

Ashley smiled and said, "Oh, okay, I get it. It's just that everyone else got here at noon, and you were nowhere to be found. We texted you and got crickets, chirp, chirp, no response. We thought you were ditching us."

"Oh, you see, when I'm on the trails, I don't check text messages. I really needed to clear my head today."

Ashley said, "No worries, we were just concerned."

At that point, Gwen chimed in. "Clear your head from what?"

"I don't know. It's just been a lot these days at home. Having three younger sisters is annoying, and they can be so loud and demanding. I just needed some quiet time, time for myself."

Gwen gave Lark a funny look, more like a smirk. Lark bobbed up and down in the water a few times and then asked Gwen, "How are things with you?"

Condescendingly, Gwen said, "You know, a barrel of fun with Mom and Dad, either not talking or fighting up a storm. Matt is locked in his room, blasting music with his headphones. It's like living with strangers."

Lark replied, "That must be hard for you. I am sorry to hear that."

And out of nowhere, Gwen blasted Lark. "What do you know about anything like this? You have the perfect family, the perfect sisters, and you get to go and run to clear your head. From what? Being temporarily annoyed? Your mom and dad actually care about your life. My parents couldn't care less if I live or die, and I can't clear my head for one second." She stormed out of the pool, wrapped a towel around her waist, stomped off, and locked herself in the cabana. Gwen was a drama queen in action.

Lark looked hopelessly at Ashley and Nikki in astonishment. "What? What did I say? I really did not mean to offend her. What did I do wrong?"

Nikki looked at Lark, shrugged her shoulders, and said, "Gwen is struggling and is like a loose cannon today. I don't think you did anything. You just might have triggered her in some way. She was looking forward to all of us being together all day, but then you were not around and didn't reply to our texts. I think deep down she thought you were abandoning her, too."

"Abandoning her? How? I'm here with you all right now."

Nikki and Ashley just shrugged their shoulders. They had no words of consolation to offer at the moment.

Lark was shaking inside. Her safe world, her friendships, were in jeopardy, so she thought. She was looking forward to a pleasant afternoon of fun and giggles, and almost immediately, things were turned upside down. Lark felt as if she had jumped into a pool with a great white shark! This feeling stunned Lark. She was totally confused with the events that just transpired, and more confused with her very own thoughts. She thought she was past these feelings of abandonment with her friends, as she dealt with this situation with Wisdom. How can this still be an issue? She attempted to hoist herself out of the pool, and her small-framed body felt like a ton of bricks. Lark's mind was racing with worry, not so much about Gwen's concerns and family problems, but selfishly about her standing with her friends. She swam to the shallow end of the pool to buy some time to think. She thought about Wisdom and what she might advise in handling the situation. *What would Wisdom do?*

A moment later, which felt like an eternity, she emerged from the pool with water dripping down her legs and the weight of the world on her shoulders. She walked to her chair and wrapped a fluffy towel around her waist. She slowly walked to the cabana, where she heard Gwen sulking and pouting like a three-year-old. She felt empathy for her friend and was also confused with feelings of anger and fear for herself. In that moment, she heard Wisdom in her mind. *It's not your job to fix anything. There is nothing to fix. It's your responsibility to be in alignment with your head and heart and let your inner guidance take the lead.* Though this felt like the right answer, carrying this out with confidence felt impossible. She felt like she was about to enter a den of hungry lions rather than confront a friend.

Lark was still shaking and in a state of fear. *How can I handle this uncomfortable conversation successfully?* The worry train was out of the gate and full steam ahead at a superfast pace. *Okay, I can breathe. Yes, breathe to calm my body.* Lark paused outside the cabana and listened to Gwen pace back and forth. *Okay, I must knock and go inside and apologize to Gwen. Though I am not sure an apology is warranted.*

Very slowly and gently, Lark knocked and opened the cabana door. Gwen gave her the stink eye, which Lark ignored.

Lark smiled softly and proceeded. "Gwen, I am truly sorry I was not here for you earlier today. To be perfectly honest, I was not thinking about your needs this morning, nor did I realize or consider how important our gathering was for you today. I did not think anyone would mind if I arrived a little later than planned. I just wanted some alone time. If I had known, I would have walked to your house, and we could have walked to Ashley's together to have some private time to talk. Please accept my apology; it was my fault."

Gwen looked her up and down with judgment. "It's just that you have been, what can I say, so weird lately. I can't put my finger on it. It's like you have been absorbed in your own personal world. It's like you don't care about us, and then when you do, you sound like a grown-up and not like, well, you know, our Lark. It's like you are there for me but then disappear for hours on end to who knows where. Oh, right, you are off on your long walks lately."

Lark became quiet and pensive. Gwen was correct on all accounts. Lark had been enjoying her alone time, the physical activity of walking, the Sanctuary of Life, and, of course, meeting Wisdom. But how to explain this to her friends and her family? *Oh no, here come those insane thoughts again. Let's keep it together, breathe, and don't explain. What does the Queen of England say? "Never complain, never explain." Sounds good to me.*

The fear that her friendship with Gwen was in jeopardy felt so real in her mind, and her body was responding with nervous energy, especially in her stomach. She breathed deeper, settled her thoughts, and had an epiphany. It was to tell Gwen the truth, not the whole truth exactly, but some truth. *This is not what the queen would do, but I am not the queen, so here goes.*

"Gwen, you are right. I have been taking time for myself these days, more than usual. Since middle school began, I tend to get overwhelmed easily. I try to keep it together, but there are some days my mind races with all kinds of random thoughts. It could be about school, my changing body, my sisters, our friends, and all the things on social media. It never stops, and I can't ever seem to catch up. Then it feels like my mind is this machine with endless thoughts that just keep going and going until I am exhausted.

"A few weeks ago, it was a nice day outside and felt inspired to take a walk on the trails. I had so much homework that day, but it was so beautiful outside, I had to get out of the house. On my walk, I started noticing things. I noticed the trees, the leaves, the birds, and even the ground covering off the paved path. I know this must sound weird to you. I even noticed the different smells. When I was there and immersed in nature, my mind stopped racing and worrying. I felt better. I wanted to feel even better, so I started taking walks as often as I could to feel better. And I do feel better.

"BUT… I feel so horrible that I neglected you and was worried you were mad at me. I know your problems with your parents are awful and worse than my silly racing thoughts. It's just that I live in my head often, and honestly, when I had some time alone this morning, I took it. It was not done to neglect you. And actually, Mom thought I had been neglecting my friends. She reminded me friendships too need love and nurturing. Maybe she sensed I was wrong to go this morning and should have come straight to Ashley's house. I guess she, too, thought I was being withdrawn. Hey, but I did see Jonah on the way home." Lark stopped her rambling explanation and became quiet.

Gwen seemed to pout a bit more. She then turned around and said, "Sorry, perhaps I did overreact a bit. To be honest, I am upset and scared all the time. I just don't know how to control my parents' fighting, and maybe I took it out on you because you feel like family. And your mom is right! You have been neglecting us."

Lark was silent and just smiled. She waited for Gwen to speak and make the next move.

And just like that, Gwen said, "Do you smell that? I think Ashley's dad started the barbecue, and I'm hungry." Gwen then raced out the door to join the other girls. That was that. As quickly as she was upset and agitated, the idea of food calmed her straight down.

She left Lark sitting in the cabana by herself, and Lark wanted to cry. She felt that Gwen was being manipulative and did not like that notion at all. However, she did get an apology, and things seemed to be okay. They both were honest about their situations and feelings, a sign of a solid friendship. She realized Gwen was struggling with a hard situation. It must be incredibly difficult to live in a house where the parents are not getting along.

Maybe Gwen was trying to be in control of at least one relationship. Lark pondered that thought; her friend wanted some semblance of control, and she became that object. But she thought silently, *it's not okay to allow friends to take out their bad moods on each other. That's just not okay.* Lark continued to think about that and had another epiphany that went even further. *Maybe Gwen was not really trying to control me. Maybe it was her strange way of seeking love—love from a friend who feels like a sister.* Ahh, now that thought felt a little better.

In that instant, she heard Taylor Swift's "Shake It Off" playing outside, and the girls were singing and dancing. Lark laughed to herself and thought, *I can and will shake this off for myself.* And with that, she joined her friends for a fantastic dance party, a delicious meal, and a wonderful evening.

When Lark rejoined the group, everything seemed to be fine. The girls were famished from the long day in the late springtime heat and all their fun-filled activities. The girls swam, played water volleyball, and had a small dance party. The girls were huge Swifties and could not get enough of this singer-songwriter's hits; it was as if they could dance for hours on end without a break.

At last, Ashley's dad appeared with a scrumptious platter of hamburgers, hot dogs, grilled vegetables, and, of course, toasted buns. Ashley's mom arrived with all the fixings, including corn on the cob, coleslaw, and homemade cornbread. What could be better? The girls assembled their plates with food and filled their cups with cold beverages. They sat and settled themselves around the backyard table, covered by a wide umbrella to block the glaring evening sun.

As they devoured their food, Ashley thanked the girls for joining her this afternoon and for their friendship. She had them raise their glasses and said, "Cheers! Cheers to fun, friendship, and Dad's cooking!"

The girls clinked their plastic cups in agreement and solidarity.

Nikki continued the conversation and pointed out how they had all been friends since second grade. Then Nikki became quiet and reflective. Her long, shiny, black hair cascaded over her shoulders, filled with natural curls from the water of the pool. She said, "You know we are all more like sisters than friends. We disagree, borrow each other's clothes, get on each other's nerves, and argue, but at the end of the day, we are always there to support each other. Let's make a pact to always be friends, in good times and in bad times. Here's to friendship, to us, the Swiftie Sisters."

The girls clinked their glasses and together said, "To us, the Swiftie Sisters."

The girls finished dinner, then enjoyed making s'mores on the outdoor firepit. Lark thought to herself that it was really a great day, a real treat. She had time with Wisdom in the Sanctuary of Life. She caught up with Jonah, then had a leisurely, wonderful afternoon with her friends. Truth be told, it was a nice change to have dinner with them rather than her sisters. She loved her friends, and being a member of the Swiftie Sisters was the best. She felt valued and included, but underneath her joy and excitement, there was that old twinge of fear and worry. She did her best to shake off those doubtful thoughts and stay present in the moment. *Yes, stay present in the moment, appreciate everything, and make Wisdom proud.*

A while later, the sun set in the evening sky. There were streaks of gorgeous colors behind the backdrop of the mountains. It was getting late, and it was time to head home.

Nikki was spending the evening at Ashley's house, and Gwen and Lark started their walk home together. At last, the two friends had some real alone time. Gwen and Lark had been friends longer than the others. They were in kindergarten together and fast friends. But there had always been a bit of a rivalry between the two girls. Truth be told, Gwen was jealous of Lark's family. She envied how her parents were supportive of all four of their daughters, how they showed up for class performances and soccer games and how they even managed to carpool all the girls to their various activities. Gwen's parents were not as involved in their children's lives, and Gwen paid the price.

Gwen would frequently misbehave to be the center of attention and was jealous of her friends in a covert way and could be mean to kids in school. Poor Molly was the last to receive Gwen's bullying behavior. But deep down, Gwen was a good person. She just wanted and needed to be loved, and who doesn't need love? The girls chatted, reflected on the afternoon, and just how great Ashley's dad is as a grill master!

As they approached Gwen's home, both promised to be there for each other and not let things get out of hand. They hugged and parted ways for the evening.

Chapter 18:

A Cuddle with Mom

A short while later, Lark arrived home exhausted. It had been a long day. The twins were excited to see her, and Grace almost barreled over Lark as she entered the house. She was so excited to share that she had scored two goals. Becca scored four goals and won the tournament for the team in overtime. But Grace felt self-assured, confident, and proud of her game performance today. She did not have the need to compare herself to Becca, because in her heart she knew she played her best and, most importantly, had fun! Lark told Grace how proud she was of her efforts and how glad she was that she enjoyed the tournament.

She then found Mom in her bedroom watching television. Lark entered her parents' bedroom and snuggled up next to Mom in the bed. Lark loved her parents' room with its bright yellow walls, a full-length mirror, and especially their king-sized bed with a luxurious comforter. It was always so comforting there.

Mom loved a neat and tidy bedroom, and everything was always in order.

It was nice to have some alone time with Mom. Mom turned off the television and inquired about her day. Lark told her all the details but focused on her interaction at the pool with Gwen. Even though all seemed to be resolved, and they called themselves the Swiftie Sisters, Lark had an uncomfortable feeling in the pit of her stomach that she could not describe. She wanted to confide in her mom, especially as she'd observed she'd been neglecting her friends lately. However, she did not share the details about Gwen's parents fighting. She wanted to respect Gwen's privacy and trust.

Mom nodded her head and said, "Girls can be moody, especially at this age with so many changes going on in their bodies. Lark, I know you are upset as you care deeply about people, and that is admirable, but sometimes you must let people express themselves and have their own moods and moments. The trick is not to take it personally, take it on, or even assume it has anything to do directly with you."

Lark frowned and retorted, "It's hard not to take things personally. Gwen singled me out and got on her high horse. She, in her twisted way, implied we are to drop everything and tend only to her needs. She snarked at me when I said I needed some alone time. And you know what is most confusing? It's that Gwen is one of my best friends, and I love her. It's just not fair!"

Mom gently stroked Lark's head. "I know it's difficult. Growing up is difficult, and teenage emotions and the roller coaster of hormonal surges are unpredictable. I get it. I was once a teenager."

Lark crossed her arms and legs under the weight of the comforter, almost in protest. "But why does she have to be so mean to me and not the other girls?"

Mom became quiet, for she really did not have a good answer about this situation for Lark. But she went on with the hopes of saying something helpful to her daughter. "You and Gwen have been friends since kindergarten. I have seen firsthand Gwen's moodiness and temper. She likes to be the center of attention, and you have gone through many trials with her in the past. But the two of you always seem to resolve situations with time and patience. I know how much you love her and value her friendship. That is why you are so affected by her moods and actions. Maybe she reacts more to you than the others because she cares about you more and values your friendship."

Lark became quiet to ponder Mom's words. Mom's advice resonated, and she felt comfortable, more at ease, and able to release the pent-up tension in her body. Maybe Mom is right; their friendship is deeper, and they challenge each other to grow and heal. Lark thought about the conversation from their walk home and shared those details with Mom. And it was now beginning to make some sense to Lark. The promise to be there for each other was indeed a promise. Lark intuitively knew deep down it would mean in good times and in bad times. Lark had the advantage of Wisdom in her life and vowed to take the high road with this precious friendship. With that notion, she turned to face Mom and said, "Thanks, Mom, I love you."

Lark was becoming quite sleepy. She thought about Mom's words about not taking things personally. She thought that would be a good journal entry for tomorrow. Within moments, Lark was fast asleep beside Mom. Mom picked up her book and read for a while as she was sleeping, stroking her back and letting her rest. Mom smiled and relished this time with her firstborn.

Chapter 19:

Ice Cream, Shopping, & Old Friends

Things felt better the next morning, especially as Lark got to sleep late and lounged in bed. Her time with Mom was nice and very comforting. It's not too often she gets alone time with Mom, especially to talk about her feelings or problems. Her sisters always seem to be right around the corner, vying for her attention. Luckily, the girls were exhausted from the soccer tournament and fell fast asleep early and slept late the next morning.

Lark was glad to have another day off before returning to school. Sundays were generally a mellow day in the Roberts' home, starting with a leisurely breakfast and then playtime with her sisters. Mom would frequently make homemade waffles, eggs, and bacon. Mom and Dad considered Sunday a Family Day. A day to connect with one another, loaf around, and relax. Mom says relaxation is just as important as work! She says you can't have one without the other. Something else she could add to her journal. Her journal was becoming a valuable resource and source of comfort and pleasure.

Sundays were also a day to go into town and do fun things. Lark always loved the town picnics and craft fairs. But this Sunday was an ordinary family day, and not too much was planned. Everyone was glad to have a day to chill since yesterday's tournament was exhausting. As everyone wanted to just hang around, she asked Mom if she could go for a walk. She told her the fresh air would do her good, and she could get some perspective about the day before with her friends. Though things seemed to be fine and settled, Lark still felt a nagging twinge of discomfort. Mom said the day was hers to do as she pleased.

As Lark made her great escape and headed toward the Sanctuary of Life, she wanted desperately to speak with Wisdom. She had that twinge right in the middle of her stomach. It was a tight, gripping feeling. She stopped, paused, and became clearly aware of the content of the thoughts causing the feeling. It was indeed about yesterday with her friends, and specifically that uncomfortable scene at the pool with Gwen. Lark was inwardly focused on her friend's interactions, anxieties, and fears. Her mind was starting to race and spiral. She noticed those feelings did not feel good at all.

Then she realized something important: she was focused only on herself and did not consider the perspective of her friend. Wisdom was right; it was the spotlight-feeling thing. And then she realized she might not be a good friend to Gwen in a way that would be supportive to her. A tear fell from her eye and rolled down her face. Lark went to the end of the block and sat down on the cold, cement sidewalk. She got out her phone and sent a text message.

Lark waited patiently for Gwen's reply. She sat on the hard sidewalk and allowed her racing mind to drop into her heart, just the way Wisdom instructed. It was challenging for her to do today, but she knew it was exactly what she must do. Lark imagined she was back in the sanctuary, admiring Goldy the tree. She breathed, calmed her mind, and waited for a reply. Lark also realized something else of importance: she had been self-centered and therefore could not see the big picture or have perspective. In that moment, she allowed herself to get out of her head and into her heart. Yesterday, Gwen told Lark exactly what she needed from her and why she needed the support. Gwen gave her a gift. She communicated clearly, if only Lark would choose to see it from that vantage point.

Several more minutes went by, then Gwen replied. "Sure, I would love to go into town for ice cream, especially if it's your treat! Meet me at my house in fifteen minutes."

Lark smiled, rose from the ground, and went back home in a frenzied rush. She pushed the door open, came in like a whirlwind, and told Dad she had a change of plans and was going into town with Gwen. Dad called her over, smiled softly, and gave her twenty dollars. Lark hugged him and was out the door in a flash.

Gwen was patiently waiting for Lark outside. She was happy to have plans and escape from her house. She was thrilled Lark suggested spending the afternoon together but, of course, had to make a sarcastic dig. She smirked at Lark and said, "You felt guilty about yesterday, didn't you?"

Lark took a breath and paused. She wanted to remain centered and poised. She looked at her friend and said, "Yes, a bit. As I told you yesterday, I was not aware of how much you were struggling, and I was sorry for not being aware or considerate.

However, it would have been nice if you could have told me what was on your mind and how to be a better friend. After all, I am not a mind reader, and your dramatic scene in front of everyone was upsetting. I am not your punching bag."

Gwen looked bashful and said, "I guess you have a valid point."

They both agreed to do better with communication.

As they strolled into town, they were both unusually quiet. It was a beautiful spring day; the air was cool, and the sky was the perfect shade of blue. It was simply enough to enjoy the view and the surroundings. They allowed themselves to have a leisurely walk into town.

Since it was Sunday, some of the usual shops were closed. They peered in the windows and admired a few garments artistically displayed. Lark eyed a gorgeous pink fleece jacket mixed with shades of denim. She was disappointed the store was not open to try it on. She thought it would be perfect for the cooler evenings and told Gwen she just had to get this jacket—it was love at first sight. This was unusual for her as she never cared too much about fashion. Gwen also thought it was quite trendy. Maybe Lark could do extra chores around the house with the hope that Mom would raise her allowance. Gwen thought it would look great on her, and Lark was thrilled. Gwen even commented that it would make a nice addition to her wardrobe. Then in unison, they said, "Ice cream time."

The girls made their way to Sullivan's Ice Cream Shop. The girls were surprised by the line, especially as it was only 11 a.m., but hey, it's never too early in the day for ice cream. The girls noticed with delight all the delicious flavors; it was so hard to select from the many varieties. There were at least eight variations of chocolate, ranging from chocolate brownie, chocolate crunch,

Rocky Road, and dark chocolate. There was caramel, vanilla cherry, pistachio, raspberry ripple, to name a few other delectable flavors.

Then there was the selection of sugar cones and toppings. *Oh, what to get, what to get?* Lark told Gwen it was Dad's treat and to order whatever her heart desired. Gwen's eyes glistened, then went back to the showcase of ice cream flavors. There were extra helpers on the weekend, and Jonah's older brother Brian was on staff today. His job was to hand out samples. *What a fun job,* thought Lark.

Gwen said a friendly hello and requested a sample of vanilla with double chocolate chips. She loved the creaminess of the vanilla with the crunch of the chocolate chips. There were both dark chocolate chips and chocolate-covered crunchies. Truth be told, it was one of the shop's best sellers. Gwen then asked for a sample of strawberry cream. The strawberries were locally grown, so the freshness in that flavor tasted like a bite of summer. Gwen went for the vanilla chocolate chip in a chocolate cone. Brian smiled at her and said, "Excellent choice."

Brian looked over at Lark and said, "Your turn."

For a brief moment, Lark was confused and startled. She was not sure where she was. *My turn?* Thoughts silently flooded her mind. *Am I allowed to have a turn selecting something for myself?* That thought confused her. She said in a hesitating voice, "I would love a sample of the same flavors."

Brian said, "Coming right up, Lark." He handed her a tiny spoon with the confectionery delight.

As she put the ice cream sample in her mouth, it was pure heaven. Lark was enthralled with the tastes and how the sweetness made her feel. That vanilla chocolate crunch was amazing. He then handed her a sample of the strawberry. That too was delicious, just in another way. Brian looked over at Lark and said, "So what will it be?"

With a tone of self-assurance, she pronounced, "Key lime pie in a sugar cone."

Brian giggled and said, "That's so different from those flavors, but it's a crowd-pleaser."

Lark loved everything about key lime pie. The flavor reminded her of a family trip to Florida, where Dad searched high and low for key lime pie treats. At every stop and every meal, Dad would ask the restaurant if key lime pie was served. It became a guessing game in the car to accurately predict if the restaurant served a variation of key lime pie or cookies. Dad could eat it at every meal, and it made him so happy. It was a happy and certainly humorous trip that the entire family remembers fondly.

The girls took their ice creams, along with extra spoons and napkins, and found a table outside under the awning. It was fun to play tourists in their own hometown and watch the people strolling in and out of the ice cream parlor. The girls enjoyed each and every mouthful of the most delicious ice cream under the sun. They also tasted each other's flavors. Gwen was pleasantly surprised with the key lime pie and noted the sweetness mixed to perfection with the tartness of the key limes. It was nice to be present in the moment, enjoying the day, enjoying friendship, and, of course, enjoying ice cream. What could be better?

When the girls finished, they took a stroll around town. It was a warm day, and it felt nice to have time to do nothing. They walked up and down the parade of shops. They did some window shopping and went into some of the stores that were open for business. It was nice that the girls knew all the shop owners and were welcomed to browse around. After a while, they returned to the shop window with the pink fleece and blue denim jacket.

Gwen turned to Lark and said, "I am concerned about my mom. She does not seem happy. She is spending so much time in her room, and she yells a lot. The yelling is not always about me, but it's always about something. I am both worried and angry at her. She is driving me crazy."

Lark smiled at Gwen and said, "Thank you for sharing. It sounds rough for both of you. How can I help?"

Gwen looked at her friend, sighed, and said, "Not sure. I am at a loss. It's been hard to talk to Mom, and Dad has not been around too much."

"Would you like to talk to my mom? Maybe she would have words of advice."

Gwen looked at Lark and said, "Maybe, not sure."

Lark gently put her hand on Gwen's arm and said, "I can't imagine how difficult this must be for you, but please talk to your mom and at the very least tell her your concerns or simply that you love her. Maybe she just needs to be heard, the way you needed to be heard."

Gwen looked at Lark and said, "As always, you are right. I owe it to her to be understanding and let her know I care."

Then the girls set off to explore the rest of the shops before heading home.

As they walked home, Lark asked if she would like to come to dinner tonight. "Mom always cooks a lot on Sundays, and you can see my sisters. Hope has grown so much since you last saw her, and I think they would love to see you, too.”

Gwen said, “If it’s okay with your parents, that would be nice.”

The girls ventured through the neighborhood, enjoying the afternoon. They stopped at Gwen’s house, and to their surprise, Gwen’s mom, Rose, was in the kitchen, organizing papers. Rose was smiling and friendly, which surprised and thrilled Gwen. The three chatted for a long while about school, the upcoming summer vacation and, of course, about the pink fleece and denim jacket in the shop window. Gwen asked if she could go back to Lark’s house for dinner, and Rose said yes. On their way out, Gwen gave her mom a hug and said, “I love you, Mom. It’s nice to see you smiling today.”

Rose whispered into Gwen’s ear, “Love you too, and I’m sorry I’ve been in a rotten mood lately.”

Gwen hugged her mom tighter and then ran out the door to catch up with Lark, who wanted to give them some privacy.

On their way to Lark’s house, Gwen commented on how much better she felt after seeing her mom smile and telling her that she loved her. And she said, “I have been holding everything tightly inside and was afraid to say anything for fear things could get worse.”

Lark looked at her friend and said, “Thoughts and emotions are so confusing sometimes, and really get in the way of happiness. I wish I could have a magic wand to make it easier.”

Gwen laughed at Lark and said, “Race you to your house. I am faster than you and will beat you every time.”

The girls arrived at Lark’s house, and Mom was thrilled to see Gwen. It had been such a long time since the girls had a playdate the way they did when they were younger. Mom asked about Rose, and Gwen was comfortable saying she was fine. It was a small white lie, but she did not want to get into the details and ruin the great day. Lark asked if it was okay if Gwen stayed for dinner, and Mom smiled with delight.

The twins came running downstairs when they heard the girls arriving. Becca gave Gwen a great big hug, and Grace just sheepishly waved. Then little Hope followed in tow. Gwen picked her up and whirled her around in crazy Gwen fashion. The girls were thrilled to have her join them for dinner; it was a treat to have company. Lark's extended family lived in a different state, and visits were infrequent.

Mom prepared a huge green salad, followed by Italian meatballs, spaghetti, and roasted vegetables. Dad grated fresh Parmesan cheese to garnish the meal. The twins flooded Gwen with questions, especially about Taylor Swift. They wanted to know her favorite songs and what she was wearing to her upcoming concert. Dressing up with just the right outfit was a must for attending her concerts. It was all about participating in every aspect of the experience, and your outfit set the tone way in advance. Gwen's mom bought them tickets for her upcoming birthday, and she was overjoyed to say the least. She was looking forward to spending time with her mom outside the house.

Though Lark loved Taylor Swift, she was secretly thrilled not to attend live, as crowds were overwhelming for her.

The meal was a big hit, enjoyed by all. When it was time for Gwen to walk home, Hope gave her a big hug and then hid behind her big sister. Lark told Hope she would be right back to read to her, but wanted to walk Gwen down to the corner.

The girls embraced in a hug before Gwen turned the corner to go home. She thanked Lark for a great day, for the food and the fun. But as she turned the corner, she said in a snarky tone of voice, "See you tomorrow at school," along with a very strange look on her face.

Lark's stomach dropped, and she was frozen. Quickly, Lark replied, "It was a fun day together," and Gwen said a barely audible, "Yup."

As Lark walked back home, that uncomfortable, familiar feeling churned in her stomach. *What the hell?* she thought silently. *We had such a great day; it was easy and relaxed. But that last comment, her strange tone of voice, and that look. What was that all about? Okay, I am just being paranoid.* But it was as if Gwen turned into her evil twin sister.

When Lark returned home, Mom commented on how nice it was to see Gwen and that it had been a while since she had a friend over for dinner. Mom recounted the days during kindergarten when their playdates lasted for hours on end. It was helpful for Mom to have Lark happily occupied as the twins were little and needed a lot of attention.

Lark said it was a fun day. She told her all about the ice cream flavors and how fun it was to spend alone time without Ashley and Nikki. Sometimes it is just easier to spend time with one friend at a time. Mom agreed and acknowledged she felt the same way, too, with her friends. As Lark helped Mom clean the kitchen, she told her about Gwen's parting remark and *the look*. She felt her comment was disingenuous, and something was behind it.

Mom acknowledged her feelings and told her not to focus on that too much. She looked at her eldest daughter and reminded her to put her precious time, energy, and attention to matters that bring her joy and pleasure. "Otherwise, it's a waste of energy," she said.

Wow. Mom sounds just like Wisdom. Something else very wise to write in my journal later today.

Lark made her way upstairs and found Hope in her pajamas and getting ready for bedtime. As promised, she pulled a book from the shelf and read Hope a story. Hope loved the way she would animate the characters. Halfway through the book, Hope was sound asleep. Lark covered her comfortably, kissed her on the forehead, and turned out the light.

Finally, Lark was able to go into her room, close the door, and have some solitude. She pondered the weekend. *That was action-packed, to say the least.* She spent time with Wisdom and the girls and had her impromptu date with Gwen. She was a good friend today but felt confused about her feelings. Honestly, she did not trust Gwen's intentions, and she was not quite sure why this distrust was surfacing. They had been friends for a long time.

Lark realized she was searching outside herself for worthiness, belonging, and confidence. She expected her friends to give her the validation and reassurance she was desperately seeking. With that epiphany, she opened her red leather journal and wrote her entire experience from the weekend. She also included Mom's words of advice. She thought it would be helpful for her next encounter with Wisdom. She journaled until her hand hurt. She highlighted her epiphanies in yellow and marked her questions for Wisdom in green. Lark spent almost two hours journaling her thoughts. Though she was exhausted from the exercise, she felt so much better. She carefully tied the journal back up and tucked it into her backpack. And now she could sleep.

Chapter 20:

The Next Day

Lark rose the next day for school, well rested and energetic. She wished she had another day off for herself, but Mondays are school days. She washed up as usual and had breakfast with the twins.

Grace wanted Lark to help her with math again, as the newer topics were becoming challenging. Lark promised to help her during the week and reminded her to become aware of her mindset. She said, "Grace, you are more than capable of learning new math concepts. Give yourself patience and promise yourself you will be persistent with your homework. Sometimes a bit of practice goes a long way."

Grace smiled at Lark and said, "Oh yes, the other set of twins, practice and patience. But I like it when you sit down with me and give me private tutoring. You are the best, and it really helps."

Lark winked at Grace and said that they needed to get to the bus stop for school. She promised again to help her during the week. With that, the girls cleared away their breakfast dishes, collected their schoolbags, and headed straight to the bus stop down the block.

The school day started out in the usual fashion. First it was homeroom followed by subject classes, then a midday break for lunch and recess.

Lark saw Ashley and Carly during the first period and then Nikki the second period. All was well until she saw Gwen sitting at their usual table in the cafeteria. She sat down next to her, pulled out her usual PBJ sandwich, and jovially said, "This is definitely not as good as yesterday's ice cream at Sullivan's."

Gwen just gave her a look and no verbal reply. She then proceeded to chat with Ashley and reminisce about the great time on Saturday at her pool party. Ashley was sitting directly across from Gwen and Lark. She noticed the obvious tension between the two friends and was dumbfounded with confusion about how to reply. Ashley was thrilled that everyone had a great time on Saturday and thanked Gwen for the compliment. Then, with poise and grace, she gently turned the conversation to Lark. She saw that Lark was struggling and that Gwen was downright rude for no obvious reason. She was just as perplexed as Lark but did not let it show one bit. She asked Lark about the twins' soccer tournament and inquired about little Hope. All the girls loved Hope as she was the baby sister they all wanted.

Gwen seemed a bit rattled as the attention went to Lark. In a huff, she gathered her belongings and left the lunch table.

With Gwen out of earshot, Ashley asked Lark what was going on.

Lark shrugged her shoulders and had no answer. "Ashley, to tell you the truth, I am very upset. I don't know what to do. She has been so rude to me over the last few weeks, but only in public. When we are alone, all is well. Yesterday we spent the day together. I texted her in the morning to see if she wanted to go into town. I know I have been a bit distant lately. I apologized again, and we spent quality time together. She even had dinner at my house yesterday, and it was great. This is the last straw. I know her parents have been arguing, and it's stressful, but she can't take this out on me any longer. It's not fair, and I won't tolerate it any longer." Lark lowered her eyes in defeat. She was on the verge of tears.

Ashley inquired if she should talk to Gwen, but Lark was skeptical that it would be beneficial. She thought it could make the situation worse. Lark wanted time to ponder the recent events. She knew she must have an uncomfortable conversation with Gwen. The problem was fear of confrontation. Lark avoided confrontation at all costs. Going down that road was worse than getting a shot at the doctor's office.

Lark was torn inside. Her mind raced all afternoon, and the final four class periods felt like an eternity. She had to use all her tools from Wisdom. She thought scripting might be effective. She knew she would see Gwen on the bus and wanted things to get back on track. Yes, scripting! I will script out a comfortable scene on the bus where everything is resolved. However, she knew deep down a difficult conversation was necessary and that Gwen could get nasty fast. Lark had to stand up for herself. She had to be strong and know her own worth. She thought she was upset over the state of their friendship, but deep down knew it was something bigger. Lark had to learn to stand in her own power. If Lark could not have an honest conversation with Gwen and share what was on her mind, the disrespectful behavior would surely continue. *But why is Gwen acting this way? What did I do to deserve such cruel treatment? Dad sometimes says, "The less said, the better." Maybe this is what to do on the bus. Hmm. All this thinking is driving me crazy.* With that thought, Lark realized something important. All the "what ifs" never help because they usually never play out the way we think or project in our minds. Lark decided to stay present and connected to her heart during the bus ride home.

Finally, the last period bell rang. The students scattered about the hallways. They either headed to afternoon sports activities or to the bus line to go home. Gwen was on the bus in her usual seat. Lark decided to be brave and sit right next to her. Gwen gave Lark that look again. Lark was calm and courageously asked her to explain that look. She breathed deeply, stayed present, and waited for an answer.

Gwen said, "That was such a weird comment you made at lunch today about the ice cream. We are not kids anymore."

Lark replied in a firm and confident tone. "Perhaps I was just stating my opinion and recalling what a great day we had together. What is wrong with that?"

Gwen obnoxiously replied, "The whole world does not have to know our private business."

In that moment, Lark knew something she did not want to know. Gwen wants a private rather than a public friendship. And that is not going to fly anymore. Lark calmly said to Gwen, "I did not realize having ice cream at Sullivan's is a private matter."

Gwen said, "Well, I think it is." Her bus stop approached, and Gwen was out the door in a flash.

Lark did everything to hold back tears on the ride to her stop. She was absolutely stunned by Gwen's remark. Was that the same person from yesterday, who was heartfelt, friendly, open, and honest? *What is going on here? Does she really think we can have only a secret friendship? We are in the same group of friends. Does she think I would be okay with this arrangement?*

Lark went up the walkway to the front door of her home. She did not want to talk to anyone. She wanted to be left alone to think about this situation. Inside, she was absolutely hurt and devastated. She felt used and abused. Lark desperately wanted to flee her house and find Wisdom. She went straight to her room, changed her clothes, and found her backpack for hiking. She knew she would have to see Mom and her sisters before heading outside. Mom would inquire about her day and if she wanted an after-school snack. But all Lark wanted to do was cry. She had no appetite for food. Luckily, Mom was on her phone on a business call. She waved to get her attention, saying she was going for a walk and would be home before dinner. Mom blew her a kiss, and Lark made a mad dash for the door.

On her way to the Sanctuary of Life, she cried and cried. Lark was totally perplexed with the events of the day but not surprised. Gwen had been nasty to her over the last few weeks. At first, it was small slights and comments, then this weekend with the girls took the cake. Lark knew in her heart she was a good friend, but she refused to be a pushover. Lark was feeling a range of conflicting emotions—sadness, anger, and fear mixed with feelings of boldness. *Where is all this coming from?*

A few minutes later, Lark reached the Sanctuary of Life and was not too surprised to see the big steel gate locked, barring her easy entrance. Lark shook the bars, almost pleading to let her in and make an exception. More tears fell and rolled down her face, and all this felt totally unfair. Lark felt defeated. She took a deep breath and, in the privacy of her own thoughts, begged Wisdom to appear. She pleaded in her mind for Wisdom to show up, help, and offer comfort.

As Lark turned around to sink toward the ground, there she was in a long silver robe and the sparkling amulet around her neck. Wisdom slowly walked toward Lark and took her into her arms. She let Lark cry and cry until her eyes ran out of tears. She held her in complete silence until she relaxed and settled down.

When Lark was calm, Wisdom said, "Crying can be very cleansing for the soul. It's okay to cry and feel your feelings. As a matter of fact, it is healthy and helps to bring the emotional body back into alignment."

Lark just shook her head, happy for the permission to cry, to feel her feelings, and release the tension. When Lark was ready to form coherent words, she said, "My eyes must be beet red."

Wisdom just nodded and said, "They are a lovely shade of red today."

Then they both laughed. Wisdom waved her hand, and the entrance gate disappeared into a thin, white mist.

They walked together into the Sanctuary of Life. Wisdom did not take Lark to the outside classroom as she suspected she might do. Instead, Wisdom led her to a beautiful waterfall. The water falling from the mountaintop looked iridescent as it cascaded down into a small pool. It shimmered with all the colors of the rainbow. This sight felt so healing for Lark. She was able to breathe deeply once again.

They found a place to sit on the soft grass. Wisdom magically produced a comfortable blanket for Lark to lie upon and rest. As she relaxed, Wisdom lightly stroked her head and forehead. Wisdom's light touch felt so soothing. She wanted to tell her all about the recent events with Gwen, but words or details were not needed, for Wisdom knew all. Wisdom acknowledged the challenging events and validated Lark's thoughts and feelings. She said, "This is one of those pivotal moments in your life that will rock you to your core, challenge your beliefs, and catapult you into growth and transformation. That is, if you let it. It can take you down one of two roads. One road contains detours of self-pity, blame, and victimhood. The other road will take grit, determination, and strength. It's the proverbial high road. That road is the way to resilience, accomplishment, self-validation, and inner peace. It's about learning to embrace your own power, spirit, and inner wisdom."

Lark looked at Wisdom with swollen eyes and said, "I have power and inner wisdom?"

"Yes, you do," echoed from Wisdom's lips.

"Well, if it's really there, it feels buried deep down," Lark retorted.

Wisdom went on to explain. "That's why you are here, in the sanctuary, to learn what you already know."

Lark was totally confused, which surprisingly felt better than being scared. "How can I learn what I already know?"

Wisdom replied, "That is one of life's grandest mysteries. It's to unlock wisdom and knowledge that is already inside. It's just like the apps on your phone that are preinstalled and are dormant. Sometimes people don't know the apps are available until they are needed. Then you learn how to use the app for the required purpose."

"Oh, I am starting to get it. It's like I instinctually knew how to ride my bike without Dad having to teach me."

"Yes, your mind knew how to help you balance, pedal, and go forward on the bicycle."

Then Lark rolled her eyes downward. "But she was mean to me, and I was trying my best to listen and be a good friend. I don't know how to sort this out."

Wisdom lifted Lark's chin, looked directly into her eyes, and somberly said, "Dear child, sometimes you can't sort out life's injustices. You just must make peace with the fact that not all friendships last forever. There is a season for everything, and sometimes seasons last for years, and other times for short periods of time. But when something ends, usually there is a new beginning, space for something new and wonderfully unexpected to bloom.

"It all starts with allowing things to be the way they are, without forcing things to be different. Like in nature, there are sunny days and rainy days. We can't control the weather, only our reactions to the weather." Wisdom paused for a moment and went on to say, "I know these are very grown-up concepts for you to understand. And to help you feel better, here is another secret: most grown-ups can't grasp or understand this concept, and they waste years in an uphill battle trying to control outcomes. They think trying to control people or circumstances will help them feel safe. Holding on too tight or trying to control is not the answer. The secret is to let go and trust."

Lark was silent for a long time. She reached for her red, leather-bound journal and wrote down everything Wisdom shared with her to review when she got home. She took so many handwritten notes that her hand hurt. When she was done, she looked up and asked Wisdom, "What should I do about Gwen? I was so embarrassed today, and I wanted to give her a piece of my mind."

Wisdom looked at her young student. "Lark, do you want to force something with Gwen? Do you think that will help rectify the situation?"

Lark bowed her head and said, "No, that probably won't do any good."

Wisdom smiled and agreed. "I wish I could offer you magic words to make Gwen see the error of her ways and return your kindness and appreciate your friendship. But no such words exist. The key is to stay in your own space, hold your head high, and know your worth. The most important relationship you will ever have is the one with yourself. Be proud of who you are and the love in your heart. Friendships are a two-way street, and if kindness is not respected and returned, it's best to seek new friends."

Lark's eyes finally brightened. She declared, "You are right! I am a good friend and if she does not want to be my friend, that's just fine. I have better things to do and better ways to spend my time and energy. Hey, I have three great sisters who love me and other friends who are way easier. Mom also said it is important to focus my time and attention on people who bring joy and laughter."

Wisdom smiled and said, "Your mom is very wise. Confide in your mother and listen to her advice."

Wisdom rose from the blanket and admired the waterfall. She told Lark she brought her to this magical spot so the energy of the water could wash away her hurt and leave her refreshed. Lark thought the spot was pristine. She remarked how the sound of the crashing water into the small pool below was a helpful distraction. She also loved how the mist of the cool water felt on her skin. Plus, the colorful rays of water were incredible to witness. Lark remarked that the experience was healing.

At that point, Wisdom encouraged Lark to head home and be with her family. She wanted her not only to be with her family but to be present with them and to enjoy the gift of their company. Lark promised to do so as she tucked her journal into her backpack. Wisdom escorted Lark to the paved path heading home. She made her way home just before the sun set for the evening.

Lark allowed herself the gift of time as she strolled home. She realized Wisdom answered the questions she had written in her journal the night before! She did not even have to ask her questions out loud. *How does she do that?*

She pondered the events of the last few days. She truly loves her friends and would do anything for them. She even loves Gwen, just like a sister. But Gwen has not been a good friend in return. She has been unkind and nasty. *I cannot allow myself to be treated in this fashion. I would certainly advise my sisters to avoid those types of people. So why should I continue to allow myself to be subject to this type of treatment? Okay, let's see what tomorrow brings and deal with events as they occur. As Wisdom says, you can't control the words or actions of others.*

As Lark opened the front door to her home, she smelled the delicious aroma of fresh, hot pizza. Pizza—a delight to all the senses. Her mouth was salivating, and she could not wait to bite into the first slice of cheesy deliciousness. Mom told the girls to wash up before sitting down at the dinner table. Lark was already steps ahead of Mom's request, and her hands and face were freshly washed. While her sisters fought about who used which sink, Lark stole a moment with Mom. She told her about the conversation with Gwen and how distraught she was about her rude and dismissive comments. Mom was shocked herself, as she had seemed at ease and right at home the day before. She was engaging and friendly with the whole family. It just did not make sense to anyone. Mom asked if she had confided in Ashley or Nikki. Lark said it was best to leave them out of the situation, at least for now, and Mom agreed. Moments later, the girls filed into the dining room, ready to devour the pizza.

Later that night, Mom went into Lark's room. Lark was rather calm considering the events with Gwen. She reviewed her journal notes and added some insights she had contemplated on her walk home. Mom asked Lark how she could help. She was not sure if her daughter needed to vent, or be given advice, or a warm hug. Lark did want to know Mom's take on the events, so she shared. She shared and shared until she felt depleted. Wisdom had advised her to trust and confide in Mom, so she allowed herself to ramble on about the events. At the end of her storytelling, Lark folded her arms and crossed her legs.

Mom was flabbergasted at what she just heard. "How could she be so two-faced? It just does not make any sense at all," she said. Mom inquired if she should call Rose. The women were not necessarily friends, but they were friendly when it came to their girls.

Lark begged her not to get involved in any way. She thought it would make matters worse, and Mom agreed. Mom asked Lark how she planned on handling the situation, as she was clueless and had no clever words to share. She was stuck with no good motherly advice or guidance.

Lark said, "Nothing. I will not beg or convince her to change her ways. She wants attention, and I am done lowering myself to make her feel better. I think my attention helps her to feel better in the moment, and then her respect for me as a friend dwindles. Perhaps I am assuming, but it feels true. I don't know why it is that way, but I'm done. And as you said, I should focus my precious energy on people who bring me joy and appreciate my friendships. I am a good friend, and it will be her loss."

Mom was pleased to see Lark so strong and determined. She looked at her and said, "I am proud of you. Growing up is challenging, especially the teen years." With that, she kissed her daughter good night.

Chapter 21:

The Day After

The next morning was rather chilly, but the fresh, cool air was delightfully refreshing. The girls found sweatshirts for the morning bus ride to school. Lark favored her black, zip-up sweatshirt, and the twins each selected their yellow soccer sweatshirts.

The bus arrived promptly on time. And as Lark boarded and searched for an open seat, there was Gwen, smiling happily. She was wearing the pink fleece and blue denim jacket from the boutique! *Unbelievable! She knew I wanted to get that jacket!!! The nerve of her to go behind my back. Okay, remain calm and take no notice of the jacket… at least for now.* Lark smiled and walked right past Gwen. The seat next to Carly was free, and she asked if she could sit down.

Carly's eyes brightened, and she said, "Of course. I had a question from science class." The girls chatted the entire way to school, and it felt great to have an easy conversation with a friend. There was no drama, just chatter.

Entering the building, the students went to their lockers to put away backpacks and jackets before attending homeroom. After Lark retrieved her books for the first period, she walked up to her friends. Nikki, Ashley, and Gwen were standing by their lockers, admiring Gwen's new pink fleece and blue denim jacket. Lark confidently circled around Gwen several times, looked her up and down, and proclaimed, "I am so glad you got the jacket we both admired on Sunday. It looks great on you!"

Nikki then chimed in, "Yes, it really is unique."

Gwen lowered her eyes and said, "Thanks."

With that, the bell rang, and the girls went to their first class of the day.

As Lark walked to science class, she felt proud of how she handled that situation. She stood in her power, spoke confidently, and did not let Gwen get the best of her. She thought about her time with Wisdom and her conversation with Mom. She realized that every time she tries to placate Gwen, she lowers herself, and Gwen has less respect for their friendship. She thought this was all too "extra," and she should not have to put up with the nonsense. Lark could not even imagine pulling a stunt like that with a friend. *How rude,* she thought.

When she entered the classroom, Carly was waiting for her with her notebook open. She wanted Lark's help with a scientific formula before the teacher started class. Carly was genuinely appreciative for the help. It felt good to assist and be appreciated. That certainly felt better than the recent experiences with Gwen. The teacher promptly started the lesson, and Lark was able to focus her mind and participate in class.

The rest of the day went smoothly. Lark called Carly over to sit with the girls at lunchtime. Gwen was actually behaving decently and noticeably left the new jacket in her locker. She was quite reserved the entire period. Lark made it a point to include Carly in the conversations, and Ashley and Nikki were friendly, but then again, those two are always kind. It was Gwen who was the wild card. They chatted about music, their teachers, and plans for summer break. Lark found it a relief to have a pleasant conversation. By the end of the lunch break, Lark thought to herself, *Friendships are meant to be easy, and low-maintenance friends are the best!*

As the school day ended, Lark found herself quietly walking to the bus. She was thinking about the events of the day and was rather proud of her resilient attitude. Gwen came up from behind her and called her name. Lark decided to continue walking and ignored her, as she was still angry and resentful from the recent events.

"Lark, did you not hear me calling you?"

Lark turned to face Gwen and said, "Yes, I did hear you quite clearly."

"I was trying to get your attention."

"I figured as much."

Gwen looked at her and said in a very low voice, barely audible, "Sorry."

Lark did not reply and made her way to the bus stop. Gwen followed her and sat right behind her on the bus and said, "Did you hear me before when I said sorry?"

Lark said, "I did hear you, and if you are really sorry, act like it."

The girls rode the bus in silence and got off at their respective stops with no further mention of the incident.

Lark raced into the house and was famished for an after-school snack. Mom had made some fresh blueberry muffins that filled the house with the delicious scent of a bakery. They were on top of the stove, cooling. Lark could not help herself and took the biggest muffin she could find with a tall, ice-cold glass of milk.

"Why, hello, Lark." Mom was sitting at the kitchen table finishing up some office work. Lark was startled as she did not see Mom quietly seated. "How was your day?"

"Honestly, it was fine, considering."

"Considering what?"

"You are not going to believe this, but Gwen purchased the pink fleece and blue denim jacket from the boutique. It was the exact one she knew I wanted to purchase with money from extra chores."

"Hold on for a moment. What jacket? From what boutique? And what is all this about doing extra chores? This is the first I am hearing about any of this, so please explain."

"Well, you see, when we were in town, I saw this amazing pink fleece and blue denim jacket. The store was closed, so I could not try it on. I thought it was so stylish and would be a nice upgrade for my wardrobe. After our ice cream, we passed by the window again, and I absolutely fell in love with it, and Gwen agreed it would look great on me. I have no idea how much it cost, but I guessed it was expensive. So, I thought I could earn some extra money by helping more in the house or tutoring Grace. I planned on asking, but did not have a chance to ask with the recent Gwen situation."

"Oh, I see," Mom said.

"She knew I loved that jacket and wanted it for the cooler evenings."

"So, what did you say when you saw her wearing it today?"

"I told her it looked great on her! I did not flinch a muscle or bat an eyelash. If she wanted the jacket so much, let her have it. It's not important. I think she may have respected me a bit more as I stood up to her today. It was not easy, but I made myself act confidently and stand my own ground. Mom, to tell you the truth, I thought it was a need to be needed and the need to do things to be a good friend. But I learned something very important over the last few days. I must be a good friend to myself first before I can be a good friend to another person or even a good sister. I was doing everything to appease Gwen, and I made myself feel sick inside. That just did not feel right."

Mom smiled with delight once again. "You are 100 percent correct. Thank you for expressing that insight so clearly. I never thought of it that way and think I, too, need to learn that very same lesson."

"The muffins are delicious, Mom. Your best batch ever. Hey, I have some homework to do, then can I go for a walk?"

"Yes, you may certainly go for a walk. I see those walks are really helping you to clear your mind. I would love to go with you one day."

"Okay, Mom, maybe on the weekend."

Lark hurried upstairs before the girls came home. They had soccer practice and stayed after school. Lark preferred when the house was quiet, as the twins often created noise. She opened her red, leather-bound journal. She wanted to jot down the events of the day and her epiphany she had shared with Mom: *You must be a good friend to yourself first before you can be a good friend to another.* This insight, her very own *wisdom*, felt great.

She finished journaling her thoughts, then proceeded to complete her homework. An hour flew by, and it was finally free time to head over to the Sanctuary of Life. She wondered what adventures would be in store for her today.

Chapter 22:

Lark's New Realization

Lark did not have much time this afternoon and decided to test out her new running shoes. Well, they were not so new; she just never actually used her sneakers to run. The faster pace felt exhilarating. She loved the way her heart felt as it pounded in her chest. Lark felt strong and very much alive and capable. As she arrived at the Sanctuary of Life, she noticed no gate. *Hmm*, she wondered, *What's up today? I guess it's okay to enter and explore.*

She went over to Goldy and admired her golden leaves. Today, there were white flowers at the base of her trunk. They were so delicate that Lark took extra care not to step on them for fear of crushing the precious petals. She felt Goldy's energy and knew she could talk to her as if she were a friend. Lark said she imagined using some of Goldy's strength during the day and being rooted deeply to Mother Earth. She also made a separate decision to stay true to her own convictions. She went on to tell Goldy that it took strength and courage to stay true to her heart.

Inwardly, she was frightened about any kind of confrontation with Gwen. The fear of humiliation was overwhelming. She felt rightfully angry at Gwen for being a terrible friend. She did not like this mix of feelings; they felt lousy in her mind and body.

Lark took a slow, deep breath and allowed her mind to settle. In that quiet and stillness, she had another thought; it was a whisper of a thought. *I am angrier with myself for playing small and not wanting to be seen. This is a sacrifice I am no longer willing to allow for the benefit of another.* Lark realized true happiness is an inside job. While others can add to your joy and happiness, lasting happiness and satisfaction must spring from inside oneself. At that very moment, Lark felt a rush of joy and energy. Her face had a glowing smile from ear to ear, and she felt peace with a sense of pure freedom. She felt free from the need to people-please and seek outside validation. Lark was getting a real sense of her authentic self, or at least a glimpse.

As she turned around to continue her exploration, she noticed Wisdom behind the elder tree. Lark was fascinated with the story of Henry and wondered if it was really true. Was this tree really the oldest tree in the Sanctuary of Life? Lark walked over to Henry, the elder tree, and admired his thick trunk and huge, deep roots. It was fun to stand and balance on his bold roots above the ground.

Wisdom went over to Lark and complimented her big smile. "Tell me, Lark, what brings that smile to your face today?"

Lark jumped off the roots to the ground below, where her feet were steady, and she was well grounded.

She grinned and said, "I stood up for myself."

Wisdom nodded in acknowledgment. "Tell me more, Lark."

"I think Gwen was trying to get the best of me or seeking attention in an underhanded way, and I refused to play the game. Fighting and debating with her was draining my energy and causing me to doubt myself. I was feeling anxious way too often, and it was really getting to me. It was affecting my attention in class and how I was interacting with my other friends. I think Nikki and Ashley noticed I was acting insecure and just not myself."

"How did you arrive at this conclusion or understanding?"

"To be frank, I am not sure. I just seemed to notice a pattern, like patterns in art, clothing, nature, and even the changes of the seasons. It would be an ordinary moment where several of us were gathered, and then Gwen would say or do something outlandish that did not make sense. It was like she was trying to get a reaction or attention. The butt of the joke was usually at my expense or embarrassment. I would draw on memories of our long-term friendship and try to help or be a friend to her. She would be receptive and friendly. Then I would believe our friendship was on solid ground once again, only to be humiliated more the next day. It was like a revolving, spiraling pattern. Wisdom, I just don't get it at all. She says she is struggling at home and needs support and friendship. I give it willingly, only for her to turn on me and be cruel. I am a loyal friend, but I don't like this pattern of friendship. It's not kind or fair to me."

"This is very astute of you, Lark! Look at you observing patterns and feelings inside yourself. Let's walk and discuss this further."

The two meandered their way through the trees that were lush and full of greenery and flowers. There was a honeysuckle scent that filled the air. It was a fragrance so sweet; you could almost taste it in your mouth. After a while, they found a comfortable spot on an old wooden log. They sat down, and Wisdom turned to face Lark. Lark noticed the sparkling pendant with gemstones that represented the elements of nature. Lark remarked how the pendant could also represent opposites, and Wisdom praised her wise observation.

Wisdom suggested she open her journal. "Let's detail how you drew your conclusion about repeating patterns and anxious feelings. What do you think about this idea?"

Lark's eyes widened, and she thought it was a great idea. Wisdom encouraged Lark to review her previous journal notes from the recent events and highlight or underline anything that stood out as relevant. Lark went through her recent entries and marked some relevant points.

Wisdom then looked at her journal and complimented her work. "Okay, next, list everything you did to help yourself through the events."

Lark looked up in her mind to remember all she did, then eagerly began to write in her journal.

- Became aware of what I was thinking and how the thinking made me feel.
- Realized my mind was a flurry of worry.
- Became aware of my breathing and slowed my breath.
- Allowed my thinking mind to drop into my heart space.
- Realized I get to be the boss of my brain.
- Imagined what Wisdom would say.
- Faced my fears and spoke honestly with Gwen.
- Attempted to trust my inner guidance system.
- Realized I was looking for validation and confidence outside myself.

- Question to self: Am I making assumptions or taking things personally?
- Confided in Mom, and it felt good to share with her.
- Scripted how I wanted things to go with Gwen the next day.
- Then the biggest realization of all: I was people-pleasing in order to hold onto friendships and not allowing myself to be authentic.

After this exercise, Lark looked at Wisdom and said, "I tend to follow along with the leader to fit in with friends. I thought going with the flow and doing what they want to maintain friendships was easier and would make me happy. I realized today I don't want to be a follower anymore. I want to be me, my real self. I want friendships that are easy and ones that go both ways. I want friendships to give me grace when bad moods strike and to call me out on my bad behavior, but with support and love. I don't want to feel judged or scared that my friends will abandon me if I say the wrong thing. I am done with hiding my real self. It's too hard faking, which makes my stomach hurt, and then I feel like a fraud. Then, when I hide myself or people-please too much, I feel incredibly anxious."

Lark paused for a while, and Wisdom remained quiet so she could process. Lark then said, "Is that why I have been so anxious for so long? Was I acting from the fear in my head rather than the love in my heart?"

Wisdom gave Lark that half smile, and she asked, "What do you think?"

Lark whispered, "Yes."

Wisdom applauded her student with her wise perceptions and observations. "You are doing well. This is where the real work and transformation begin. This is what is considered the long road. It will take some effort, but it's the way to freedom and happiness. You see, every person is born unique. There are no two people the same, nor should anyone have the same experience as another. You were born to be unique, different, and that is why everybody is precious and special. People were meant to follow the way of their heart, not the path others have traveled. One cannot emulate another and expect true inner happiness. Each person has their own song to sing, their own book to write, their own path to follow. That is what makes this world beautiful. I am happy you discovered the call of your heart and now promise to stay true to its whispers."

Lark looked at Wisdom and said, "Wow, this has been a lot today."

Wisdom agreed and suggested she take a moment of quiet reflection for herself before heading home. Lark thought that was a great idea. "But Wisdom, I have one more question for today."

She turned to look at her prize student.

"May I tell people about you? May I tell people about the Sanctuary of Life? I want to share this place with them."

Wisdom replied, "If you could share this place with only one person and one person only, who would that be?"

Lark pondered and replied, "Jonah. I think he will be open to this, and you could really help him."

"That is very interesting," remarked Wisdom.

Wisdom started walking toward the elder tree, and Lark followed. She turned to Lark and said, "Remember, this place exists in your mind, in a way that is friendly and receptive to your imagination. You were ready as a student, and I appeared to you in this form and fashion. I know you have a heartfelt desire to share this place with Jonah, but this is not a real place, the way your school has a specific address. This place exists in your mind, and you have been receptive to its calling. When you walk in this direction, it is a welcoming invitation for you to enter this realm and absorb the love and knowledge being offered to you.

"In the same way, when bedtime approaches, you begin a routine of winding down from the hustle and bustle of the day. You wash up, brush your teeth, pack your bags for school, and maybe clean up your room a bit. Then you like to read before sleep. This helps your mind relax. You notice the night sky or maybe hear the chirp of crickets out your window. When it's time for sleep, you get into bed and feel the familiar comfort of your pillow and blanket. Then, when you turn off the lights and close your eyes, you begin to naturally enter the realm of sleep. Do you understand how you naturally enter these different realms of consciousness?"

"It's beginning to make more sense now."

"You may certainly share your experiences of being mindful and connected to nature with Jonah. Do bring him here and show him this place, then allow him to reflect to you what he experiences. Nature itself is a wonderful teacher. I encourage you to drop small breadcrumbs and see if he is eager to follow the trail. One day, you will be a teacher, but now you are still a student. Enjoy being a student and avoid rushing the process." With that, Wisdom winked at Lark, and they found themselves by the paved path, and Lark knew it was time to head home.

She walked for a while in silence, and just before she turned the corner to head toward her home, there was Jonah. He was riding his bike. *Wow, what a coincidence,* she thought. The two stopped and chatted for a while. They spoke about school and Brian's new job at Sullivan's. Truth be told, Lark really liked Jonah and valued his friendship. He was always kind and respectable. Before they each left to head home, he asked her if she would like to walk the trails on Friday afternoon. Lark smiled at Jonah and said she would like that very much! Jonah blushed and said, "Okay, let's meet right here at 4 p.m. on Friday."

Chapter 23:

A Walk with Jonah

Yeah! School was finished for the week. Time for the weekend! As promised, Lark arrived at the corner promptly on time. It was a few minutes later when Jonah arrived. He apologized for being late. The two acknowledged it was nice to spend time together without their parents within earshot. They giggled in unison. As they walked the path toward the trails, Jonah mentioned their conversation from last Saturday was very inspiring. He appreciated sharing he was struggling with fearful thoughts getting the best of him. He did not realize others deal with similar intrusive thinking.

Lark turned to Jonah and said, "I get it completely. Sometimes my mind races and won't shut off. Usually, it is about what others could be thinking about me or if my friends really like me or not. When I get in those ruts, my stomach hurts, and I feel so off and dizzy. But it's been better lately, and these walks help to clear my mind and settle anxieties. Being amongst the trees and nature is so peaceful and soothing."

"I can't wait to get there, so let's hurry up."

The two amped up their speed. When they arrived, the trees were in all their glory. It was a picture-perfect day.

Lark guided Jonah through what she perceived as the Sanctuary of Life. But today, it appeared more ordinary to her, except for Goldy. She was there with all her magnificent golden leaves. She stopped by her favorite tree and introduced her to Jonah. He looked at her and was confused. Was he supposed to talk to the tree like a person?

Lark giggled and said, "Just feel her essence as if she were a person. After all, trees are alive and have an amazing life force."

Jonah agreed with that notion and looked at Goldy more closely than before. He noticed her bark, her deep roots, her gorgeous golden leaves and, of course, the knothole that looked like a human eye. He even put his arms around her and was shocked that the width of her trunk was larger than the span of his arms. "I never hugged a tree before, and honestly, it feels good!"

Lark was pleased. "Jonah, I was reading online that trees are interconnected under the forest floor and support each other in a variety of amazing ways. When a tree is ailing, maybe it has a fungus or lacks a nutrient, it can ask for help from the surrounding trees. One way is by blooming early in the season, a way to signal it's experiencing weakness. It gathers nutrients while it's able, hoping for more time to spread its seed, to extend its cycle of life. It sends a special signal to the surrounding trees that it requires support to survive. That tree holds no shame for having a moment of illness, difficulty, or weakness. It instinctively knows asking for help is a good thing, a natural thing. Trees would not give asking for help a second thought, but then again, trees don't think, or do they?

"When I read this, it made me pause and think. I was afraid to ask for help or tell anyone I was hurting inside. I have a great family and friends, but I was ashamed to ask for help. I thought they might judge me or tell me it would go away, or not to be concerned. But when I read about trees, I wanted to be like this one right here, Goldy, who shines all the time and knows she is worthy and beautiful. I wanted to be strong and grounded. So, when I am here, I feel connected to this ecosystem, and all feels right with the world. What can I say? This must sound so weird."

Jonah took Lark softly by the hand, smiled, and said, "It sounds just right, very helpful and hopeful."

Just then, Lark asked Jonah if he would like to venture a little bit further. She wanted to introduce him to Henry, the elder tree. She was fascinated with the legend surrounding this tree and thought Jonah would be intrigued as well!

He was eager and said, "Lead the way."

The two made their way to the elder tree. She told Jonah it was believed that Henry was the oldest tree in these woods. She pointed to his super wide trunk that seemed to be squashed down by the weight of his heavy branches, which were twisted in all directions. Jonah was fascinated that she gave names to the trees.

Beside Henry they found a rather large, fallen tree trunk. Jonah marveled at its smooth surface. He let his hand gently swipe the surface and was fascinated with what the elements of nature could accomplish. They wondered if this tree trunk was as old as Henry. The two sat down next to each other and placed their hands on their laps.

Lark encouraged Jonah to close his eyes and breathe. She said, "Take a long inhale and feel the cool, fresh air entering your lungs. Now hold the inhale… and when you are ready, exhale twice as long. I will be quiet as you continue to breathe deeply like this for a few minutes."

Jonah loved the experience and remarked that he never takes time to simply breathe.

"Great, let's sit here for a few more moments in silence and just breathe deeply."

And that they did. They were quiet and breathed the crisp afternoon air for several moments. They gave themselves the gift of time and silence. When Jonah opened his eyes, he shared how calm he felt in his mind and body. He said it reminded him of Thanksgiving with his family several years ago, when they were all playing tag football together and having a great time. Everyone was laughing, enjoying the outside family experience followed by the delicious meal his father prepared. It was one of his favorite family memories. Lark was thrilled that he had a positive experience.

She asked if he was ready to head back, and Jonah agreed it was time to head home. As they made their way back out and past the Henry, Jonah stopped and turned to Lark. He said, "This may sound strange, but when we were over there breathing deeply, I heard a voice from within that I had never heard before. It was very, very soft, almost inaudible."

"Oh, tell me more." Lark thought she sounded just like Wisdom and giggled to herself.

He went on to say it was very subtle and that all he heard was "You're okay." He heard this repeating in his mind a few times, and each time it was softer and gentler.

"Well, how did that make you feel, Jonah?"

Jonah smiled and said, "That I really am okay. It gave me a sense of hope, and I liked it."

Lark hugged Jonah and said, "I am so glad!"

The two made their way back home with less chatter than before, each contemplating their experience. Lark was thrilled to share this space with her friend. She did not need to share about her rather unusual experiences with Wisdom, or that she refers to it as the Sanctuary of Life. It would probably sound goofy and take away from his own mystical experience. Lark, of course, was correct to share but not share. *It was great to share this place in the woods with Jonah, as it is real and known to all. And it was also rewarding to not share my special secret. It truly feels good to have something all for myself.*

Jonah was happy to have a special day with Lark and get the gift of inner peace. He asked if he could accompany her again soon, and Lark nodded her head in agreement. "That would be nice. Now I've got to get home before Mom starts calling, asking about my whereabouts," she said.

The two laughed, then went their separate ways.

Chapter 24:

Henry, the Elder Tree

Lark woke up Saturday morning refreshed from a good night's sleep. All felt right in her world. She spent some lazy time lounging in bed, reflecting on her time with Jonah. She loved sharing her experience in nature, particularly in her favorite spot—the Sanctuary of Life. She thought it was interesting how she could share a personal experience without sharing all the specific details. She had something all her own she could privately treasure and share at the same time. She would have her experience in the sanctuary, and Jonah would have his own unique experience. Maybe that was the real secret of the sanctuary, its life force reveals itself personally to the individual in the most meaningful ways.

She loved that Jonah had a transformative experience and heard a helpful message that was uniquely his own. Wisdom was spot on with her advice about not sharing all the details. It was way more powerful for Jonah to have his own unbiased encounter. It's like seeing a rainbow for the very first time; the awe and wonder of the marvel of a beautiful sight in nature is to be experienced with one's eyes. It's just like the saying goes: A picture is worth a thousand words. Jonah's time settling his body, completely immersed in nature, was exactly what he needed on that day. Lark's personal experiences might have only added pressure on Jonah for it to be her way. In that moment, Lark realized something, *There really is no one right way.*

With that notion, she put on her bathrobe and headed downstairs to see what the family planned for the day. Grace greeted her with a big frown. "You promised to help me with math again, and you were too busy for me this week. I really need your help again. My mind is all over the place, and you are the only one who can help."

Lark smiled softly and agreed she did drop the ball and promised to help this weekend. In the meantime, she prompted Grace. "Write down the thoughts that are floating in your mind, getting in the way, and bothering you. Give yourself just five minutes and jot down all the random thoughts. Then we will talk about the thoughts and the math. How does that sound?"

Grace looked at Lark and said, "Weird, but if you insist, I will do it."

When Lark returned to the kitchen hoping that Mom had whipped up a batch of her famous pancakes, Becca reminded everyone she had plans with friends. Mom remembered and promised to drive her into town. Meanwhile, she was cooking up a storm and made enough pancakes for everyone to have second helpings. Lark loved the weekends and the simplicity of the mornings. There was no frantic rushing, no school, just breakfast with her family.

After devouring three huge pancakes with a side of scrambled eggs, Lark texted the girls to see if anyone wanted to hang out later in the day. She thought it would be fun to go into town or ride bikes. She finished making her bed, washed up, and got dressed for the day. An hour or so passed, and no one replied. She thought it was weird, checked the text and noticed the message was indeed sent. *Hmm, okay then, I will get some homework done, and by then, someone will respond and be free to play.* Another hour went by, then two hours and no reply. *Well, that is strange. Alright then, if no one is around, I'll go for a walk to my happy place.* Lark laced up her sneakers, packed her lightweight hiking backpack with the red leather-bound journal and off she went.

She was in bliss as she hit the trails. Lark was practicing running and thrilled her endurance was improving. She was able to go much longer stretches without a break. She was proud of her progress. A few moments before approaching her favorite spot, she noticed Jonah heading back home. The two stopped to catch up. Truth be told, she was thrilled to see him again so soon.

Jonah blushed when he saw Lark. "I can't tell you how happy I was that you shared your magical place with me yesterday. I loved it! And last night I had the best night's sleep, the best in months. For the first time, I trusted I was okay and that there was nothing wrong with me. I realized I just care deeply about people and want to be liked in return. The breathing really helped to settle my mind and relax my body. So, I wanted to come back alone as soon as possible to see what else could be experienced, all on my own. I hope you don't mind. Is that okay?"

Lark looked deeply into Jonah's gorgeous blue eyes and smiled. "Why would I mind? This place belongs to everyone, and I am genuinely happy for you. That's why I shared it with you. It was my joy to see you happy. One of the biggest lessons I have learned here is that happiness is an inside job. I too was so consumed trying to make others happy, going along with the crowd, that I squashed my own needs and as a result felt awful inside. It was very confusing to understand this for myself. It took me a while to really get this concept. Would you want to share your experience or prefer to keep it to yourself?"

Jonah looked at Lark. She smiled and patiently waited for his reply.

"It's hard to explain, and I think if I told you, you would think I have lost my grip on reality."

"Jonah, I promise not to judge anything you say, and besides, you have no idea what I am thinking; that's simply impossible!"

Jonah looked down toward the ground with an embarrassed look on his face. "You promise not to laugh."

"I cross my heart and promise not to even comment until you are finished."

"Okay. Do you have the time?"

Lark, beginning to get frustrated, said, "I don't think it's a coincidence I am here right now, just as you had your first personal experience. I just wanted to be in the fresh air and would love to listen, and honestly, it would be an honor. Want to go back and sit on the bench by Henry, the elder tree, where we hung out yesterday?"

Jonah nodded.

The two made their way quietly back to the bench that was polished smooth as marble, yet surprisingly comfortable.

When they arrived, Jonah took a nice, deep breath. "Where to begin…? When I woke up this morning, it was such a strange feeling to be relaxed. I have been so tense for so long that it was hard to even recognize feelings of calm in my body. What a concept! To wake up refreshed and renewed. Since it was Saturday, and I had no other pressing plans, and I was so curious about your personal adventures after yesterday, I just had to return. The day was gorgeous, and my parents are always encouraging me to spend more time outside rather than playing video games. I finally realized, maybe they are right. So as quickly as I could get myself ready and out of the house, I came straight here! It was tricky to remember where to enter, but then I saw her and knew it was the right path." Jonah paused to breathe.

Lark just had to interrupt. "Saw who?"

Jonah smiled and said, "Goldy. Who else?"

They both giggled, and Lark replied, "Of course!"

"I turned left, and I swear she bowed to me with her branches and golden leaves that seemed to sparkle in the sunshine. I bowed back and said a polite good morning, and that it was great to see her again. And I swear she said, 'We have been expecting you.' I was dumbfounded! Expecting me? Seriously? Okay, well, it's nice to be wanted and welcomed. She then motioned in a northern direction, so I followed her guidance and walked in that direction.

"As I walked, I observed my own breathing. I slowed it down, sped it up, and just noticed it with a curious mindset. I kept walking through the trees and took your advice to notice the beauty all around. It was quite remarkable. And then I came across the enormous tree you showed me yesterday. I observed its trunk, the intricate roots, the thick branches, and its foliage.

"Then, you are going to think I'm crazy; I heard it talking to me. I swear the tree was talking to me. I looked around, and there was no one else in sight. I looked to see if there were speakers attached to the tree, and I could not see anything electronic. But the sound did not sound like anything I had ever heard before. It's hard to explain. It was as if the voice was an inch from my own ears. Okay, this must sound ridiculous and completely absurd. Even though I feel so peaceful right now, right here talking with you, maybe I've lost my mind."

Lark took a deep breath and shone love from her heart directly to Jonah's heart, and he settled down. She smiled at her friend and deep down appreciated him and his friendship more than she appreciated any other friendship. Lark finally spoke with a sparkle in her eyes. "What did the tree say to you?"

"You believe me? You don't think I'm crazy?"

"Not at all. I think you had a mystical experience. And I know exactly what you are describing. I, too, thought I was losing my marbles when all this started, but it has been transformative. So, are you going to share or keep me in suspense?"

"He said, 'I am Henry, the elder tree, for I am the oldest living tree in these parts of the woods. I have been here for thousands of years. I know your parents, your grandparents, and their grandparents. I am here to help humans, to be a reminder to be grounded and authentic. Grounded means to walk with your feet firmly planted on the ground and your mind to be fully present in the moment. I am here for awe, pleasure, and admiration. I am here to teach all who wish to know about courage, humility, and strength. I have weathered storms of all forces and have endured many events where my physical form has been squashed. That is why visitors think I look squashed, wrinkly, and haggard. I do not take offense at these words. I have learned to embrace change and all the harsh elements in my environment with strength and dignity. I am here to be a source of strength to you today and share unconditional love and acceptance.'

"He then went on to tell me, 'I know all about you, your struggles, thoughts, and dreams. I know you want to be accepted for your gentle soul and kind nature that is unique and different from other boys in your life. I know you have been hiding your distressing thoughts and trying to be tough on the outside, especially at school with your friends. This faking it for fear of what others think is causing your inner turmoil. I am here to help ease your mind and teach you how to be unapologetically, authentically yourself, for everyone else is taken.'

"I thanked him for speaking with me and sharing his wisdom. I asked him what he wanted me to do, and he simply replied, 'Relax in your own body, breathe deeply, and walk with your feet firmly planted on the ground. Stop pretending to be someone you are not. Speak to your friends with ease and remember to laugh. Then each day, look into the mirror and find something to appreciate about yourself and say it out loud.' After that, all became quiet.

"I was speechless and at the same time overwhelmed with joy. I always thought I could hear nature speak to me heart to heart, but this confirmed my suspicion. I guess people would call it intuition, or if it's not intuition, maybe I am going crazy. I am so glad you showed up here today."

"Jonah, you can be assured you are not going crazy. You are right; it's a form of intuition that others refer to as a sixth sense. In a way, it's like a combination of all the senses. Besides, what was relayed to you were messages of hope, truth, and love. Let's face it, you are a gentle soul who is kinder than other boys we know. You have been trying to fake it to seem tough on the outside, but that faking is causing you sleepless nights and distress that you have been hiding from your parents and, most importantly, yourself. Every time you attempt to mask who you are, you feel anxious. I think you were given a gift by meeting Henry. Let him teach you what you need to know and what will be helpful so you can be who you were born to be!"

Jonah looked at Lark and sighed. "I guess you are right. What should I do now?"

"Exactly what he told you to do. Follow his instructions and maybe keep a journal of what you notice."

Jonah smiled and exhaled with a huge sense of relief. "Do you have time to show me around today?"

"Absolutely, let's go!"

And together the friends explored the Sanctuary of Life until their legs hurt.

Two hours quickly passed by as they observed the trees, the colorful leaves, and the species of birds whose chirping was a natural acoustic. The two talked, explored, and took time to breathe in the fresh air, which felt delightful. Jonah even noticed a tree with purple leaves, and he named her Miss Tree. Lark was flattered he gave her a name. The two commented on how they never saw a tree with purple leaves and thought Miss Tree was extraordinarily beautiful. They both promised to visit her again on their next trip. It was at that moment that they agreed it was time to return home.

Lark hoped the girls replied to her text to hang out, and Jonah promised that he would visit Brian at Sullivan's.

As they made their way past Henry, the elder tree, Jonah bowed as a sign of respect and promised to relax, breathe, walk mindfully, and appreciate something about himself every day. He heard Henry praise his good intentions.

Finally, the two were on the path heading toward their homes. Lark said, "Race you. I bet I'm faster than you are today." And that she was. Lark surprised herself with her agility and speed today, and Jonah was impressed.

As the two were ready to go their separate ways, Jonah reached over to hug Lark. Lark accepted his gesture, and the truth was, it felt good to be embraced physically by her friend, who now shared this special, secret part of her life.

Chapter 25:

Crickets

As Lark reached the end of her block, she checked her phone and, to her surprise, not one of the girls replied to her text message about getting together. This was strange, and she was not sure how to feel or if she should send another one. She felt bewildered inside herself. The girls always promptly reply, especially if it's to socialize. *What should I do?* Then there it was those old fears–racing thoughts, creeping back inside her mind. Finally, she thought, *I can't take this anymore. Something has to change.*

She decided to circle around the block another time before going home to give herself time to think and reflect. She checked her text messages again to make sure she did not overlook a message, and there was indeed no reply from the girls, just crickets. Lark found herself going down the rabbit hole of despair, and thoughts of abandonment filled her mind. Within seconds, a river of tears streamed down her face. Her heart was racing so fast she thought it would pop right out of her chest. How could her friends ignore her like that? What was happening? Lark was confused and frightened that it was the end of her friendships. The more she thought, the worse she felt.

She stopped at the corner, took a deep breath, and began to intentionally settle her racing mind. All this thinking was just causing anguish. It did nothing to solve this friend problem. Lark desperately wanted to feel relief. She then deliberately dropped her thinking mind down into her heart center, exactly how Wisdom taught her to do. She breathed deeply and allowed her heart to expand. As she did this mindful exercise, she calmed her mind and body. She started to feel a bit better. She dried her eyes with a tissue from her pocket, then took some more deep breaths. Lark composed herself as best as possible, but she was still a bundle of raw emotion.

As Lark made her way home, she remembered her realization from the other day. She remembered, *I am angrier with myself for playing small and not wanting to be seen.* She also remembered her other epiphany of *not wanting to be a follower to fit in with her friends.* She wanted friendships to be easy, accepting, and most importantly, kind. If her current friendships no longer met these criteria, something would have to change, and she most likely would have to be the one to change the dynamics. Lark stopped at the walkway to her front door; it was as if she was frozen and couldn't even move a muscle. Though she knew this was her true desire, it hurt so very much. She feared the difficulty ahead in navigating school without these friendships in place. *Who will I hang out with? Who will I sit with at lunch? Will everyone know what happened, judge me, and not want to be my friend?* The unknown was scary.

Lark slowly made her way up the paved walkway to her home. She quietly opened the front door, hoping nobody would notice her return. She attempted to go up to her bedroom when Mom spotted her and inquired about her walk. She tried as best she could to hide the tears, but it was no use; she burst into tears once again and became hysterical. Lark was happy Mom was there to console her, but felt so weak and embarrassed.

Mom was stunned by her sudden burst of emotion and walked her calmly to the bedroom and closed the door. "Honey, tell me what happened. I am concerned about you."

Lark took a tissue and wiped away the tears. She sat on the bed next to Mom and lowered her head. She cried until there were no more tears left to cry. Finally, she shared that the girls did not reply to her message about getting together. She felt left out and alone.

Mom lifted Lark's chin and asked, "Are you jumping to conclusions?"

"Maybe, but why didn't anyone reply to me today?"

"Lark, you told me the other day you sometimes intentionally do not reply to all the texts you get. Maybe they were busy and just did not reply because they had other obligations."

"Mom, I just have this feeling in the pit of my stomach that they are all together and purposely ignored my text."

"Okay, let's say you are right. What does that mean for you?"

"That they don't want to be my friend anymore, and it hurts."

"Didn't you tell me the other day you were angry at yourself for playing small, and you wanted to have some new friends in your life?"

"Well, yes, but I don't want to be excluded either."

Mom scooched closer to Lark and gave her a hug. "I wish I had words of comfort. Growing up is hard and challenging. Remember, you are a great person, sister, daughter, and friend. It may be hard in school for a while, but you will make new friends and feel a whole lot better. Maybe not today or tomorrow, but I promise you will feel better, and things will get easier."

"Thanks, Mom. I do feel a bit better. And I promised Grace to help her with math."

"I am so glad. I love you. Another thing… There's an old saying, 'Don't put all your eggs in one basket.'"

Lark crinkled her face and said, "What does that even mean?"

Mom laughed. "Well, I guess that means if you put too many eggs in one basket, there's a good chance some will break. I think you're spending too much mental energy worrying about these friendships. I know the girls are important to you, and I understand you don't want to stop being friends. But all this worrying is robbing you of your happiness. I've noticed this pattern lately of you worrying or trying to control how things will turn out."

"What have you noticed?"

"Lark, every time you are upset these days, it's always about Gwen, or your interactions with the girls. On the other hand, you have also told me you have had some nice times with Jonah, Carly, and even Molly. I would encourage you to get busy with other people, so the girls take up less room in your head. I do get it, honey. Gwen, Ashley, and Nikki have been your besties since grade school. I know how much you love and care about them, but sometimes friends outgrow friendships. It's a normal part of maturing."

Lark turned to Mom and said, "You sound just like Wisdom."

"Who is Wisdom?"

Lark caught herself and said, "Oh, she's a character in a great book I'm reading."

"Well then, I like sounding like Wisdom! Are you feeling better?"

"Yes, much better, but it's still upsetting."

"How about finding Grace and helping her with math homework?"

"Good idea, and I did promise to help her again."

"I tell you what, after you help Grace, let's go for a walk into town and go to that boutique. I would love to buy you something special. There is a lot to be said about retail therapy."

Lark's eyes widened, and she smiled with joy.

Chapter 26:

Grace

Lark washed her face with some cold water and calming lavender soap. It felt good to cry, talk with Mom, and then wash away the tears. She went downstairs and found Grace playing with Hope.

"I know it's Saturday, but would you want me to help you with math now?"

"Oh, now you have time for me, what? You've got nothing better to do now?"

"Okay, I deserved that. Do you want me to help you? Maybe we could even go outside and sit at the table in the backyard. It's a beautiful day."

"I'm sorry. I did not mean to be nasty. Yeah, that would be fun to go outside. Let me get my books and the list you asked me to make."

Lark was confused. What list was she talking about? Oh, she quickly remembered she had encouraged Grace to make a list of what specifically was upsetting her about math.

The girls each got a drink of lemonade from the kitchen and made their way to the backyard. It was a picture-perfect day, and the sisters were glad to have some time together.

Grace opened her class notebook and textbook to the troublesome math lesson. Then she went into her pocket and showed Lark her list, which was beautifully written and decorated with doodles. On her list were four items…

- I still think math is hard.
- I forgot how to change my mindset.
- I'm worried the kids will think I'm dumb, not smart like Becca.
- If I'm not smart, I won't have any friends.

Lark silently read over Grace's list and was quiet for a moment. She then looked over at Grace, who had an embarrassed look upon her face, and said, "I get it."

"You do?" Grace was relieved.

"Yes, to be honest, I've been struggling myself with overthinking, it sometimes feels like a runaway train in my mind. I'm learning to calm my thoughts, and taking long walks in nature has been a big help. This morning, I walked through the trails and noticed how the sunlight filtered through the trees, and it made me feel a little lighter.

What I'm discovering is that it takes time and effort to find real peace of mind. That's why I, too, have had to lean on what I taught you: to utilize the other set of twins, patience and practice. I have had to constantly remind myself that developing peace of mind requires both working together, just like you and Becca, supporting each other. For example, there was a day when I felt especially anxious, but I practiced patience by taking a few deep breaths and gave myself time to work through my feelings. It didn't make everything perfect, but it helped me get through the moment, especially with my friends."

"I thought I was the only person in the world to feel this way."

"Grace, so many people who seem confident on the outside worry on the inside and think they are not good enough or that people will not like them."

"Where did you hear this?"

"Mom shared this with me the other day, and it helped me to chill out."

"I am so glad you shared this with me. I feel a bit better and not so weird. Do you think you can fix my mindset again?"

Lark went quiet. She let everything sink into her mind. By sharing these mindfulness ideas with Grace, it helped her absorb the teachings on a much deeper level. Wisdom was right; the student will one day become the teacher. "Let's give it a shot. We will start with your list. Is it okay if we write on it? You did such a nice job with this assignment."

"Yes, of course."

Lark put the list on the backyard table between them. "Okay, let's go through each one and change the statements. What would feel better? What sounds more truthful?"

- I still think math is hard → Math takes patience and practice.

- I forgot how to change my mindset → Lark is helping me to have a better mindset.
- I'm worried the kids will think I'm dumb, not smart like Becca → The kids don't care about my math grades, only their own grades.
- If I'm not smart, I won't have any friends → I do have friends who like me.

"Now, how do these improved variations feel to you?"

"A whole lot better! You are right. Since math does not come naturally to me, I do have to work a bit harder and practice, and it's okay to ask for help."

"Yes, you can ask for help. Grace, I am also sorry it took so long for me to give you my time and attention. You are my sister, and I love you. Will you please forgive me?"

"Of course, silly!" Grace leaned over and gave Lark a hug, exactly what the big sister needed in that very moment.

The girls opened Grace's math books and got to work. Just like last time, Lark showed Grace how to solve the equations and reminded her to use the formulas. They did a few examples together, then Lark got out her phone and set a timer for fifteen minutes. By the time the timer was complete, Grace had finished her math assignment with a big smile on her face.

Lark reviewed Grace's work and gave her an unofficial A+ grade! Lark realized that Grace needs to feel relaxed and safe, and when these conditions are in place, Grace excels!

Grace promised to practice with a few more examples the next day to reinforce the learning.

Lark agreed that it was a great idea and said, "Hey, since it's still light outside, let's ask Mom if we can go for a walk on the trails. It will be fun, and we deserve some playtime."

The sisters quickly found themselves on the trails, and Lark pointed out her favorite trees that were blooming with springtime flowers. Grace was quick to notice the scent of honeysuckle in the air. It was a bit overpowering but a delight to the senses. It felt special to share the trails with Grace. Lark relished being a big sister, and as the two continued to explore together, Lark had another epiphany. A *sister is a friend for life, so why not spend more time with the three wonderful sisters I will have forever?* With that notion, she smiled to herself and enjoyed the time mindfully with her little sister, Grace, who showed her what real grace is all about.

Chapter 27:

Let Me

The girls truly enjoyed their walk, and when they arrived home, it was late in the day. Since no one had evening plans, Mom suggested the older girls help her make the family's favorite dinner, spaghetti and homemade meatballs. Of course, Hope wanted to join in the fun and got the privilege of sitting on the barstool at the high-top counter. Mom showed the girls how to make and form the meatballs and even shared the secret ingredient she learned from Grandma to make them extra tasty and delicious. They all had so much fun together as a family, cooking and laughing.

Lark thought, *It is strange the way things tend to work themselves out. I was so stressed that the girls did not want to hang out today. If they did, I would not have had my release-cry with Mom or that special time with Grace. And who would want to miss cooking with Mom and the twins when she's usually rushing frantically to get dinner on the table? It really was a great day.* She continued to think about her realization, her sisters are her friends and will be for a lifetime. With that notion, she was able to put the relationships with her three main friends into perspective. She made a note to herself to journal today's experience in her red journal to share with Wisdom.

During dinner, Mom remembered she had promised to take Lark shopping to the boutique. However, by the time everyone settled down, it was too late in the day, and the shop was closed. The good news was that the boutique was going to be open this particular Sunday, and Mom promised to take her first thing in the morning.

The Roberts family had a great meal together. There were no cell phones, just conversations and laughs. Lark felt so grateful to be a part of this family and loved her role as the big sister.

The next morning was perfect in every way. The air was cool and crisp, and the sun was shining amongst a gorgeous blue sky. After family breakfast, Mom and Lark made their way into town. It was nice to stroll around before the shops opened and the streets got busy with people either shopping or looking forward to a casual meal or a delight at Sullivan's.

When Main Street Boutique opened its doors, Lark was the first to enter and felt like a kid in a candy store. Nan, the shop owner, greeted them with a warm reception. Mom knew Nan for years, even before she opened her clothing boutique. They chatted while Lark explored the clothing and all the exquisite accessories.

Mom was exceptionally patient today. She wanted Lark to relax, enjoy herself and forget about the drama with her friends for a bit. She was so glad Lark confided in her and told her of her predicament. She knew firsthand that growing up is hard and friend dynamics are challenging. Lark browsed the clothing in the shop and enjoyed looking at the new items so beautifully displayed. Lark looked around for a while and wanted to find that jacket, but knew she could not show up in school with the exact same one as Gwen. Meanwhile, Mom filled Nan in on the situation without giving away too much information. Nan looked at Mom and said, "I have some new merchandise in the back room that I have not been able to unpack or put on the store floor. I can take Lark back there and give her first dibs on anything she likes, if you could watch the store for me?" Mom was thrilled and quickly agreed.

Nan called Lark over and escorted her into the back room, where the new clothing and accessories were stored. Lark felt proud and privileged. She eyed a few new jackets and even some trendy sweatshirts, but had a hard time deciding, as nothing really appealed to her the way the pink fleece and blue denim jacket did when she first saw it. Nan enthusiastically wanted Lark to find something special and brought her to another section of the back room. She had just received a shipment from a new company that made athletic leisure wear and wanted Lark to be the first to see the new items. Together they opened the box, and Lark was in heaven. The shipment contained zip-up jackets with matching capri leggings. The material was the softest fabric, and the garments had pockets. She could not believe all the fantastic colors, and it was hard to choose which she liked best. Lark decided to try on a pair of navy-blue capris with an ice-blue matching jacket.

When Lark emerged from the fitting room, she had a huge smile on her face. Mom and Nan loved the way the outfit looked on Lark. Mom was pleased to see Lark happy. It was a perfect fit. Since it looked so great on Lark, Nan asked her to model the other colors. They all looked great on Lark, and she took pleasure in helping Nan. She modeled the pink and purple combination, then the sage green and espresso brown set. They all looked terrific on Lark. It was finally time to choose, which was almost impossible. Mom and Nan said the choice was hers to make. She could not decide which she liked best, then decided to go with her first choice.

Mom believed she would get more use from the athletic wear than a jacket and thought it was a great purchase. They brought the items to the register, and Nan gifted Lark a matching ice-blue tank top to complete the outfit. Lark was overjoyed with her kindness.

As the two left the boutique, Mom thought Lark could use a fresh haircut. They went over to the salon to see if they could get a last-minute appointment, and they were in luck. Carolyn, Lark's favorite stylist, had an opening in one hour. Since they had some spare time, Mom said she would treat Lark to lunch at… where else but Sullivan's. Lark felt so special and loved today. It was a good day, and she took delight in the act of gratitude and appreciation, especially toward Mom.

Brian was working today and found them a table inside by the window. It was the best seat in the house. They decided to share a deluxe sandwich and then indulge in some ice cream for a treat. Mom looked across the table at Lark and said, "I am glad you are feeling better. What changed in the last day for you?"

"It was Grace. I promised for days to help her with her math homework. She was rightly upset because I pushed her off several times. When I felt guilty and finally sat down to work with her, I realized it felt great to help her feel capable and confident. I could see how much she appreciated my attention and how much she genuinely loves me. Then I realized a sister is a friend for life, and I have three great sisters. I was spending so much time worrying about my friends, I overlooked what was truly important. Then yesterday, I focused my attention and really enjoyed being at home with our family. I loved that you spent time with us, and it was a blast to cook with you. And thanks for sharing your secret ingredient!"

Mom took a slow, deep breath. She had to really focus and take in all Lark was sharing. She was impressed with Lark's new perspective on life and shocked that a fourteen-year-old could be this wise. She looked at Lark and inquired how she came to this wonderful conclusion.

Lark wanted to blurt out about her encounters with Wisdom. It was challenging to keep all that inside. "Let's just say my walks are really helping; the fresh air and exercise help me to shrug things off faster. It was fun to walk and talk with Grace. I think she liked that it was just the two of us and that Becca had other plans. And I gave myself permission to like hanging out with my kid sister."

"Nothing makes me happier; all I have ever wanted for my children is to be friends. You will see as you get older that there is nothing better than having a sister for a friend."

"I know, Mom, and thanks for giving me three friends!"

On that note, Mom and Lark finished their sandwich. Brian gave them special treatment and brought over an assortment of ice cream flavors to sample. Each flavor was decadent, rich and creamy. Mom went for Cherry Burst, and Lark indulged in Double Chocolate Crunch. Brian brought over four spoons so they could share. They savored their ice cream as if tasting it for the very first time. Every mouthful was rich, creamy, and delightful.

Finally, they made their way back to the salon, and Carolyn was ready for Lark. She delicately unbraided and washed her hair with luxurious shampoo and then conditioner. Lark silently thought, *this is the life. Mom is the best. Shopping, lunch, ice cream, and a haircut.*

Mom patiently waited while Carolyn cut Lark's split ends and styled her hair. Once Lark approved the haircut, she blow-dried her hair with curls on the bottom, which bounced off her shoulders. Lark looked lovely, and more importantly, she was relaxed. It had been a while since Lark felt that way, and Mom knew she really needed some TLC.

On the way home from the salon, Mom and Lark ran into Gwen, Nikki, and Ashley on Main Street. Mom became instantly worried about Lark's reaction, but held in her thoughts and put on a poker face. Lark smiled brightly and went right up to her friends. She acted calmly and confidently. Ashley commented immediately about her haircut and blowout and said she looked stunning. Nikki had to bounce her curls, and Gwen managed to give her a compliment as well. They all chatted for a while, and Mom walked into one of the local shops to give them privacy. All acted as if nothing had happened the day before.

Then Gwen inquired what was in the shopping bag.

Lark beamed and said, "You will have to wait and see. Mom treated me to a new outfit for tutoring Grace in math."

Nikki replied, "Can't wait to see it on you."

Mom emerged from the store with another shopping bag. Lark was surprised as Mom rarely shopped, especially for herself. Mom showed the girls her purchase, a chic black V-neck top with eyelet sleeves. She thought it would be great for work and the occasional date night with Dad. The girls complimented her taste and gave her their seal of approval.

With that interaction, Lark said to the girls, "Have a great day. Got things to do."

Ashley said, "See you in school tomorrow."

And Nikki and Gwen smiled.

On the way home, Mom noted how cool, calm, and collected Lark acted. She thought Lark might have inquired as to why they did not reply to her text the day before, or why she was not asked to join them in town today. Mom too was surprised by her friends' behavior.

Lark looked at her mom and said, "Let Them! My teacher was listening to a podcast by Mel Robbins the other day. She was talking about something called the Let Them Theory. I stopped to listen because it sounded cool. Basically, if people want to do their own thing, you just let them, without getting upset or taking it personally.

"So, if the girls want to go into town without me, I'll let them. I mean, I get to hang out with the world's greatest mom. I'll let myself have fun with you today instead. I still get to be happy, have other friends, and enjoy my sisters.

"It's kind of simple, and when I tried it in my head earlier, it actually worked. Mel said it takes practice and it does feel way better to say, 'Let Me' enjoy the day, rather than think worrisome thoughts."

Mom looked at Lark once again, gave her a big hug, and said, "You never cease to amaze me!"

Chapter 28:

Get Comfortable Being Uncomfortable

The next day started off with a quiet bus ride to school. When Lark arrived at school, there was the typical hallway commotion getting to homeroom for attendance. She waved hello to Molly and Carly. Lark could not wait to start the day. She felt calm and eager for a great day. After the next bell rang, signaling time for the first period, Lark saw Nikki by their lockers and stopped for a quick chat. She was rather cool and a bit casual, not her typical chattering self. Lark asked about her weekend, and she gave a very short, unusual answer. It was as if she did not want to answer at all.

Nikki simply replied, "Um, it was fine, you know, I hung out with the girls."

"Yes, it was nice to run into everyone yesterday in town. I texted to see if everyone was free this weekend and did not hear back."

Nikki gave her a half smile and said, "Talk later, late for class."

Then, suddenly, it was back. That feeling, that feeling of uncertainty, she knew it in her bones; she was getting blown off by her friends. The dynamic she had since elementary school with her friends was changing. She did not want anything to change. She wanted things to remain just the way they had been for years. Lark wanted to break down and cry. All of it was so confusing to her, as she had such a great weekend. She recounted the great time she had with her family, her time with Grace, shopping with Mom, and more importantly, the huge realization about what is really important in life. But in that moment, it all slipped away and did not matter one bit. She felt abandoned and alone and did not understand what she had done wrong. Her mind was racing, but she had to get to class. If she skipped class, it might make her look weak, and things could get worse. She tried to remember just one piece of advice from Wisdom, but it all seemed to have faded away.

In class, she was evidently not paying attention. She tried to recall how she had explained the Let Them Theory to Mom. She was feeling like a big, fat fraud! She felt undeserving of Wisdom's time and attention. How can I let them get away with this? Lark felt herself seething with anger. All this is so unfair. What did I do to be blown off by my friends? Lark's face was getting rather pale, and Mr. Nally approached her desk to see if she was okay. She smiled at him and said, "Yes, just a bit hot today. Sorry, I will focus now."

Lark did her best to recenter her attention and pay attention in class. She took notes and was mindful of her breathing. That seemed to help and give her a bit of relief. But those thoughts about her social status in school were pervasive. Let's face it, Gwen, Nikki, and Ashley were considered the cool kids. They are pretty, dress well, and Gwen has that mean girl, don't-mess-with-me attitude. Lark was always a bit more bohemian and marched to her own beat. She typically did not care about fashion or if every hair on her head was brushed to perfection. She was more 'go with the flow.' The girls always accepted her for who she was, especially during their younger years. But the tide was turning, and it was evident that change was in the air. Lark realized she had a choice to make, and she could make it first or be forced to accept a decision made for her by others. Even with this clarity of perspective, it still hurt inside. A small, single tear rolled from her left eye. She gave herself compassion and wiped it away with her shirt. She wanted to save the tear, though the idea seemed silly, but it brought a smile to her face.

Finally, the bell rang for the next class. Lark packed up her bag and was first in the hall, ready to change classes. Carly happened to be right outside the doorway, and it was so nice to see a friendly face. She walked Lark to her locker, and there was nonstop chatter the entire way. Lark was appreciative of the distraction, especially for the fact that Carly asked to have lunch with her today. She accepted the invitation proudly, then Carly headed down the other hallway for her next class.

As Lark walked to her next class, she ran into Gwen. She hated the fact that she could not be casual and spontaneous. Lark knew her guard was up, but had to act calm and collected. She disliked this faking-it business and preferred her easy conversation with Carly.

As Gwen approached, she looked at Lark and inquired about her new outfit. She said in a slightly sarcastic tone, "I was looking forward to seeing the new outfit that you did not want to show us yesterday."

Lark, to her surprise, was quick-witted. "Nope, it was a bit too warm to wear today. You'll just have to wait. See you later." She smiled at Gwen, then casually walked to class.

Lark thought it was such a shame to play mind games with friends. Friendships are supposed to be easy, tolerant, and forgiving. Let's face it, everyone has off days, goes through hard times, and has their own quirks. These recent interactions with her friends, the Swiftie Sisters, were not making her feel so great, and it was becoming harder to shake things off and let things slide. Just as she approached the door to math class, she remembered something Wisdom said to her weeks ago. She told her that friendships have a time and a season. With that awareness, Lark made a firm decision to prioritize friendships that felt genuine and where she felt relaxed and appreciated.

The next few classes seem to drag by slowly. Lark did her best to focus, but the inevitable change in her social life and social status in school caused her to feel sad and gloomy. She was grateful to have plans to sit with Carly at lunch. When she got to the lunchroom, Carly was already seated with Molly and Anna. A seat was saved for her right next to Carly. She found her way over, breathed a sigh of relief, and sat right down. Truth be told, she felt a bit awkward sitting with them, as she always sat with the girls. She felt in a way she was using these new friends, but was relieved to have this new experience so fast. These girls chatted about school, their teachers, and the current streaming TV series. It all felt so comfortable, and nobody was trying to impress anyone. Anna loved listening to Lark and loved the fact that she had three younger sisters. Anna was also the oldest, but of two brothers. She thought sisters were way more fun.

At the end of lunchtime, the students were allowed outside for recess to enjoy the fresh air. Lark went outside with everyone from her table. It was a picturesque day. The sun was shining, and it was not too hot. The temperature was great, warm with a soft breeze. It felt great to breathe in the fresh air, and it helped Lark to clear her mind. A few moments later, Gwen, Ashley, and

Nikki approached. Lark politely excused herself to converse with them privately. Ashley started the conversation by inquiring, "Hey, why didn't you sit with us today?"

"Carly invited me to sit with them today, and I thought it would be fun."

There was silence from the three. She knew then she had to ask the dreaded question. She was tired of making assumptions, letting things pass, and being made to feel like she did something wrong. She looked Ashley right in the eyes and asked, "Why didn't any of you respond to my text this weekend about getting together?"

The girls all looked at each other, hoping someone would respond first. Finally, Ashley said, "Because we just wanted to hang out by ourselves. It doesn't always have to be the four of us all the time."

"Is that all? Anything else?"

Nikki looked down and said, "Sorry, I guess that was not really a nice thing to do. Then we felt bad when we saw you in town with your mom."

Gwen looked at Ashley and Nikki, then turned to Lark. "I went with you into town the other weekend and wanted to spend time with them this weekend. Besides, you have been hanging around with Jonah."

"What does he have to do with you all not replying to my text?"

"You two seem to be so cute talking together."

"Again, I don't see what Jonah has to do with that. I have been family friends with him forever, and we have been hanging a bit on our own. Please tell me what is going on and if you are upset with me for something specific because I am clueless."

Gwen eyed Lark and said, "Okay, the truth is you have been acting weird lately, and we wanted a break from your quirkiness."

"Weird in what way? Please enlighten me, Gwen."

"I can't quite describe it, but you have been odd, saying all these strange things, such as 'enlighten me.' What does that mean? You seem to act like you are better than us. You have changed, and well, we are not liking the new you so much."

Lark looked at Gwen and said, "Thank you for your honesty. I was only trying to be a good friend, finding the right words to help you with your family situation."

Lark continued to talk to Gwen while deliberately stepping away from Nikki and Ashley so they would be out of earshot. She then stared hard at Gwen and said, "It's funny that you and I are great friends in private, then once we get to school or somewhere in public, it changes. That is the thing that is weird, and honestly, it's hurtful. Now, I want to get back to Carly and Molly." Lark confidently and deliberately turned away from Gwen and started walking back toward her other friends.

Gwen stood there, almost frozen, shocked that sweet, kind Lark spoke so abruptly. For once, Gwen was speechless! She could not respond with any sharp words because deep down she knew the truth. She knew Lark was right and only trying to be a good friend, and that she herself was not being a good friend in return. Gwen knew she was acting like a spoiled brat to get the attention she no longer receives at home. But in typical Gwen fashion, she refused to admit she was wrong or apologize.

In a flash, everything backfired on Gwen, and she knew she was responsible for the events. She could not blame her parents or anyone else; she was solely to blame for this mess.

Nikki ran after Lark and said, "I am sorry. It was wrong."

Ashley followed Nikki and said, "Yes, we were insensitive and ghosting you was not right."

Lark smiled at the girls and said, "Yes, it was, and I am done settling for scraps of attention from my closest friends."

As Lark made her way back to Carly, Molly, and Anna, she was proud of the way she spoke with her old friends. She was outwardly brave to ask the uncomfortable question and remained strong during their dialogue. She told them the truth about how she was feeling and being treated over the last few weeks. But inside, she was sad and fearful. She remembered how Wisdom explained about growing pains, how sometimes, when the human body is growing, it can physically hurt. It's the same when changes in life occur, as they too can be emotionally painful.

Lark knew she had to grow and become more resilient. This cycle of fear was getting in the way of her happiness and negatively affecting her mental health. It was even taking its toll on her family dynamics. The truth was, she was changing; she was learning things about life that she could not ignore or deny. Wisdom was blessing her with gifts of knowledge. She was chosen for some reason beyond her grasp. She still had no clue why she experienced Wisdom or the Sanctuary of Life, but instinctively knew to trust the process. She also knew deep down that Jonah was a part of this story. She was not sure how or why, but Jonah would be a part of this private chapter of her life. Lark knew in that very moment she had to be comfortable being uncomfortable. She took a few long, deep breaths and rejoined her new friends before the class bell rang.

Chapter 29:

Return to the Sanctuary

Lark could not get home from school fast enough. It had been days since she had time with Wisdom in the Sanctuary. She changed into her brand-new outfit, tied her sneakers, grabbed her backpack and journal, and was ready to head off to the trails. Mom had a sneaky feeling Lark was going to go for a walk today. She had an after-school snack and drink waiting. Lark thanked her, grabbed the snack, and was out the door in a flash.

As she started her walk, Jonah texted to see if everything was okay. He saw her talking with the girls during the lunch break. He observed that it looked rather heated. She appreciated his concern immensely. Lark quickly replied that all was okay and she needed some private time today in the sanctuary. He respected her space and said he was there if she needed to chat. Lark replied with a purple heart emoji.

As Lark approached the sanctuary, the large steel gate was up. She figured it would be, as her energy was scattered, and emotionally, she was not in a good place. She paced in front of the gate for a while to burn up some of her energy and to think. She knew she had to become clearly aware of her upsetting thoughts and breathe deeply and rhythmically to slow down her racing mind. She looked around at the gorgeous trees while she mindfully started to breathe long, complete breaths. With each deep breath, she deliberately focused on some beautiful aspect within her surroundings. She looked at the colors of the leaves, the bark on the tree trunks, and the knotholes, and smelled the scent in the air. This noticing practice helps to settle the mind, Wisdom taught. It was about twenty long minutes before the large gate would evaporate into a mist, and she would be allowed to enter and explore the Sanctuary of Life.

As she entered, she felt relieved and proud of her accomplishments. She was learning to master her mind, but knew it would take plenty more dedicated work. She also wanted life to be easy, without all this emotional fuss. Lark wanted to become the lark and soar over the sanctuary to bring joy to all.

Mom told her she was named Lark as she was born with a cheerful spirit. As Mom held her firstborn for the very first time, she had a wonderful sense that this baby of hers would soar to new heights and bring joy to all those she would meet. Lark smiled at all the nurses. They all said she was the most beautiful baby in the nursery. Mom said her smile symbolized larks bringing joy and hope into the world. That is what she wanted for her firstborn baby girl and gave her the unique, fitting name of Lark. Lark loved hearing this story again and again. It brought a smile to her face, and she loved the fact that Mom knew she was special right from the start.

Another ten minutes passed by, and Wisdom finally appeared from behind Goldy. Lark smiled with relief and, at the same time, she wanted to curl up into a ball and cry. It had been a rough few days for her with lots of emotional challenges.

Wisdom said, "Let's go for a walk. It's good to move energy, and a walk will be just the right medicine for what ails you."

Lark wanted to regurgitate everything that happened over the last few days with her friends, Grace, and Mom. She wanted to tell Wisdom every last detail. Lark wanted her to understand how hard it had been and all she had done to be resilient. Wisdom quietly looked at Lark with those big, blue eyes. She said nothing but placed both hands on her shoulders. It was as if to ground Lark to the present moment. Lark too became quiet.

Wisdom said, "I know every detail about the last few days. I know of the interactions with your friends and how you were so mature and comforting to Grace. I also know your mom is spiritually awakening, thanks to you and your growth. You are giving her new ways to view the world, and she is so proud and grateful to you. You get well-deserved kudos. You are rocking her world in wonderful ways, but let's keep that to ourselves."

Lark smiled and laughed out loud. "But how do you know everything that recently happened? How can that be?"

Wisdom turned to Lark. This time she took both of her hands in her hands. "Because I AM You. I am your highest aspect. You can think of me as your nonphysical self, or like a guardian angel if you wish; the name you give makes no difference. It's what feels right for you."

"But how can I see you? You are separate from me. You look different, act different, you are much older, your eye color is different, and, well, you have blue hair, and I have brown hair."

Wisdom laughed out loud heartily. "Not everything is as it appears. There is so much more to life than humans comprehend. This is why I have been teaching you to get quiet and settle your mind. Just like you are teaching Grace about math with practice and patience. Do you think it is a coincidence you are teaching her about those traits?"

"Well, I guess not."

"Being a teacher presents opportunities in many ways. Your mom was teaching her daughters how to cook meatballs, but more importantly, she was showing you how to bond with family. Your teachers in school share their knowledge of subject matters while helping the students learn how to learn. Waiting in line at Sullivan's teaches you how to be patient. The act of waiting your turn to select something delicious can be a frustrating experience for many. Humans live in an age of immediacy and want everything instantly. But patience and consideration of what is really important are necessary for true joy and happiness.

"You, my child, are a teacher as well. You are teaching Grace how to open her mind to hard subjects and how to be successful and resilient. You are teaching Nikki and Ashley all about complacency and the consequences of being complacent. They follow Gwen around for acceptance, approval, and validation. They fear that outshining her will lead to rejection and are afraid to rock the boat of social acceptance. Gwen is the so-called popular girl, and they like their perceived status with her. You are showing them what will happen if you become too independent. You are mirroring their innermost fears, and they have no desire for anything to change. That is fine for them, as everyone is on their unique path. I mean this with sincerity. "They are free to cultivate friendships as they see fit. Everyone grows at different speeds and times in their life. It is the judgment of another's path that causes emotional upheaval.

"Now let's talk about Gwen. You have become Gwen's biggest teacher in the form of what we call a 'mirror.' You are mirroring her inner fears. It is similar to the way a mirror reflects a person's appearance. You two have been friends since kindergarten, and up until now, the dynamics have remained the same. The friendship has weathered storms and, for the most part, has worked. She has been the more commanding friend in the relationship. That is part of her natural personality and what makes her popular in some sense with friends.

However, now the currents are changing, and you no longer like the rules of this game. Gwen is becoming more dominant in controlling what she thinks she can control, and that is you. That is what people do; they do what is familiar, hoping for the same results. She thinks if she bosses you around enough, you will eventually comply and fall back into the familiar patterns, and all will be well again in Gwen's world. Her parents' fighting is causing her to feel unsafe, and her brother has a different way of managing the conflict. All this is shaking her world, and she is not happy. She has been putting on an act for the sake of others to maintain something familiar. Today, you called her out on her bad behavior, and she froze. She felt guilty inside but would do anything to save face and avoid embarrassment. This is a common behavior for many.

"Lark, deep down, Gwen cares about you and values your friendship more than you will ever know. She feels threatened that you are changing, and it's reminding her of the changing dynamics with her parents. She fears they will never work things out or be able to get along. This is causing her a great amount of uncertainty about her place within her own family. Gwen just does not understand any of this on a conscious level. Secretly she fears the two of you will not be able to work things out, and she will lose you too, and this scares her on the inside."

Finally, Wisdom paused and became very, very quiet.

"Take a breath, as I know this was a lot to comprehend."

Lark took a breath as instructed and found a large stone rock on which to sit and think.

"Oh my gosh, Ashley and Nikki were rather complacent, especially Nikki, when I asked her point-blank why she did not respond to my text message about getting together. Why was that?"

"I cannot speak to their intentions, nor will I judge their lack of a response as good or bad. It's best to stay neutral. Remember, everyone has their own perspective from their own life experiences. Sometimes, people will react or be highly triggered by a situation where another person would not give it a second thought. It's all about someone's inner programming, past events, their parents, family, friends, teachers, and so much more. This is the cause of much conflict between people. Remember, everyone comes into this world wired differently and has different life experiences."

"I am starting to see and understand."

"Now let's chat more about Gwen since that is the friendship causing you all this inner turmoil. What did you think about my observation regarding your interactions?"

"Honestly, that was quite a lot to take in and comprehend."

Wisdom nodded her head in agreement.

"I do think your observation was clever. She has been the bossy one in the friendship from the very beginning. I did not mind because I prefer being more introverted, so I let her take the lead. Now, she is just becoming manipulative, and I no longer want to be bossed around by Gwen. It hurts, and it's not fair!"

"Remember when you completely forgot Gwen was upset because her parents were fighting? She reminded you of that fact, and you apologized and promised to be more understanding of the stress in her home life. You also promised to be a better friend. It became easy for you to forget her troubles because your parents get along and parental fighting is not part of your daily life. Her current home life experience is completely different from your home situation."

Lark retorted, "I have tried over and over to be a good friend, but she does not make it easy. She judges me, calls me weird in public and has excluded me from our friends. She has not been a good friend. It's been upsetting and, on the other hand, liberating. She has forced me to see what and who are important. I have been forced to reevaluate my priorities and even friendships."

Wisdom smiled as if to imply she sees Lark and all her efforts. "Yes, you are doing quite well, and I am very proud of you. What else do you think is going on with Gwen?"

"I don't know. She has just been so mean-spirited lately, but it seems only mean to me."

"Why do you think she is being that way only to you? Take a breath and carefully consider the answer."

Lark did as she was instructed and took a long, deep breath before responding. "Okay, maybe she does not feel loved at home with all the fighting and saw the love in my family. I know her mom loves her, but does not share it openly the way my mom shows love. Maybe that upset her in some way?"

"That's an interesting perspective. Go on."

"Well, she called me quirky. Maybe she is afraid of letting herself be quirky or vulnerable. Maybe she is afraid of change or rejection, so she is deliberately pushing me aside. Maybe I am mirroring her own fears."

"That is a very good observation, Lark. As we have spoken about before, change is a natural part of life. It occurs daily in nature and can be a good teacher if you choose to see it that way. There are rainy days followed by sunny days, cold months, and hot months. I could go on and on, but I gather you get the point."

Lark nodded respectfully.

"Let's talk about something that needs to be discussed, and that is your blind spot. Especially when triggered by Gwen."

"What is a blind spot? I can see just fine."

Wisdom smiled. "Everyone has an emotional blind spot, meaning where one gets easily tripped up or emotionally triggered by someone or something frequently. It is difficult for one to see their own blind spot; it's kind of sneaky. And I am not talking about the way someone looks, but about the way they perceive the world and their unique place in the world. Yours is a common one, and one many teens and grown-ups contend with the same thing. Your blind spot is a fear of abandonment and a need for certainty. This is showing up in your life with the need for things to remain the same within your social network of friends. If things begin to shift, you start to mentally catastrophize and think the worst will happen. It's like a fear of not being good enough, leading to inevitable and automatic abandonment by those whom you love and trust the most.

"This is what has been getting in your way lately. It's like an annoying pebble in your shoe. Every time something happens with Gwen, you start to mentally spiral down a path of fear and worry of rejection. Then you catastrophize the worst possible outcome.

"You are learning so much about being your wonderful, authentic self. You have been journaling, grounding yourself, breathing deeply, and being mindful. I know how much you appreciate the Sanctuary of Life. We see who you are and are helping you to awaken your natural abilities and strengthen your connection to your true self. But every time Gwen does or says something upsetting, it is as if your whole world is rocked to the core and will explode, causing you to be frightened and feel alone. I am sorry if this sounds harsh."

Lark looked at Wisdom with tears in her eyes. "Yes, it was brutal... but... accurate and truthful. Maybe I do have a blind spot."

"How does this make you feel?"

"Like I am a fraud, and you will stop loving me and disappear if I don't get it right soon." More tears streamed down Lark's face.

"Oh, dear Lark, this is another common fear people have frequently, that somehow, they are unworthy of continued love. Nothing could be further from the truth. Just because I pointed out your blind spot does not mean I don't love you anymore. As a matter of fact, it's impossible to stop loving you. Love will always be and can never cease to exist. It's because I love you that I pointed this out, so that you could become aware of it in the future and not let it pull you down. Awareness is key. It's essential. I want you to live your best, most beautiful life, and I'm here to give you the guidance to do that, beyond your wildest dreams. Besides, I am you, and you can never stop loving yourself. It's impossible not to love oneself, though people claim not to like or love themselves all the time. Keep this in mind: it's a human tendency to want to feel safe to survive. That is why people harbor so much inner anxiety; it is a fear of dying before living fully, joyfully and authentically."

"What can I do to fix this blind spot? Do I need glasses or something?"

Wisdom giggled with Lark. "This is not something that can be fixed or repaired quickly in the way you imagine. I wish it were that simple. Here is my wisdom: Practice doing the ABCs. Become aware of your thinking. It's always best to do this step when you feel neutral, meaning cool, calm, and collected in your head. Just observe what you are thinking without any commentary on right or wrong. This can be done by writing your thoughts in your journal or the mere act of noticing the specifics of what you are thinking in the moment. Then breathe deeply into your belly, just the way you have been taught for a few moments. Observe your inhales and exhales. This deep breathing calms the mind and body. Then realize something super important: You have a choice in the way you respond. This puts you in charge and in control. There are always options, and sometimes doing nothing is doing something. Remember, this takes practice. Observing thoughts and even recognizing something might be in your blind spot is empowering and the key to feeling better fast.

"So, the A is about awareness, the B is a reminder to breathe deeply, and the C is about your power of choice.

"I know this is a lot for you to understand. You can take some time to journal everything into your red, leather-bound journal. Do you have any more questions or concerns?"

"So, you do still love me and won't disappear?"

"Yes, I love you; always and forever. Do remember that, as things may change in how you experience me during different stages and times of your life. Take a few moments now and journal all we have discussed. I have a good hunch you will find the exercise very helpful now and in the future. It will be something valuable to reference."

Lark journaled and journaled until her hand hurt. She wrote down what Wisdom defined as a blind spot and how she described Lark's perpetual blind spot. Maybe she was right that if she knew the blind spot existed, she could be on the lookout for it in the future and deal with it more rationally and with self-compassion. When she was finished, she showed Wisdom all she wrote. Wisdom was impressed with her use of different colors, highlighting and underlining key points.

She then rose from the rock and noticed her bottom hurt from the hard stone.

Together they walked around the sanctuary and noticed more trees and the sanctuary's wild inhabitants. Lark felt blessed and loved beyond measure.

She then turned to Wisdom and asked, "What should I do about the girls?"

"Is there really anything to do?"

"I guess not. I should just be me and be thankful I am making new friends, expanding my social circle. It would be great if we could all be friends. I would love to have a party and invite everybody Gwen; Ashley, Nikki, Carly, Molly, Anna, Jonah, and some other kids from school."

"Yes, now those are uplifting thoughts! I think it's time now for you to be on your way and head home to your family. I have a feeling your sisters are waiting for you, especially Becca."

"Okay then. I trust your guidance. I love you."

And as those words came out of Lark's mouth, Wisdom disappeared into a thin, blue mist.

Lark walked home in complete silence. She could not even remember her steps or how she arrived home that late afternoon. It's as if she were in a trance. She recounted the events of the day, her talk with Wisdom. It was a lot to take in and understand. She knew she could no longer backtrack. She had to be sure of her convictions, or she would appear weak and needy. The truth was, she was a loving and joyful person and wanted to soar like a lark. It was time for her to leave the nest, spread her wings, and prove to herself she could fly. But that first step, the first jump from the nest, seemed scary. What if she falls and flops on the ground? Lark took a deep breath and had an inner knowing. That was just not going to happen. If she were daring enough to spread her wings, she would indeed fly.

Chapter 30:

Becca

When Lark returned home, she was shocked to see Becca doing homework in her bed with her bedroom door closed. A feeling of confusion was setting in, and she felt that in her gut. This was unusual, a big surprise, as Becca always did her studying in the den, where everyone could observe and compliment her academic dedication. "Um, hello, what are you doing in my room, in my bedroom, in my bed, and under my covers?"

"I did not think you would mind, as you are rarely home these days. Grace and Hope were loud, annoying, and running all over the house. I needed a quiet place to study."

"Did you ask Mom if it was okay to barge into my room?"

Becca sheepishly replied, "Nope, I did not ask Mom because it's your room. Please don't be mad at me. I just wanted to study in quiet and then wanted to have some alone time with you today."

"It's okay, I don't mind. I was just surprised to see you here. Actually, I'm glad you wanted to spend some time with me. That's rather nice."

"You are? Why is that?" Becca inquired.

"I don't know. I guess I have been spending more time with Grace and had a sinking feeling I had been neglecting you. Plus, it's nice to be needed as the big sister."

"Well, glad you are not mad. I like your bed; it's quite comfortable. What I would not give to have a room to myself."

Lark looked at Becca and said, "That's what you get when you are a twin, the pleasure of sharing a room." Both girls giggled.

Becca looked at Lark and said, "I wanted to say something to you for a couple of days now, but did not think it was my place or that you would even take me seriously, as you are the older sister."

"When did that ever stop you before?"

"In this case, it's different, because it's about your friends." Becca took a deep breath before proceeding. "I just have to say this: Gwen is a bitch. There, I said it! She has been stringing you along, and I don't like it one bit."

"Why do you say this?"

"Come on, Lark, you have been moping around the house for weeks, you take off on these extra-long walks, and cry in mom's bed. You are like a volcano ready to explode. Can't you see what she is doing?"

"Wow, you have been rather observant. I did not realize I was that bad.

"Becca, I love that you are looking out for me and want to protect me. Your sentiments fill my heart. You are correct. She has been driving me crazy and making me feel terrible. I think this has been happening slowly for years, and I am just becoming aware of it now. It's confusing because I don't really know what to do, what to say, or how to handle the situation. It's not just about Gwen; it's also about Nikki and Ashley. However, I can tell you, I am becoming stronger and getting to know myself much better on a whole new level.

"Friends have flaws. People are not perfect. I see Gwen for who she is, deep inside, and the truth is, I love my friendship with Gwen and don't want to lose it. I just don't want to lose my self-respect in the process. So, I am learning to stand up to her. It's been a good experience for me, and I think it's good for her too. She has challenged me on so many levels recently: my emotions and even my reactions. I realized something important; I don't want to play small anymore and would love some new friends in my life."

"Whew, I am so glad to hear you are onto her games. That night when she came for dinner, she felt phony, like a fraud. I honestly think she stayed for dinner to feel like a part of a family, and you provided that experience. You know, as I am saying all this, I kind of feel sorry for her. She only has a brother who is much older, and she has no cool sisters, like us."

"I am glad you feel that way. Look at you being all grown up and mature."

"Hey, I might not be the oldest sibling in the family, but I am the oldest twin, and that comes with rank and privilege."

"I'll give you that one."

"Lark, can I ask you a question? Um, how did you realize you no longer want to play small? And what does that mean? I have a clue, but I'm not sure what you mean by that remark."

"When I am with the girls, I feel like I do whatever they want, on their terms, whenever they want, and not much concern is given to my needs. I shrink my needs to give them what they want, and if I do, they will still need me, and we will all stay friends. This behavior did not happen overnight; it subtly kept getting worse until I was ready to burst. I did not realize it for a long time. Then I slowly started to push back, and they were not used to this at all. I would speak up, and it seemed like they just did not care and started to exclude me. That exclusion hurt and felt so unfair. We have been friends since elementary school, and I wanted them to be nice to me. When Nikki and Ashley sided more with Gwen, I had a big realization."

Becca looked wide-eyed at Lark and inquired, "What was that?"

"It was time to expand my circle of friends. The truth is, I like my alone time, but do want friends who are easy, you know, low-maintenance friends. I think friends should be kind and considerate and be compassionate when someone is having a bad day. It's like give and take. Mom and Dad always encouraged us to take turns. We each get time to speak at the dinner table, and they rotate who goes first every night. We all get a voice, and let's face it, we can be loud sometimes and interrupt each other. I think it's a nice ritual and taught us all patience and how to listen to each other."

"Now I know why you are the big sister. You are much wiser than us."

"I'm glad to hear that! Let me tell you, it's not always easy."

"What do you think is going to happen with Gwen and the girls?"

"I wish I knew, but I can't let their moods interfere with my happiness anymore. It's hard, and I am trying my very best." Lark let out an audible sigh. "Let me fill you in on a secret. The act of journaling thoughts and feelings has really helped me to put things in perspective!"

"You keep a journal? Where do you keep it?"

"That, little sister, is none of your business. That's private! I'm just saying it has been helpful to write down thoughts and feelings. It helps to sort out all the thoughts in my mind and get a grip on life. You'd best not snoop around in my things. It's okay you took over my bed today, but next time, please ask. I love you and will always say yes… well, most of the time."

"If I kept a journal, I'd be afraid Grace would find it and read it. I don't have a room to myself to afford me such a luxury of a hiding place. Grace is always there and always in my business."

"Hey, give her some more credit, please. She really is a good sister, and she is envious of you. Things come easier to you, like school and sports, and she thinks she must keep up with you. She probably says the same thing about you and would love her own room as well. I bet if you two made an agreement about privacy, it would do you both a world of good. Everyone needs to feel safe about their personal possessions, especially in their own house. Maybe you could each have a locked trunk with a heartfelt promise not to snoop. You know what, that could be a great birthday gift for each of you." Lark looked pleased with her idea and smiled.

Becca looked down and said, "I know, she really is the best, but it's fun to give her a hard time." Becca then leaped off the bed, hugged Lark, and said, "I am glad I barged into your room today."

"Me too!"

Chapter 31:

Nikki & Ashley's Crazy Dreams

Nikki decided it was a beautiful day to walk to school. The sun was shining, and the weather was crisp, clear, and cool. She loved being outside, when at all possible, especially early in the mornings. Her mom was surprised she declined the usual car ride to school. This was a routine they established at the beginning of the school year to have a few quiet moments each day to catch up and talk. Nikki assured her mom that this was just an exception because she needed to be active before sitting in school all day.

As Nikki walked to school, she pondered the strange dream that had left her baffled and perplexed. She had strange dreams before, but this one was unlike any other dream. She felt like she had traveled to an alternate universe. In her dream, Nikki was walking to school on a day very much like today. It was a picture-perfect day with a clear blue sky and a slight chill in the air that felt refreshing to her senses. But her walk to school was on a road she had never seen before. The road felt illuminated in some unusual way. There were lush trees with purple leaves along both sides that had a mysterious fragrance, like lavender. As she walked down the road, she felt as if she were walking to school with an eager anticipation to see her friends. She remembered admiring the trees that seemed out of place and rather unusual. She also felt as if she was gliding along the path, and there was no effort or strain on her physical body. It was all so lovely and delightful.

And there she was, a mystical woman waiting for her at the end of this road. She had shiny, long purple hair with beautiful, cascading waves. Her hair reminded Nikki of her own hair, just that it was purple rather than silky black. This woman also had an exquisite shawl around her back and covering her long, thin arms. The garment was colorful and radiant and adorned with a beautiful amulet around her neck. Nikki admired all the colors of the shawl, and as she did, she felt transported to another realm. When the two approached, there was nothing but a peaceful silence. Nikki remembered the absolute peace she felt in her presence. And then she spoke in a low, demure voice. All she said was these ten words: "It's time to be brave. Be part of the solution."

In the dream, Nikki knew exactly what this meant. She realized she was being complicit with her friend Gwen over Lark. By doing nothing, she was indirectly making Lark's problems with Gwen worse and hurting her friend. She knew Lark was struggling, but instead of helping, she deliberately chose to brush her off to gain favor with Gwen. In the dream, she lowered her head in regret. She knew she was a better person, and truth be told, Gwen's treatment of Lark had been unfair and downright mean.

The purple-haired mystical women put her hands lightly on Nikki's shoulder and said, "You can do this and will feel better for doing what is right. You will all benefit from the right words and the right actions. Trust yourself and let your heart lead your path and guide your decisions. Let your true self guide your words, deeds, and actions."

Nikki looked up to acknowledge her advice, and as she did, the path lined with the trees with the purple leaves vanished into a mist. Then Nikki was on the road right in front of her school, and all seemed normal again.

A moment later, Nikki awoke from her spectacular dream. As quickly as she lifted her head from the pillow, she found her cell phone and typed those powerful words in an app so that she would never forget them. "It's time to be brave. Be part of the solution." She knew in that very moment that things would never and could never be the same. It forced her to look deep inside herself to evaluate her priorities.

Nikki entered the doors to school and went straight to her locker in silence. She was baffled by the power of her dream and the mystical woman. She retrieved her books needed for the first two periods and put away her jacket. As she turned around, Ashley was at her side. Nikki smiled and greeted her quietly. Ashley looked at her as if she had seen a ghost. "Can you be late for homeroom today? I've got to tell you something very strange."

"Sure, I guess it would be okay."

"I've got to tell you about this strange dream I had right before I woke up this morning. It was bizarre, and I don't want you to think I am going nuts or anything."

Nikki's eyes bugged out. "Guess what? I had a crazy dream too."

Both laughed.

"You go first."

Ashley took a deep breath and said, "I think we're going to get in trouble for cutting homeroom and part of first period. But I must share this with someone, and it's you."

"Okay, spill it. Tell me all about your crazy dream."

"I was having trouble sleeping last night. Not sure why, but I was tossing and turning. It was late, and I played a few games on my phone and finally was tired and fell asleep. Before I fell asleep, I knew there was not much time before the alarm would go off to get up for school. Maybe I was feeling anxious or something."

"Are you going to get to the dream in this lifetime?"

"Yes, I wanted to preface what was going on before the dream. Okay. I was dreaming I was late for school and did not have a ride, and Mom had already left the house. I found myself walking to school, but the streets were not our streets and looked completely different. I was so confused and delighted at the same time, as the road leading to school was absolutely magnificent. It was lined with the most colorful trees. The leaves of these gorgeous trees were in all the colors of the rainbow, and one was brighter and more vivid than the next.

I found myself walking leisurely, forgetting where I was going. There was also a fragrance in the air, like a light, refreshing lavender. The scent was intoxicating. I was walking and noticed so many different trees, flowers, and even rocks. I knew they were all leading me to school. And then I looked straight ahead, and there was a woman standing in the middle of the road. She was just standing there looking at me. She looked magical and looked like she had secret powers. Her hair was flowing down her shoulders and was green. She had a cape or a shawl around her back and down her arms. This shawl was so colorful, like the colors of the trees. It was as if she blended in with nature. Around her neck was an exquisite necklace with colorful stones. She just stood there, and I had a gut feeling she had a message for me, and I should walk toward her to listen closely.

As I approached, she said, "Ashley, it's time to be brave, be part of the solution." I froze as she said those simple words, and I knew what she meant. In the dream, I wanted to break down and cry.

"The green-haired, mystical woman put her hands lightly on my shoulders and said, "You can do this and will feel better for doing what is right. You will all benefit from the right words and actions. Trust yourself and let your heart lead your path and guide your decisions. Let your true self guide your words, deeds, and actions."

"I looked up to acknowledge her advice, and as I did, the path lined with the colorful trees vanished into a mist. Then I was on the road right in front of school, and all seemed normal again. A moment later, I heard the alarm clock ringing to get up for school. I wanted that dream to go on forever.

"Can you believe this? It's so weird."

Nikki looked stunned and astonished. "Um, I had the exact same dream, well, almost the same dream. In my dream, the leaves were purple, and the mystical woman had purple hair. What do you think this all means?"

Ashley looked at Nikki and said, "I think we both know exactly what this means. It's about Lark. Let's face it, Gwen has been extra obnoxious these days, and we have done nothing about it. We have ghosted her on more than one occasion and made it worse. We must face the fact that we, too, have not been good friends. I think this is a big-time wake-up call for both of us to do the right thing. It can't be a coincidence that we had the identical dream. I feel spooked by the whole thing."

"That's exactly what I was thinking as you were describing your dream. Okay, Ashley, we should get to class to avoid detention. But let's find Lark today and start with a hug and a huge apology."

"Okay, Nikki, that sounds like a plan. Fingers crossed we can make things right."

And with that, the girls were off to class with inspiration starting to brew.

Wisdom certainly works in mysterious ways.

Chapter 32:

Hugs from Friends

Lark was surprised, if not stunned, by her pleasant mood today. She was happy inside and able to focus her attention on class. Even though the last few days were eventful and emotionally challenging, she was doing better overall. Her mind was starting to settle as she was really absorbing and putting into action all she was learning from Wisdom. She was becoming less reactive and felt proud of her strides. And as Wisdom says, "It takes practice and patience." She was also noticing that insight and ah-ha glimmers come in random moments, and emotional healing occurs in the simple awareness of new and better feeling thoughts.

Lark realized she was ready for a fuller life and wanted to embrace new friendships. The thought of an expanded social circle made her heart smile. She did not have to stop being friends with the Swiftie Sisters; she could expand her social circle with joy and enthusiasm. She also realized that she did not have to take on Gwen's moods. She could let Gwen be Gwen and stand up for herself in those tense moments. She would not be abandoned if she allowed herself to use her voice to advocate for herself.

As Lark thought about this while walking to her next class, she thought of something important to discuss with Wisdom. She wanted to understand why Gwen's moods really took a toll on her mental health and why she was so triggered by this particular friendship. There was significant improvement, but still emotional work to be done. She knew she had already spent much time on this subject with Wisdom, but this was an issue that was not totally resolved.

Ah ha! Maybe this is the blind spot concept Wisdom tried to explain the other day. Gwen is in my blind spot. As Lark had this huge realization of who and what was in her blind spot, it suddenly dawned on her that she had the power to change her perspective and thinking about their friendship. If she did this, the discomfort regarding Gwen would be in plain view and no longer catch her off guard. There was significant improvement, but still emotional work to be done. With that thought, she held her head high, went to her next class and took her seat.

She was thrilled when Carly sat right next to her in science class. Carly was always in a good mood and loved to chat before the teacher started class. Lark just let her talk and talk while appreciating the good feelings she felt in the moment. She felt valued as a friend for who she was, and the feelings were mutual. She liked Carly's energy and easygoing spirit. As the teacher clapped her hands to commence the class, Lark took a long, deep breath and focused her attention on the front of the classroom. Carly followed suit, opened her notebook, and prepared herself for class.

The last period before recess seemed to fly by quickly, and before she knew it, Lark was on her way to the cafeteria for lunch. She planned to sit with whoever she saw first. Her new motto was "Go with the flow." She wanted to let go of the need to control and have lunch with whomever she wanted to in the moment. Before she entered the cafeteria, she ran into Nikki and Ashley, who were super friendly and happy to see her.

Ashley started the conversation, and Nikki nodded in consent. "Hey, Lark, it's such a beautiful day, we were thinking of going outside before eating lunch. Want to come with us?"

Lark looked around for Gwen, but she was nowhere to be seen. "Sure, that sounds good, and besides, I'm not hungry yet."

Nikki took Lark by the arm and quickly escorted her outside. Ashley and Nikki were hoping to avoid Gwen to speak with Lark alone.

They went around the side of the building, where typically no one goes. Lark thought this was peculiar, but went along with the girls, as they seemed to be on some kind of a mission.

There was a ledge along the building, and Nikki quickly hopped up and sat down. Ashley stood next to Lark and took her books and placed them down on the floor rather deliberately.

Lark finally spoke and inquired, "What's up, guys?"

Nikki looked over at Ashley and said, "You start."

Ashley looked at Lark with her eyes toward the floor and said, "We are sorry. We have not been good friends to you lately. We have noticed you have been rather upset and are trying to hold yourself together. Nikki and I wanted to talk to you privately and say how sorry we are for not being nice and considerate. We promise to do better."

Lark was speechless and did not know how to respond. "Thank you. Can I ask what made you realize this now?"

Ashley looked at Nikki, and Nikki shrugged her shoulders. "Um, well, it's hard to explain. We just realized we have not been good friends and feel bad about what has been happening over the last few weeks."

Lark looked at Ashley. "Why do you think you have not been good friends?" Lark was beyond curious at this strange turn of events.

Nikki jumped down from the ledge and said, "The day we saw you in town with your mom, we knew we ignored your text. Okay, we admit we ghosted you. We decided it would be just the three of us. We could tell you were upset and did not want to show it. We noticed you trying to be super cool, especially to Gwen. Then, when you deliberately sat with Carly and Molly in the cafeteria, it became clear you were trying to be brave and to save face."

"I was not trying to save face from anyone," Lark replied in a matter-of-fact tone of voice. "I recently realized I want to expand my circle of friends. Besides, I like Carly and Molly; they are genuinely nice people. And with Gwen being moody, it was the perfect time to make a change. It had nothing to do with either of you. I adore you both, but I must agree it was upsetting when you all ghosted me that weekend. I thought I did something wrong. I was going over it in my head and could not understand why no one replied to my text. So maybe I was acting cool to seem okay on the outside."

"We thought so and wanted to make things right," Ashley replied.

"I appreciate that admission more than you will know. But this is what I want to understand: why today? Was Gwen occupied with something that gave you the opportunity to sneak away from her prying eyes? Does she know you are talking to me about this?"

Nikki replied in a low voice, "No, she knows nothing about this."

"Okay, what gives? I have a sneaking suspicion there is more to this story."

Ashley looked at Nikki and then back over at Lark. "You see, we had this dream last night. Actually, we both had the same dream, and it's quite weird. It was really bizarre. Let's just say we each had a hunch we were being bad friends by going along with Gwen all the time. We felt guilty… since we are being honest."

Lark thought to herself, *Okay, now this is really getting good.* "Go on, tell me about your dream."

Nikki said, "Don't worry about that. Just know we love you and are really sorry."

Lark looked at her friends and took a deep breath. "I truly appreciate your sincerity. I am glad you shared this with me today. However, you piqued my interest when you said you had the same dream, which is strange. How is that possible?"

Nikki replied, "We have no idea, but our dreams last night were almost identical and left us freaked out and confused."

"Why were you freaked out?"

"Because it was weird and beautiful at the same time. It was like being in a fairytale."

Ashley said, "I am hungry. Can't we go back inside and eat lunch?"

Lark replied, "Not now. Your stomach can wait. I won't think you are strange, but please tell me about your dreams. I am beyond curious. And did you share any of this with Gwen?"

"No, not a word to Gwen. We spoke before homeroom this morning, and we each felt awful about how we were treating you. Our shared dream helped us to see just how inconsiderate we have been toward you. Can you forgive us?"

Lark replied, "Yes, of course, but please do tell me all about this dream. I have all the time in the world and don't care about the consequences of being late to class. This is way better."

Nikki started with the details of her dream. She told them all about the beautiful path with the trees and their purple leaves. Then she told them about the mystical woman with the long purple hair. She said the woman appeared to be from a different world, as she did not look like any other person she had ever seen in her life. Nikki said she was not scared in the dream and even felt a sense of reverence toward the woman. Then she shared the words the purple-haired woman uttered just before Nikki awoke. "It's time to be brave. Be part of the solution." I knew as soon as I woke up what she meant and realized I had not been a good friend to you. That made me feel awful."

Lark simply said, "Thank you for sharing; sounds like a memorable dream. So, Ashley, what was your dream about?"

Ashley looked at her friends and said, "Believe it or not, my dream was identical to Nikki's dream. However, the trees I noticed were trees with multicolored leaves, and the woman had green hair. The message at the end of the dream was the same, and I woke up with a huge sense of regret and guilt. I knew in that very moment I could and should do better, especially by you. Your friendship is important to me, and I am truly sorry. I am also sorry it took a dream for us to come to this realization. Do you think we are crazy?"

Lark simply replied, "Not at all. I think that was absolutely fascinating. You are not crazy." She knew deep down how and why they shared the same dream; it was Wisdom!

"Okay, now that you have told me about your dream, how are you planning to be brave and be part of the solution?"

Nikki looked at Ashley, then back at Lark. "We only had the dream last night and thought the first thing we should do was talk to you and apologize. And if it's okay, can we have a group friendship hug?"

"Yes, please. I love hugs from friends."

And with that, the girls walked back into the school cafeteria, ready to devour their lunch. Nikki and Ashley promised to stand up to Gwen and not give in to the pressure of her whims or moods.

When the three returned to the cafeteria, Gwen was sitting with Alex, eating lunch and talking about their science lab project. The girls joined them, and all was well. Gwen was unusually subdued, and that was a welcome relief for Lark. Since there were only a few minutes left before lunchtime was over, the three ate their sandwiches in silence.

Before the bell rang for the next class period, Gwen quietly inquired about their whereabouts. It was Ashley who responded first. "We took a walk with Lark to apologize for our bad behavior. We admitted we were avoiding her and promised to do better. We love Lark for who she is—quirky and lovable. If you think she had become too weird, that's your issue, not ours."

Gwen just looked at them and had nothing to say. She simply glanced in Lark's direction and gave her a half smile.

225

Chapter 33:

Coincidences Galore

When Lark arrived home from school, she was flabbergasted by the events of the day. She felt a sense of expansiveness like nothing she had ever experienced. Lark was exhilarated with all she had experienced in the last few weeks. She thought to herself that life was working for her in strange and mysterious ways. This felt much better than thinking her long-time friendships were falling apart and that all was lost.

She remembered Wisdom explaining about the nature of change and that it's normal for there to be metaphorical storms and upheavals in life. These natural cycles were necessary for growth and new life. Lark pondered this sentiment and thought that all this recent drama with her friends created the start of new friendships with Carly, Molly, and Anna. She was excited to have some new friends and adventures in the future. She could keep her old friends and have new ones as well.

Lark's thoughts returned quickly to her private conversation this afternoon with Ashley and Nikki. She knew deep inside, without a shadow of doubt, it was Wisdom who appeared to both Nikki and Ashley in their dreams. But how did she do it? Why did she do that? Lark knew better than to even inquire about the answers to those questions but had every intention of asking anyway. She just had to know how Wisdom managed to influence Nikki and Ashley's dreams in the exact same way, the same night, with similar imagery. It was mind-blowing to even consider how Wisdom managed to accomplish this feat. It gave her a sense of relief that things were working out with her friends, even if she did not comprehend the specifics. Lark realized that being stuck in her own head with a swirling stream of negative thoughts does nothing to help a situation. But she also knew firsthand that in those moments of being triggered, it's just so damn hard to break free from old patterns.

With that notion, she laced up her hiking sneakers and headed toward the trails. Lark had to find Wisdom, even though she had a ton of homework and a few tests the next day. She had to know why and how she got her friends to have the exact same dream. How? Why? Those were the two questions on her mind, and she was burning with excitement and the curiosity of a cat.

On her way to the Sanctuary of Life, she ran into Jonah. He confessed he, too, has become hooked on walking the trails and immersing himself in the sanctuary. He shared that he is feeling a whole lot better and mindful breathing during the day is helping to settle his mind. Jonah was also thrilled that his brother Brian noticed the improvement in his mood. For Brian to give a compliment, things really must be turning around for the best.

"Lark, I can see that you, too, have been better, and I am happy for you. You just seem more confident and self-assured. I knew how challenging it can be when you are at odds with friends."

"Yes, it has been upsetting, especially with Gwen, as I really don't understand why she has been so cold with me. Nothing really happened between the two of us, and it really does not make sense. I have tried to be a good friend. But maybe that is not what she wants right now. I just wish she would be honest rather than unpredictable with her actions and attitude. I have come to the realization it is her decision, and I cannot let her rob me of my joy one day longer."

Jonah smiled at his friend. "I do have to confess something else; I love that we get to share this special place. It's nice to have something just for us, a treasured secret of some sort."

Jonah then reached for Lark's hand. She first pulled away and then, suddenly out of the blue, accepted the gesture and took his hand. The two journeyed to the Sanctuary of Life, hand in hand in peaceful silence.

When they reached the entrance to the sanctuary, she asked Jonah if it was okay to go in different directions. There was something important she needed to do on her own. Jonah agreed and asked if they could meet up later to walk home together. Truth be told, he did not like Lark walking alone. And he loved her company more each day. Lark agreed, and they decided to meet by Goldy the tree in forty-five minutes. If Lark was late, she promised to send a text message.

Lark ventured through her favorite parts of the sanctuary. She greeted Goldy with a pleasant smile and praises of gratitude. She was always grateful for her simple presence and gorgeous golden leaves. Goldy became a healthy source of stability for Lark, and she liked having something she could always rely upon to ground her energy and uplift her spirits. As she waved goodbye to Goldy, she meandered effortlessly through the sanctuary and directly toward the outside classroom. As she did, she realized the big steel gate was not up today and was delighted she was granted immediate access without effort. She thought her energy must be in a good place for that to occur. Lark was all smiles as she took in the beauty of her private sanctuary. She listened to the sweet sound of the chirping birds, as if they were personally welcoming her home. She breathed deeply and appreciated the scents of nature, the dried leaves, as well as the fragrant aroma of honeysuckle. Off in the distance, she could also smell wild lavender, which always calmed her mind. She wondered what Jonah was experiencing today and looked forward to comparing notes on the walk home.

As she reached the outdoor classroom, there was something written on the board between the two large trees. The message was five words, "Trust You Know the Answer." Lark walked up closer to the board to see if there was anything she might have missed. There was nothing else to see or read, just those simple words. She backed up and looked at the board again and reread the words, but this time out loud, "Trust You Know the Answer." Well, I know for sure Wisdom knows the answer, but how can she know that I know? That thought made Lark laugh inside. *Wisdom knows all, and if she believes that I know the answer, it must be true. But how exactly do I know the answer?* Lark started to pace up and down until the ground was worn beneath her feet. She then wondered where Wisdom was today. She looked behind the trees, for certainly she must be here waiting for me if she wrote those words on the board. But Wisdom was nowhere to be found, and Lark was clearly disappointed.

Okay, this must be a trick or something. Yes, ma'am, this must be a trick of some sort. Then another thought occurred faster than the first… *Wisdom does not do tricks; she is my teacher and trusts in my abilities.* She read the board again and this time sat down and steadied her breathing. Lark allowed her thinking mind to drop into the heart center. As she did, she settled herself and allowed herself to become ONE with the sanctuary.

At that very moment, she became one with the trees, the ground beneath her feet and even the chirping birds. She let herself mentally soar like a lark. She imagined flying high in the air. She felt connected to everything and felt blissfully free. As a lark, she flew over to Goldy and perched herself on top of her high branches. Goldy welcomed her and let her rest safely on her branches to allow her consciousness to soar to new heights. Goldy was proud of Lark, but no words were necessary for Goldy to convey her love and reverence for Lark. Lark was indeed becoming who she was born to be, a light in this world to share the love in her heart. As Lark had this knowing in her heart, another truth surfaced. Everyone was born to love. She remembered something she once heard, "We are here to love each other. The more we love, the more we get." Lark really did understand a simple truth: everyone was born to experience love uniquely and to share their love and passions differently, for love is the highest vibration of them all. She thought this world certainly needs more love.

In that moment, it was as if Lark became nothing but pure love that transcended everything. She realized her friends were just like her. They too wanted to be happy and loving. They were good friends and always were good friends. But sometimes people do make mistakes or fall short of their good intentions and need a nudge along the way. Lark knew she certainly was not perfect, not by a long shot. She had her moods, fought with her sisters, acted out, and could be a brat just as easily as she could be an angel. Her friends were just as deserving of Wisdom's guidance as she was. *Wisdom was not just for me but for everyone.* Lark was starting to understand and trust herself, just like the message on the board suggested.

Lark realized Nikki and Ashley do love her, and that love transcends all and has no limits. Lark was overjoyed with the possibility that all humans have access to higher realms and possibilities. Lark was understanding this at a deeper level, and it was mind-blowing. She also knew the struggle of overthinking was real, and it's easy to get hooked on the content of the thinking mind and spiral down a rabbit hole of negativity. Lark knew that all too well. She knew overcoming these habits takes practice–lots of practice and patience. She knew she would have to continue settling her thoughts and practicing what she learned from Wisdom. This would have to be a lifetime practice. Lark became grateful in that moment for all she was learning and who she was becoming.

After a few more moments of quiet bliss, Lark slowly opened her eyes, and Wisdom appeared. Lark smiled from ear to ear. "Hi! I am so glad you are here. I thought maybe you would not be here today after leaving those words on the board."

"I am always here and present if you choose to tune into me."

"Is this another riddle for me to solve?"

"No, just a simple truth. I AM always here. It may not be in this form or this way, but I AM always here. The truth is to trust this connection by deliberately tuning your attention to your awareness, your true self.

"It's like choosing a program to watch on television. There are many program options for entertainment. First, you select the show to experience in the moment. Just as there are a multitude of shows to consider, there are unlimited thoughts to think and capture your attention. You get to choose which thoughts to focus your attention on. You have the free will to choose where to place your thoughts or spend your precious time. This will determine your mood and your personal energy or vibration.

"When you focus your attention and trust I AM and WILL BE here for you, you will experience me, in some form or another. The trick, as you like to say, is to be open to possibilities and not limit your imagination. I can appear to you in different forms, like answers to questions. When you trust this truth, you will feel uplifted."

"What would be some ways for you to appear to me or make yourself known when I am not here with you in the sanctuary?" Lark inquired.

"Good question! First, remember to communicate with me frequently and trust that I do hear you, even if you cannot hear or see me. You can talk to me, write to me in your journal or even think of me. You may ask for guidance or signs. You can also be as specific with your requests as you wish, so you can be aware when they appear. It could be a song on the radio with meaningful lyrics, seeing a special number on a clock, finding a particular coin on the floor, noticing a random object, or even words said to you by another. The key is to be aware and recognize the signs. Then offer me gratitude for the support, so I know you received the guidance. This is a two-way relationship, and validation of signs is important."

"I like these possibilities and will start to notice more coincidences." Then Lark became quiet. She was still burning to ask Wisdom her questions. She wanted to hear from Wisdom's lips how exactly she appeared to both Ashley and Nikki. *Hmm,* she thought to herself. *What is the worst Wisdom would do if I asked the question? Okay, I know better, but here goes.*

"Wisdom, how did you appear in the dreams of both Nikki and Ashley on the very same night?"

Wisdom looked at Lark, smiled, and pointed back to the words on the board. She then took Lark by the hand and placed her hand on top of her heart. She then simply said, "Trust the wisdom and knowledge in your own heart. For there are things I cannot explain to you, but you do know in your heart. Trust yourself."

And just like that, Wisdom vanished into a thin blue mist. Lark frowned.

Truth be told, Lark was a bit upset she disappeared without warning. *But maybe this was to reinforce the message of the day, to trust myself.* Lark had a momentary pang of fear that she would never see Wisdom again, but she quickly let that thought, an untruth, fade away. She knew deep down in her heart she would see Wisdom again.

Lark glanced at her cell phone and realized that forty-five minutes had passed. She quickly texted Jonah, who was relieved to hear from her. He had been patiently waiting by Goldy for an extra twenty minutes. Jonah instinctively knew she was not in any danger but wanted to escort her safely home. A few minutes later, she emerged from around the tree, and the two were back on the trail heading home.

Jonah was playing it safe and did not attempt to hold her hand, though he desperately wanted to reach for her hand to feel that special connection. He felt butterflies in his stomach every time he was around Lark. Instead, he asked if she wanted to share her experience.

Lark looked into Jonah's eyes, then glanced down toward the pavement. "Not right now. I really need to journal everything that happened today first. If I start speaking of them out loud, it may alter my recollection."

"Oh, that makes so much sense. I should start journaling myself, but it just seems so weird, and I would be afraid of someone finding it. I'd be mortified."

"I get it. I too was afraid of my sisters snooping. The other night, Becca surprised me by waiting for me in my bed. She was on a mission to talk privately. At first, I was so mad, but realized it was sweet. It was a bid for connection, so how could I stay mad for longer than a minute? After we chatted, I told her about my journal and that it was private. She promised to respect my privacy and not to snoop. I trust her at her word and know that Grace would never even consider going into my room without permission. I think being upfront and setting healthy boundaries and expectations can help a relationship bloom. I would not want to do something or not do something from fear. Well, of course, I would not jump off a moving train or anything dangerous like that."

"Hmm. That makes sense to me. I will consider keeping a journal for myself."

"Hey, we have a few more minutes before we get home. What did you do today with your time in the sanctuary?"

"After we went our separate ways, I found myself walking toward Henry, the elder tree. I did that breathing thing again and suddenly began to feel a strong connection to everything surrounding my body. It felt like my legs were becoming tree trunks, and I was super tall. It was so much fun, almost magical. My feet felt like they were becoming tree roots, grounded deep into the earth. It was not scary or anything. I let my arms shoot up toward the sky, as if my body were in the shape of the letter Y. Then I imagined my arms and hands becoming branches with delicate leaves. It felt so free to become a tree. I just stood there silently for what felt like a long but actually was a short time. I could almost hear Henry talking to me."

"What did he say?"

"Trust your inner knowing."

Lark was about to burst, and she barely let Jonah finish his reply. "Seriously, is that what you heard?"

"Yes, that is exactly what I heard him say. 'Trust your inner knowing.' I thought it was kind of cool that he said that because I have been unsure of my answers on tests at school. I study efficiently and do my very best to prepare. Then, when the teacher passes out the test papers, I freeze or find myself thinking of too many answers. I know you should go with your first answer, but I get so nervous, like I'm being judged, and become too focused on getting the wrong answer, and all I have studied goes right out the window. It's frustrating."

"Well, then, you got exactly what you needed today. You should trust your inner knowledge. You are smart. Let yourself excel."

"Thanks, Lark!" Jonah smiled. "Can I share what else I imagined?"

"Of course. I would love to hear it."

"After hearing those words, I imagined becoming a bird and flying above Henry, the elder tree. I felt light and free and could see everything from a new perspective. Then I flew over to Goldy and sat upon her branches." Jonah giggled and had a look of sheer embarrassment on his face. "I imagined you too were a bird, and we were perched next to each other on one of Goldy's highest branches. It was fun to pretend we were birds and could fly! This must all sound ridiculous."

"Not at all, please don't be embarrassed. Okay, I will share something about my experience today. It's only fair as you shared with me."

Jonah turned to look at Lark with relief in his heart and gave her his full attention. "Let's hear!"

"You are not going to believe this, but I got almost the exact same message and had a very similar experience! My message was not about school; it was about trusting my intuition with friends and various situations. I did not understand the message at first. I became doubtful I could really know the answer I was seeking. Then I settled my attention and grounded my energy into the earth. Then I felt like a bird, a lark, soaring through the air and landed on Goldy's branches. Sorry, I did not envision you there with me as a bird perched on her branches. Then some other stuff happened; I will journal all in my book later tonight."

"This really is crazy and even a bit creepy. How is it that we both had such a similar experience today? We did not plan on meeting on the trail; we just happened to be walking over there at the same time."

"Maybe there is something in the air today. There have been several coincidences that have been life-changing for me. Listen, Jonah, would love to stay and chat about this some more. Actually, that is all I want to do but I must go home. Got a ton of homework and need to journal everything that happened today. I don't want to forget a single moment. There was so much good stuff to capture on paper to remember. We will catch up on the weekend, okay?"

Jonah reached over and gave Lark an awkward, teenage-boy hug. "Okay, see you tomorrow in school."

237

Chapter 34:

A Day to Remember

Just as Lark walked through her front door, Mom yelled. "Where have you been? It's late, and you did not check in to let me know your whereabouts. It's a good thing there is tracking on your cell phone. I saw you were walking home, or I would have been worried about you. I really do appreciate it when you text in advance."

"Sorry, Mom. It was a busy day, and time got away from me. I walked home with Jonah and, honestly, just forgot to check in with you."

"Okay. Please be mindful in the future. It really is helpful to know where you are and when to expect you to arrive home."

"I promise to check in earlier and not worry you."

"It's nice to see you spending time with Jonah. He was always so nice, and I think he had a soft spot for you."

"Don't be ridiculous, we are just friends. He, too, has been hooked on the trails, and we enjoy them together. Listen, Mom, I have a lot of homework tonight, so if it's alright, I would like to eat a fast dinner then head upstairs."

"Sure. I will make you a plate and sit with you. Dad is working late, so the rest of us will have dinner later."

Lark finished her dinner, made small talk with Mom and raced upstairs. She organized her books and her assignments for the evening. She had to get work done before bed, as she likes being prepared in class. But on this evening, she opted to journal first. She had to get the events of the day into her red, leather-bound journal. This was certainly a day to remember.

She settled herself comfortably at her desk and began to write and write until her hand hurt. An hour later, she was surprised at how many pages she had filled with the events of the day. She started with the conversation with Nikki and Ashley, and then her experience in the sanctuary. She used the next blank page, and on the top line she wrote the five words Wisdom wrote on the board in the outside classroom. Below the headline, she penned what she knew to be true...

Wisdom's Words: Trust You Know the Answer

- Settle thoughts
- Begin to breathe deeply
- Ground your energy
- Be present in the moment
- Connect with surroundings completely
- Become a bird, a lark
- Trust everyone was born to give and receive love
- People generally want to be happy

- Nobody is perfect
- Wisdom is for everybody and has no limits
- Overthinking does not help and magnifies the illusion of problems
- Always be grateful
- It's a choice to tune in or away from Wisdom
- Wisdom is always here with me
- Recognize signs from Wisdom and offer verbal gratitude
- I get to choose where to focus my attention
- It is good to trust myself
- Coincidences are little miracles

Lark took a breath and reviewed all she wrote. She was super proud of her own efforts. She felt inspired to list and summarize the learnings from the day to use them as a quick reference in the future. This was certainly a day to remember. She put a small sticky note on the side of the page for easy access. With that task complete, she wrapped up her journal and put it in its safe place. Now onto class assignments. She had only ninety minutes before bedtime and was confident everything would get done with her focused attention and positive intent.

Chapter 35:

Stand Proud

Lark was grateful for bedtime so she could decompress from the day. She wanted to sail into a nice, deep sleep and did so the moment her head hit the pillow. It was a long day, and her mind and body welcomed the peace and solitude of sleep. She slept deeply and barely heard the alarm clock ring the next morning. Mom had to help her wake twice more, which was rather unusual, and she had little time to get ready for school and get to the bus stop.

She made it to the bus stop just in time. As she walked down the aisle to select a seat, she noticed Gwen sitting with Alex. Gwen had the aisle seat. Lark went toward the back of the bus and found an empty row. She placed her book bag next to her and waited for the other kids to board and for the bus to be on its way. A moment later, Gwen appeared and asked if the seat next to her was taken.

Lark froze momentarily but moved her bag out of the way to make room for Gwen. This bought her a few seconds to compose herself and settle her energy. Gwen looked at Lark and cheerfully said, "Hi. Guess what?"

"It's too early for guessing games; fill me in."

"My parents are not fighting as much, and things are getting better at home."

"That's great to hear. I am happy for you and especially your mom. I could see how distressed she was when I was over at your house. I bet you feel relieved."

"I sure do feel better. We even had dinner together as a family last night. Hey, I know it's early in the day to think about lunch, but do you want to sit together today?"

Lark hesitated for a moment. She was not sure how to reply. At that moment, the bus was pulling up to the school's main entrance. Feeling relieved, she gathered her backpack and said, "Let's get off the bus." She then silently thought, *I guess it's also time for me to get off the roller coaster with Gwen; this is just too stressful. This is as good a time as any to speak up for myself.*

After they disembarked the bus, Gwen pulled Lark off to the side and asked, "Well, do you want to sit together at lunch?"

Without hesitation and in an even tone, she confidently replied, "Not today."

"Why not? Are we not good enough for you anymore?"

Lark turned toward Gwen. "I'm confused. Are you asking for yourself, or are you speaking for Nikki and Ashley too?"

"Umm, you know, we always sit together. I just wanted to know if you would sit with us today. You know what, Lark? Just forget about it. Do what you want; you always do."

"Gwen, I only said not today. You don't have to get so annoyed with me. This is why I have chosen to sit with other people lately, because you have been rather rude to me. Honestly, I don't quite understand this recent change of attitude. So, I may choose to sit with Carly and Molly. It's nice to have variety and sit with different people. You sat with Alex yesterday."

"I sat with him because you all were nowhere to be found when I got to the cafeteria. Lark, are you seriously still upset with me?"

"Here is the truth," Lark whispered so that the world did not have to overhear their conversation. "I am not upset, but yes, I am hurt. I do not like the way you have been treating me lately. One day, we are best buddies, and the next day, you are an ice queen. I never know which Gwen will show up. We have been friends for years, and frankly, I deserve better. I get that you have been struggling because your parents have been fighting, but that's not my fault. I, too, have stuff going on in my life and have apologized several times if I have not been there to support you. However, you have not been a good friend either." Lark straightened her body, looked into Gwen's eyes, and said, "Actually, you have been rather mean to me, and enough is enough."

Gwen must have been in a state of shock that Lark spoke up and stood up for herself. *This is new behavior for Lark,* she thought. She had no words other than, "Well, maybe a little."

Lark looked into Gwen's eyes and said, "Glad you can admit that to me."

The girls noticed the time and headed into the building, as they were most likely going to be late for their first class.

244

Chapter 36:

The Lure of Blueberry Muffins

When Lark arrived home from school that day, the house was filled with the scrumptious aroma of freshly baked blueberry muffins. Her mouth salivated with anticipation. Mom's muffins were famous around town. She baked them for holidays, gave them as presents to neighbors, and when the school had bake sales to raise money for events, she always baked a fresh batch.

Mom was waiting for her in the kitchen and brewed a fresh pot of English breakfast tea. She had a plate ready for Lark and motioned for her to sit. The twins were at after-school activities, and Hope was in the den watching a movie. As she poured Lark a cup of tea, Lark knew Mom wanted to talk. Mom's parents always served tea in their home, especially when someone was going through a hard time or seemed upset. Lark did not particularly care for this tea; she found it bitter. But she wanted to please Mom and added a spoonful of sugar and fresh milk to her cup.

"Sweetheart, catch me up on what's going on with your friends. You have been in and out so much, and we have barely had time to talk. I wondered how you are coping and if I can help in any way."

Lark took a huge bite of the muffin and grinned with delight. "Mom, this is your best batch ever!"

"I am glad they have your seal of approval."

"You are not going to believe what has been going on these days." Lark wanted to spill the beans and tell Mom everything, but knew there was only so much she could share. "Ashley and Nikki pulled me aside yesterday and essentially apologized. They realized they had been going along with Gwen for far too long and were wrong to brush me aside. They even felt terrible about ghosting me on the weekend we went shopping in town. They really felt regretful and promised to do better. I think they are seeing right through Gwen."

"Wow, that was quite mature of them. How do you feel about that?"

"Well, it was a genuine apology. They really seemed remorseful, so of course, I forgave them. I love my friends and don't want to be on awkward terms.

"I have also been spending more time with Carly and Molly. I have been sitting with them at lunch, and it has been a nice change. I decided it would be good to expand my social circle and have really enjoyed spending time with them. Carly is in my science class, and she is so friendly and funny. It's been nice to laugh."

"Lark, I am so glad to hear all this. It's wonderful news. You are right. It's good to expand your circle of friends. Having a variety of friends in your life is healthy. You will see that friendships with different people will meet different needs in your life. People enter your life when you need them, bringing new adventures and experiences. People will also leave your life at certain times. Sometimes that can emotionally hurt and bruise the ego, but it will make space for new opportunities and friendships."

Lark thought, *that's something Wisdom would say.* "I have also been spending more time with Jonah."

"Yes, I have noticed, and I'm very pleased. I have always liked Jonah and think he is good for you."

"Mom, stop! It's not like that. We are just friends."

"I know. I'm just saying he is a really nice person."

"Well, I'm glad you approve. Okay, here is the best part… Gwen apologized today."

"I would expect she would. You have been friends for years."

"Mom, you don't understand. She has changed, and I am not sure what to expect from her anymore. It's sad, but true. She has this attitude in school. At first, I was so upset and afraid I would lose all my friends. I was in a bad, negative headspace for quite a while. Then, after feeling so anxious, I realized it became an opportunity to move on and make new friends. As you always say, I am a great sister and friend and deserve to have nice friends. When I shifted my attitude, everything became easier socially. I also think when I decided to be stronger, it changed the dynamics between us."

"You never cease to amaze me with your wisdom and kindness." Mom got up and gave Lark a big hug. "When did Gwen apologize?"

"This morning. She sat with me on the bus. She started off with small talk, which was fine, as I do want to be on decent terms with her. Then she asked me to sit with her at lunch."

"What did you say when she asked about lunch?"

"I said not today, as I wanted to keep my options open and go with the flow. I told her I enjoy the variety of sitting with Carly and Molly. I also clearly expressed she has been rude to me lately."

"What did she say next?"

"Well, she did not exactly apologize but conceded to how I had been feeling lately. I'll take the win. When I arrived at the lunchroom, the girls were sitting with Alex and some of his friends. Gwen waved me over because she'd saved me a seat. I sat down, chatted with everyone for a few minutes, then got up and told them I had plans to sit with Carly and Molly. The girls were all friendly and said we would catch up later. Ashley texted after school and invited me over on Friday night. Her dad is cooking some new recipes and said to invite her friends. She invited Nikki and Gwen as well."

"Are you going to go?"

"Of course, if it's okay with you?"

"Yes, you may go. Weekends are for fun. I'm truly happy and so very proud of you. You have a good perspective on your friendships and are doing a great job setting healthy boundaries for yourself. I especially admire how you found the courage to share your feelings with Gwen calmly and honestly. That takes real strength. I can imagine that conversation wasn't easy, but you handled it with maturity and grace. Lark, having that conversation was great practice in standing up for yourself.

Confrontation is a challenge for many people, but holding onto hurt can lead to resentment and inner turmoil. I'm glad you chose to speak with Gwen and clear the air.

"I'm curious and have a question for you. What do you think helped you most to express your feelings to Gwen?"

Lark had to think quickly about her answer to Mom. She knew it was from all her time with Wisdom. "I have to say walking on the trails has been a game changer. Being outside and surrounded by nature is so peaceful and helps to put things in perspective. I have also been journaling my thoughts. Remember, Grandma bought me that red, leather-bound journal? I figured I should put it to good use. I even told Becca about my regular journaling practice, and she was impressed. She might even try journaling for herself. I made her promise and pinky swear she would never snoop around my room."

Mom laughed and gave Lark another hug. She just could not help herself and took advantage of every opportunity to hug her daughters. "Is there anything else you would like to share?"

"Nothing else to share today. May I please have another muffin? They are delicious."

Chapter 37:

Rainy Days are for Reflection

The next few days were rainy and dreary outside. Lark preferred days where the sun was shining on the backdrop of a picturesque blue sky. She loved having the freedom to be outside at her own discretion. However, she used these days to be reflective and journal her recent friend interactions. There was much to capture in the private pages of her beloved journal. She believed in her heart the rainy days were needed as much for her mental well-being as for the plants and trees.

The last few months were a fantastical, mystical ride. From the moment she dreamt about Wisdom, everything in her life changed rapidly and certainly for the better. She reflected on all the emotional growth and resiliency she developed. As she thought about the distress with her friends, she realized she would not change a thing. She would do it all over again in a heartbeat to embody the teachings from Wisdom. She became quite aware that growing up is difficult and challenging. She also counted her blessings. She was grateful for her family. She has the best parents and awesome sisters. She loves her small town, her teachers, and all her friends. She also is ever so grateful to Wisdom, Goldy, and the Sanctuary of Life for welcoming her into their realm.

She wondered contemplatively why she could see Wisdom and the elements within the sanctuary. Lark was starting to realize that even though she could see all of this, others could also experience this mystery in a way that would resonate with them. Then there are others that cannot experience anything beyond what the human eye can see and perceive. She knew now from her time with Wisdom that there is no one right way to view the world or experience life.

Lark quickly came back to reality and looked at her messy room. She decided it would be best to use this rainy day to organize her space. After her room was in better shape, she went into the closet to find her prized journal. She took out her special purple pen and started the entry for the day. Lark reflected and then detailed how much better things were going at school and with her friends. She loved addressing her journal entries in a variety of ways. It made each session unique and fun. Today, she decided to address a letter to Wisdom.

Dear Wisdom,

You are not going to believe how things have been going this week. Ever since my talk with Gwen, I feel liberated, like I have been let out of an inner jail. I surprised myself by just how confident and assured I felt when we had the opportunity to speak privately. I told her what had been on my mind, and I believe we cleared the air. I was upset with myself for way too long for holding in my feelings to maintain peace. I realized that holding in my feelings and not saying what needs to be said did nothing to improve the situation. That was eye-opening because I always thought it was best to keep everything inside and not rock the boat. In the past, things would usually blow over, and I was glad about keeping quiet. I realized by staying silent, I was betraying myself and not being kind to myself. I gave myself permission to speak up and be heard. It felt good to hear my own voice advocating for myself.

Things with Nikki and Ashley are great, too. We are talking about our feelings and topics that are important to us. They also told me more about their shared dream and how it has impacted their lives in wonderful ways. I giggled silently because the woman in both of their dreams was definitely you, Wisdom. They also sat with me at lunch along with Carly, Molly, and Anna the other day. I am happy we are all becoming friends.

I did have lunch with Gwen, Ashley, and Nikki the day after my talk with Gwen. Things are back to some kind of normal. I am happy we spoke honestly, as her friendship is important. However, it will take some time for me to regain trust with Gwen. In the meantime, I will continue to enjoy my new friendships because they make me happy.

Ashley invited us for dinner on Friday night! I can't wait to hang out with the girls again now that I am feeling and acting more confident.

That's all for now.

Love,

Lark

Lark finished up with her journal and placed it back in its hiding spot in the closet. She felt it quite cathartic to write down events and her feelings in her private book. It helped her to sort out her thoughts and put things into perspective. She wanted to share her practice with the world, but knew it was fine to have rituals just for her own well-being.

Lark then finished her homework and went downstairs to be with her family. *I wonder what Mom made for dinner. Maybe I could help her this evening. I bet she would appreciate my assistance without her having to ask.* When she arrived downstairs, her sisters were thrilled to have their big sister join them for a great meal and an evening of fun.

Lark allowed herself to be fully present with her family. She savored Mom's meal, the easy dinner table conversations, and the warmth of being together. Her thoughts were still. She quietly appreciated the moment.

Chapter 38:

Scripting in Action

Friday night came quickly, and Lark was thrilled to be done with school and head over to Ashley's house. Lark had been experiencing a different set of emotions this past week that felt both unusual and wonderful. She was stepping into her authentic self and owning her self-worth. Her air of confidence was becoming noticeable. Mom commented on how much lighter her energy felt when engaging with the family, and her teachers praised her improved class participation. She contributed more to classroom conversations and was easy-going when answers were incorrect. She stopped criticizing herself if she was not perfect. Her new inner dialogue was, "Nobody is perfect, and people make mistakes." This felt a whole lot better than when she berated herself for answering incorrectly.

Lark also noticed Nikki and Ashley were a whole lot easier to be around and were nicer to other kids in school. She knew their dream with Wisdom had a positive effect on each of them. They seemed to be more tolerant and relaxed. It was a nice change to witness firsthand.

She felt compassion for Gwen, who still seemed to be struggling on the inside, even though she would always have a brave face and a sarcastic tone. Lark wanted things to be good with Gwen; after all, she felt like they were sisters. Sisters argue and misunderstand each other, but at the end of the day, they can resolve their differences and be friends again.

Lark was curious how Friday night would play out. Would it be a fun and relaxed evening, or would Gwen pull a stunt? Lark quickly became mindful of her negativity and used the scripting process she learned from Wisdom. She set the intention that Friday night at Ashley's would be wonderful and memorable. How could it not be a great evening? Her dad was a master chef, and her mom always made everyone feel welcome in their home. Ashley's house was like a second home to girls. She imagined everyone smiling, laughing, and dancing to Taylor Swift music. The truth is there is nothing like old friends and tradition! Friday night will be a great night and an evening to remember.

Well, that is exactly how the evening played out; it was a fantastic evening. It was even better and more special than how Lark imagined it would be.

When Lark thought about the evening, she thought the best part was just how comfortable she felt in her own skin with her oldest friends. She did not have to pretend or hold back her needs or feelings. She showed up with a relaxed and carefree demeanor. Her energy was contagious, which, in a way, allowed her friends to be relaxed and carefree, even Gwen. It was certainly a great night!

Chapter 39:

A Little Patience Goes a Long Way

Lark slept late Saturday morning, and when she finally made her way downstairs, everyone was finishing breakfast. She was still stuffed from eating dinner at Ashley's and could not even consider eating another bite. She opted for some peppermint tea Mom had freshly brewed. Grace finally asked Lark, "Well, how was last night with the girls? We want all the juicy details."

Lark was still tired and really wanted to go back to sleep, but did not want to be rude to her sisters. Besides, it was late, and there were things to accomplish.

"Don't keep us waiting," Becca proclaimed.

"It was the best! We were all back on track and had a great time." It was fun to arrive in pajamas and slippers and have this feast with her family. Her dad is seriously a great cook. Her parents are hosting a dinner party next month for some of his business associates, and he wanted to practice cooking some new dishes.

He started with a fancy charcuterie board and amazing tiny, hot appetizers.

Becca chimed in quickly. "We could care less what her dad cooked for you all. What happened with Gwen? Did she behave herself?"

Grace giggled with delight.

"Yes, Gwen was rather chill. We could all see Ashley's dad was a bit nervous, so we just wanted to be supportive and eat the scrumptious food. He prepared things I had never had before last night. That was a real treat."

"Enough with the food. Please tell us before we burst."

"Right, okay. Gwen was rather mellow. Let's say she was a reserved and relaxed version of herself. She took a back seat and listened more than she spoke. Ashley was rather curious about how I have been spending my time. She really listened with an open mind. I shared about enjoying time on the trails and how it's been helping to calm my racing mind. I explained how this past year, I have been struggling with lots of negative thoughts and did not understand where they stemmed from because all is well here and in school. I told them the fresh air and the break from the cell phone seemed to do wonders very naturally. It's almost impossible to be on the phone and on the trails at the same time. I shared how the break from technology was life-changing. It is something I now enjoy.

"Nikki was impressed I had been able to cut down time on the social media platforms so easily. She also got why I just did not reply to all the random text threads. She realized it was not personal. She felt so bad that she did not realize I was struggling because I seem to have it together all the time.

"My friends really listened to me last night, and it felt nice to be heard. Even Gwen noticed I seem to be in better physical shape. I told them I had been learning to run, and it's been fun, even if I can only keep it up for short sprints. They all laughed.

"Then we had a sit-down dinner with her parents. It was fun for us all to be in pajamas. We gathered around the table in the living room and discussed things about school, plus what has been going on in the world. Her parents commented on how grown-up we were all becoming this year.

"After dinner, we danced in the living room for her mom, then hung out in Ashley's bedroom, just like when we were younger. We flopped around in her bed, surrounded by her stuffed animals. She can't bring herself to get rid of any of them. She said they are all sentimental and bring her comfort at night.

"Honestly, it was just fun to hang out with them and feel relaxed. I was able to be myself without any pretense, judgments, or expectations. We just had a nice night. That's about it, nothing else to share."

"So, no nasty remarks from Gwen?" Becca inquired.

"Nope, I think she was glad we spoke privately and respected the firm way I expressed my concerns. I had to stand up to her for the benefit of both of us. Not speaking up created this weird dynamic between the two of us that just was not healthy. We got back on track once I stood my ground, which was easier than I thought possible. It was the fear of the fear getting in the way the whole time. I guess I had to learn that lesson for myself. Things were nice with Gwen last night, and I am happy. We even walked home together, just like old times. She made no mention of the past few weeks. We talked about our favorite shows and raved about the food. It will take me a while to completely trust her again. Perhaps things will never be quite the same, but that is just fine. I am not the same person I was at the start of this school year, and I like myself a whole lot better."

Grace interjected. "I am glad you had fun last night. You see, a little patience with yourself and your friends goes a long way."

Lark winked at Grace. "You are wise, little sister."

Chapter 40:

A Golden Nugget of Wisdom

Sunday morning came quickly, and Lark awoke to the sounds of chirping birds outside her window. She loved their melodic chirps, like an orchestra in perfect unison just for her delight. She got out of bed, opened the curtains and was thrilled to see a spot of sunshine peering through the grey clouds. It had been a long stretch of rainy days, and Lark was thrilled with the chance to be outside. Her loud sisters were already downstairs with Dad this morning. Mom was eager to head over to the new yoga studio for an early morning class to enjoy some peace just for herself.

Just then, she heard the text alert ping. It was Jonah inquiring if she wanted to walk and catch up this morning. The smile that came to her face surprised her. Did she like Jonah? That could not be possible; they were old friends. Lark flew downstairs and asked Dad if she could meet up with Jonah for a walk on the trails. Dad inquired if all her schoolwork was ready for Monday. Lark promised she would do her homework later in the day.

"Okay, Lark, schoolwork is your job and must be a top priority. I trust you will give it your best effort and get everything done on time."

With Mom gone, Dad could be over the top. "Dad, I always get my work done. You will be impressed with my next report card."

"I am always proud of you. Just giving you a hard time."

"That's what I thought." Lark went over and gave him a big hug, and he smiled with delight.

Lark replied to Jonah and agreed to meet at their usual corner in thirty minutes. She washed up, made her bed, straightened up her room and scarfed down one of Mom's famous blueberry muffins. Little did Lark know Mom snuck protein powder into the batches she made for the family.

She arrived wearing her new outfit this morning with a long-sleeve layering top, as there was a crisp chill in the air. Jonah commented on how great she looked. Lark pretended not to care, but inside she was all smiles. Jonah started the conversation casually. "I see you have been sitting with Molly, Carly, and Anna during lunch this week, and I was completely shocked to see Nikki and Ashley joined you as well."

"It's been a nice change. It's boring to sit with the same people all the time. Too bad your lunch period is different. It would be nice for you to join us, too."

"It's fine. My lunch period is not as crowded in the cafeteria. Sometimes I can get my homework done. What's the deal with Nikki and Ashley? They always sit with Gwen and follow her around like puppy dogs."

"That's not nice or even true, Jonah. I had a long, rather interesting conversation with them last week. It was the day you saw us going outside during lunch. Let's say they had a big wake-up call. They were sweet and admitted they had not been good friends, complying with Gwen's demands way too much. They saw firsthand how hurt I was when we ran into each other in town after ignoring my texts. It was an awkward moment in front of my mom. I held myself together, but they knew I was devastated. No one likes to be excluded or ghosted. We worked everything out, and things are now even better with them.

"Then the other day, I hashed out things with Gwen. Long story short, I had the opportunity to straight out tell her I did not appreciate the way she has been treating me lately. It was empowering to speak up for myself. In that moment, I think she had more respect for me than at any other time. She is usually the one setting the tone and the rules. I had to change the rules of the game once and for all. Let me tell you, it felt liberating. Ever since that day, things have been better, at least in my mind. It's only been a few days since our talk, and I am taking things one day at a time. Then on Friday night, Ashley had us all over for an incredible dinner, and we had a super fun time together."

"I am glad to hear that news. I must say you have really matured this year. You seem much more resilient."

"My walks on the trails and spending time in the Sanctuary of Life have been, well, life-changing. I am learning things in there that I could not have learned anywhere else. And I think you know exactly what I mean, don't you?"

"Yes, and I think it's so special that we get to share this place. Got a question for you. I've been wondering lately, do you think others know what we know?"

"That's a tough question to answer accurately. I do think others have gotten glimmers of what we have experienced. There is an expression, 'When the student is ready, the teacher will appear.' I think you and I were both eager and ready, and our teachers magically appeared. They manifested themselves to us in ways that would personally resonate with us."

Jonah looked over at Lark, "I guess that makes sense. You have been at this longer, so I trust your judgment."

As the two arrived at the sanctuary entrance, Jonah paused to give Lark time to settle her thoughts. She appeared to be on a mission today. "I have a hunch you want to go on your own for a while, to have some private time."

"Yes, that would be great. Let's meet by Goldy in forty-five minutes."

"Sure, that's perfect. Text me if you need to or are running late. I have a feeling today is going to be very interesting for both of us," Jonah replied.

"Why do you say that?"

"I'm not exactly sure; just have a gut feeling."

Lark winked at Jonah as she made her way quietly into the depths of the sanctuary. This is the place she felt most at peace. It was the most familiar feeling in the whole world. She did not need a thing in this place. It's as if every time she entered, she was bathed in tranquility. Lark walked ever so slowly and allowed herself to enjoy the crunching sound of the leaves with every step. She smelled the sweet scents all around her and marveled at how adept she was at deciphering the different smells, even with the change of the seasons. She looked at the various types of trees as well as the little critters running up and down their tall trunks. She was fascinated with the variety each time she experienced the sanctuary.

As she made her way toward the outside classroom, Wisdom was waiting for her with a fresh pot of chamomile and lavender tea. Lark was becoming fond of this tea to her surprise. Wisdom motioned for her to sit beside her and sip the tea slowly. Wisdom wanted Lark to experience the tea with the same mindful awareness as walking through the sanctuary. She wanted her to be completely present while enjoying her cup of soothing tea. Wisdom explained that mindful consumption of food and drink is a way to respect the human body. Through mindfulness, you will become a master of your body's needs. Wisdom went on to comment on how she felt it was odd that people need electronic devices to be in tune with the rhythm of their own bodies. Nature has provided all that is needed. I would advise people to slow down to observe, listen, and notice their own unique patterns.

"I am learning this for myself firsthand," Lark said thoughtfully. "I am paying closer attention to how different foods feel in my body. It's been an interesting experiment noticing the foods that give me energy compared to the ones that make me feel sluggish. I definitely ate too much at Ashley's house. The food was great, just way too much for my stomach. Thank you for being such a good teacher."

Wisdom turned to Lark and said, "That is very astute of you to recognize and appreciate all you have learned. Focusing on gratitude is a wonderful habit to practice often. It will help you have feelings of well-being. Here is another secret: you manifest what you focus on in your life. That is why it is important to be aware and mindful of your thoughts. Notice how the stories in your mind make you feel. The more you are in tune with what you are thinking and how you are feeling, the easier it becomes to shift into positive states with good feelings. Do you understand this?"

"Yes, it's all coming together for me, and I have been putting this into practice, especially this past week."

"What have you practiced that was most helpful?"

"Well, I noticed several things. It was like putting puzzle pieces together. I realized my monkey mind of worry does nothing to help and only makes me feel anxious. On the other hand, trusting things will work out helped me to feel both curious and optimistic. I liked the idea of curiosity. It was fun, like the anticipation of receiving a surprise birthday gift from someone special.

"I was curious how you managed to appear in Nikki and Ashley's dreams and marveled at how they were so positively impacted by the shared experience. They were certainly transformed by their dreams. They took the time to deeply listen to the message they received. I believe they felt better, too, when they acknowledged my feelings.

"I know their shared dream was somehow a gift for all of us, even if I don't understand everything. Maybe understanding all the details is not necessary. I do know life is good, especially when I focus on good things. If I give and show love to others, I will be open to receiving love in return.

"I then realized something important. I am the one who creates my life experiences. That thought felt playful and empowering. I had a deep desire to expand my social circle without leaving anyone behind. I started using the scripting process you taught me when we first met. I scripted out enjoying lunch period with both new and old friends together, and it happened. I also scripted a wonderful, relaxed Friday evening at Ashley's house and that worked like a charm, even better than imagined.

"All these realizations are helping me to feel settled, relaxed, and playful. I can be the creator of my experience and direct my thoughts appropriately."

"Bravo," Wisdom proclaimed. "You are a fine student. I have a final concept for you to master. This will summarize all you have learned in one simple concept."

Lark looked at Wisdom with curiosity and sadness. "Does this mean you will leave after you have taught this to me?"

Wisdom looked compassionately at Lark. "What have you learned, Lark?"

"That you will always be with me in one form or another. I am to trust myself, this wisdom, now and always."

"That is correct. Hold onto this truth, even in the darkest of days. Now, let's have some fun and teach you the golden nugget that will help you now and always. This will propel you forward and teach you the art of mastering your consciousness."

"This sounds very serious and difficult."

"That is the farthest from the truth. It is the easiest and most profound concept of all to learn. Once you understand this principle, you are to practice often with compassion and patience. Let's go for a walk while we talk."

Wisdom guided Lark around the sanctuary. They went past the waterfall, Henry, the elder tree, and of course Goldy. Lark was amazed at how her leaves sparkled with golden shimmers. They listened to the sounds of the chirping birds and other animals that inhabited the sanctuary. Lark inhaled the clean, cool air into her lungs. She felt exhilarated and ready to learn something new.

"Lark, the golden nugget of wisdom I always want you to remember is simple. The human mind is like a receiver of information. It's just like your smartphone with unlimited capabilities to download all types of data. The mind is either inwardly focused on one's mental thoughts, chatter, memories, or it's expansively focused. Expansively focused means connected to aspects of your grander self, the true self. Sometimes this is also referred to as your nonphysical self or spiritual self.

"Please do listen carefully. You have learned to become aware of your thoughts, feelings, and beliefs. The quality of mental thoughts, the thoughts between your two ears, creates feelings in the body, also referred to as emotions. There is a subtle difference between emotions and feelings. Emotions are perceptions such as anger, sadness, or fear. Feelings are how they are felt in the physical body.

"As you are practicing becoming aware of what your mind is thinking, this puts you in a state of awareness. This gives you the ability to make choices. In this awareness state, the golden nugget is to become aware of where your attention is focused. Is your attention on thoughts generated between the two human ears? Or is your attention with your higher self or true self? The important key is to decipher <u>where</u> your thoughts are coming from, not <u>what</u> your thoughts or stories are all about.

"If you are focused on thoughts coming from the thinking mind, it becomes an invitation to notice and then redirect to your true self. How you do this is your wonderful choice. There is no one right way to connect with your true self. As a matter of fact, humans have many grand ways to feel that connection. The best one is the one that feels right, productive, or loving. People have lots of great ways to connect to their true self. There is no right way, and there is no wrong way. It's the one that feels good, calm, or peaceful in the moment. The connection will have a loving or settling feeling."

Wisdom paused to give Lark time to absorb this golden nugget of wisdom.

"I also want you to know that it's impossible not to be connected to your true self. Your true self is always there. It's not pushy and stays patiently waiting in the background. People tend to forget this bit, and this is what causes anxious feelings. It's like the human heart. It is always beating; we just don't pay attention to this natural process.

"Here are steps to help grasp this concept. First, notice where your thoughts are in the moment. In times of distress, they are most likely from the thinking mind. This awareness gives you the advantage of choice. It's an opportunity to be at one with your higher self, your true self. Remember, a person is always connected to their true self; it's like having a patient guardian angel always on the job, ready to provide help or assistance. The key is to ask and trust!"

"Wow, that does help to simplify everything you have taught me. My job is to recognize if I am in my head in a worry loop or doing something mindful like breathing or appreciating something, allowing me to feel my true self."

"Excellent job; you are understanding this concept wonderfully. Here is a good analogy for you to remember to help absorb this concept at a deeper level. Think of an ordinary room lamp. A lamp must be plugged into an electrical outlet, or it will not work to illuminate the room. When the lamp is connected to its source of power, it works perfectly. If the plug is disconnected from its source of power, it cannot work. That is the way it was designed.

"It is the same for people. When one is connected to their true self or source, life has a way of flowing in wondrous ways, and life feels good. Yes, there will be hardships and sadness in everyone's life. Life and death, good times, and bad times are all part of the human experience. Just like the weather, there are beautiful, sunny days as well as rainy, gloomy days. It's a part of nature.

"Let yourself practice connecting to your true self frequently, and eventually, this connection will be your natural, preferred state. Remember, you have free will and choice, and there is no one right way to do anything. The best one will feel good inside yourself. Be playful and allow yourself to be guided by loving whispers of inspiration.

"I like your lamp metaphor. That really helped to illuminate this concept even more." Lark giggled at her own pun.

Wisdom giggled as well! "Very good, Lark. You are a fine student, and you will continue to be a good teacher."

"Do you really think I am a teacher now, or do you mean I will be a teacher when I grow up?"

"Yes, you certainly are a teacher now and might be a teacher in the future. It may not be a classroom teacher, but a teacher of wisdom or knowledge. That is your journey, and it will unfold as you mature. You are practicing being a teacher in your life now. Look how you helped Grace not only with math but with her mindset about math."

"I never thought about that in that way. I guess I am a teacher." Lark felt proud of herself.

"We have covered so much today. Do you understand this golden nugget concept?"

"Yes, I believe I do understand." Lark picked up a stick from the ground. She turned to Wisdom and said, "I am either focused on thoughts between my ears," then pointed the stick toward her forehead, "or I am connected to my true self and the Universe." She then pointed the stick upward toward the sky.

"Very good. You have grasped this concept very well indeed. Here is another secret: it makes no difference in the content of the thoughts. We do understand mental thoughts can feel very real and are at times justifiably upsetting. What we are focusing on today is the repetitive nature of thinking that disconnects one from the wisdom of their true mind or true self. The awareness of too much thinking becomes an invitation to pause and choose wisely."

"Let me see if I understand your words. What you are saying is that the habit of negative thinking is the culprit that disconnects a person from their true mind and their very own *Wisdom*."

Wisdom smiled at her prize student and embraced her into her arms. "I am so very proud of you. I trust with all my heart you will have a beautiful, inspired, and purposeful life. I wonder what you will create with your heart and mind connected to your true self."

Lark smiled from ear to ear and became quiet. She took a few moments to absorb the golden nugget of wisdom from Wisdom. It felt way more than just a single golden nugget; it was a world of information. They both enjoy the stillness of the sanctuary for a while.

Several minutes later, Wisdom took off the amulet necklace from around her neck and placed it around Lark's neck, so the pendant was perfectly centered by her heart. The colorful stones sparkled from the sunshine peering in through the trees. "Ah, this amulet has found its true owner and forever home. Wear this pendant close to your heart. Let it be a reminder to connect to the elements of nature, your breath, and your true self. This amulet does not have magical powers but will awaken your memories of me now and always."

Lark looked at the amulet she always admired on Wisdom. Tears of happiness streamed down her face. She thought this was the most precious gift and would treasure it forever. "Thank you so very much. I love it. But who shall I say gave me this beautiful necklace?"

"You will say very simply that you found it at the foot of your favorite tree in the sanctuary. You may show them this note attached to its box. "The finder of this amulet shall wear it proudly as a reminder to connect to the beauty of nature and all its inhabitants." Wisdom slipped the box with the handwritten note into Lark's hand. She looked at the pendant around her neck and admired how it sparkled brightly and how the stone's colors illuminated Lark's face. She hugged Lark one last time, kissed the top of her head, and vanished into a colorful blue mist.

"Wisdom, where are you? Where did you go? I want to thank you again for this beautiful present." Lark looked in all directions. Wisdom was nowhere to be found.

As Lark settled her thoughts, she heard Wisdom clearly in her mind saying, "I did not go anywhere. I am where I belong—at home inside you and all around you. I will always guide your words, deeds, and actions. All you have to do is ask and trust. You can feel my love and guidance now and always. I appeared when you asked and were ready. You are now ready to fly solo, like a lark."

Tears streamed down Lark's cheeks. She loved coming to the Sanctuary of Life and spending time with Wisdom. Lark knew in that moment things were changing, and she would no longer see Wisdom in this form again. Or would she?

Lark knew she could always come to the sanctuary, and she would learn new ways of connecting with Wisdom. Lark allowed herself to feel the sadness while holding the amulet around her neck in her hands, giving her joy. She would always know the truth about who gave her this special gift. It was real and tangible. She was excited to show it to Jonah.

She glanced down at her phone; it was time to meet Jonah by Goldy. She said a soft goodbye to Wisdom and trusted with all her heart it would not be the last time.

Chapter 41:

Embrace Changing Times

Lark picked up the pace and hurried to meet Jonah. She knew how punctual he was and did not want to keep him waiting. As she made her way through the trees, she felt the sadness again. She would miss Wisdom immensely but knew it was time to be the lark and fly solo, away from the comforts of the nest. Lark felt ready for the next chapter in her life. She had her journal with all the lessons and learnings from Wisdom to treasure forever. She would be adding one of the most important entries later today and title it, "A Golden Nugget of Wisdom."

Jonah was so excited to see Lark appear from behind the trees. Her natural sparkle made him smile inside. She had an uplifting presence, and he loved her company and friendship. He even felt grateful to have experienced so much anxiety earlier in the year. The struggle led him magically to rekindle an important friendship, even though he did not know that at the time. Jonah reflected on how his struggles helped him grow spiritually, becoming a happier person. He knew deep down that one day the story of his inner battles would assist another. This notion filled him with a sense of joy and purpose.

On their way back home, Jonah sensed something was off with Lark. He wanted to reach for her hand but resisted the temptation. Instead, he dramatically walked a few paces in front of her, jumped around, and stopped. He was going to ask her about her time in the sanctuary, but as he turned in her direction, he noticed the exquisite necklace around Lark's neck. He was curious and looked closer. Lark too looked down and admired the amulet. "That's beautiful, Lark. I've never seen anything quite like that. Were you wearing that earlier, or is it new?"

"I just received it today. It was a gift."

"From whom?"

Lark wanted to share the real story of the amulet with Jonah. She could confide in him more than anyone else in the world. But she decided to keep the story of Wisdom privately to herself. She was not ready to share Wisdom with anyone just yet. She wanted to preserve this part of her life.

"I found it in this gorgeous, colorful box resting on the tree roots of Goldy. This note was attached to it. Maybe it's from Goldy." Lark showed Jonah the note, and he read it carefully.

"It's stunning, and you're right; it truly is a gift. I think it's a gift from the Universe to thank you for all the light you bring to others. You have certainly helped me in so many ways.

"Are you going to show it to your parents?"

"Oh, I have not thought about that yet. I just found it a few minutes ago, right before our meeting time. Maybe I'll show it to them, but no one else. I will keep it at home in a safe place, next to my red-leather journal."

"Good idea, it certainly looks beautiful on you. Wear it proudly."

"Thanks, Jonah. How was your time today?"

"It was amazing! This place really is magical. I can't believe others in town don't know about this place."

"Jonah, we can't be sure others don't know about the sanctuary. What I have learned is that things happen right on time, when a person is ready. It's not a race. Everyone progresses at their own pace." Lark giggled at her own rhyme. It's like we get private lessons from our very own private tutors, who show up at just the right time. There's a saying, 'When the student is ready, the teacher appears.' I feel very fortunate our lessons are conveniently orchestrated."

"I've never heard that expression before, but I like it! It feels so true."

"So, tell me what happened for you today?"

"I first passed by Goldy as usual. When I arrived today, there was the cutest yellow bird chirping. It was as if she were singing a song just for me. I admired her fine feathers and the sweetness of her song. She flew over my head in a circular motion and then slowly started flying in the direction of Henry, the elder tree. I wanted a few more minutes with Goldy, and she flew back and again flew overhead in a circle, then again in the direction of Henry. She chirped a bit louder. I think she was trying to get my attention, so I decided to play along and follow her lead. We went past a few more trees I never noticed before. There was even a tree with blue leaves. That was an incredible sight to see. I will take you to see it next time. Then we arrived at Henry, the elder tree.

"I literally heard him welcoming me back to the sanctuary. It was like he was singing to me in a unique harmony or melody. I never heard anything like that before today. He said it was good to see me and to be proud of my accomplishments. He noticed I am breathing more deeply and allowing myself to be myself without all that intrusive worry. He commended my dedication to feeling better and said I was doing quite well."

"That's amazing, Jonah! It must have felt great to know Henry sees you. What else did he say?"

"Not too much after those words. He encouraged me to keep practicing all I have learned every day. He sounded so wise. He then went on to say it's not a marathon; therefore, there's no need to rush progress. He said he has been around for centuries and has all the time in the world for me. All the while he was talking, or at least, I thought he was talking, I heard that beautiful melody emanating all around his wide trunk. I even looked to see if there were electronic speakers buried inside him. It was hypnotically blissful.

"I thanked him, bowed before him as a sign of respect, then wandered around before heading back to the tree with the blue leaves. I had to see that tree again with my very own eyes."

"That is incredible, Jonah. Next time, I would like to come with you and hear Henry's melody for myself. That will be fun to experience firsthand."

Lark and Jonah continued their walk home, side by side at a leisurely pace. Both were reflective and refrained from any further conversation. The quiet silence was peaceful and gave them space for contemplation. Lark thought to herself, *There is so much more out there than we will ever understand, and it's amazing.* She was still sad with the belief she would not see Wisdom in the same way again. She loved her time in the sanctuary with Wisdom in her full form. She also trusted with total conviction that she would interact with Wisdom in a new, magical way. She wondered with a sense of curiosity and delight what was next. How would Wisdom continue to be a part of her life?

When it was time to part ways, Jonah summoned his courage and gave Lark a hug. She melted in his arms and wondered what those feelings were in her stomach.

Chapter 42:

Trust Your Wise Mind

Lark headed right for her room, dodging Mom and Dad, who were always inquisitive about the events of her day. She loved that her parents cared so much about her well-being, but sometimes she yearned for more privacy. She took off the amulet from around her neck and admired the pendant with the colorful stones. This was something real and tangible from Wisdom. She could hold it in her hands and feel the essence of Wisdom. She could hear her voice, feel her encouragement, and even see her etheric figure before her eyes. Lark promised to keep the necklace safe and would treasure it forever.

She retrieved her red leather-bound journal, ready for an important entry. She dated the page and titled it "A Nugget of Wisdom." She began to detail how Wisdom explained this pearl of wisdom so eloquently just a little while ago. She knew this was a very important concept to grasp and master. *Notice where thoughts are coming from, the thinking mind or the true self. Distressing thoughts are typically from the thinking mind. This awareness becomes an opportunity to connect and ask our true self for guidance. By asking and trusting, I will be guided and loved.* She then poured her heart out onto the pages about her conversation with her beloved guide, Wisdom, and how she gifted her the amulet necklace. Lark journaled her thoughts and feelings beautifully, using her special purple pen. Then, to her surprise, she wrote about her time with Jonah. She wrote about their unexpected hug and her innermost feelings.

Lark then put down the pen and naturally allowed her mind to drop into the center of her heart, just the way Wisdom taught her all those weeks ago. She went into a quiet, meditative state, and it was blissful. Her heart, perhaps her true self, echoed these words to her mind, "Peace starts when you trust your wise mind and show up authentically as yourself. As you do this, your life will bloom and flourish. You've got this."

Almost an hour later, she finished her entry and heard Mom calling her downstairs for dinner. She tied the ribbon around her journal, put the amulet necklace into the box, and safely put her treasures away in the secret hiding place in her closet. Lark was not ready to show the necklace to her parents quite yet. She wanted something just for herself to relish and treasure.

Chapter 43:

Emotional Freedom

Lark entered the school building on Monday morning, cheerful and refreshed. She embodied a new sense of emotional freedom that awakened her inner confidence. What a great way to be as the school year was coming to an end in a few weeks. As she walked through the hallways, she greeted her friends and teachers with a big smile. It felt good to simply be herself without putting on an act to impress others. She thought, *This is the way life is supposed to be, easy and harmonious.* She wished others could have this same feeling of contentment. She felt proud to be Wisdom's student and vowed to keep the memories of their time alive in her heart and imagination. *Today is going to be a great day*, she thought.

She entered her English Language Arts class and sat up front, right next to Gwen. Mrs. Givens allowed the students to select their own seats. Mrs. Givens was a serious teacher and always got right to work when the bell rang. The girls only had a quick minute for small talk. They reminisced about their time on Friday night at Ashley's house and commented on her dad's delicious cooking. This teacher had no tolerance for stragglers or idle chitchat. When the bell rang, they quickly ended their conversation and sat up straight, ready for class.

Mrs. Givens was a progressive teacher whom Lark admired. She had them read interesting books, and class discussions were active and dynamic. Mrs. Givens encouraged the students to immerse themselves in the literature for a deeper understanding. She also had a knack for recognizing each student's potential and was highly motivational.

Immediately, she instructed the class to open their books to the assigned chapter for discussion. She called on Lark to summarize the chapter and give her interpretation of the plot. Lark smiled and eloquently gave a succinct summary of the main points. She was confident in her perspective and delivery. Lark was a naturally bright student and prided herself on being prepared for class. Mrs. Givens complimented her thoroughness and asked her to continue with a personal analysis. Lark looked down at the passage, then at her homework notes. She gave a remarkable perspective that impressed her teacher and the other students. A few of them even clapped softly. She felt confident speaking to the class, and it filled her with pride, as this was not always an easy task. Once again, Mrs. Givens thanked Lark for her impression of the passage.

Just then, under her breath, Gwen retorted with a nasty comment. "Look at you being all academic and Miss Smarty-Pants. Are you trying to be the teacher's pet again?"

Without hesitation, Lark turned around, met Gwen's eyes, and gave a small shrug.

"I'm not trying to impress anyone. I just like learning." She turned back around, smiled, and refocused her attention on class just as Mrs. Givens reprimanded the two for talking in class.

Where in the past, Lark's mind would have raced with worry, there was just a mere hint of the old anxiety, which faded quickly. She was calm and composed as Gwen's words no longer had the power to cause her mental anguish. She remembered what was most important. They are friends, and this friend finds it humorous to pick on others. This time, Lark refused to take Gwen's comments personally. She used Wisdom's golden nugget of wisdom to stay in alignment with her true self.

After Lark refocused her attention, she was surprised by how quickly the class time passed, as she enjoyed the discussion. Lark was well prepared and loved the intellectual conversation about the book. She enjoyed hearing different points of view from her classmates. Mrs. Givens always listened to different perspectives and never made anyone feel inadequate during her class. In fact, she always inspired her students. She was a tough teacher, and Lark respected her immensely.

Right after class, Anna went up to Gwen and Lark and complimented Lark's knowledge of the passage. She was impressed by how she spoke in front of the class. Anna wished she could be more comfortable speaking in public. Lark told her it was a skill she had been working on this year and finally got more comfortable raising her hand and answering in class. Anna looked at the girls and said, "Hopefully, it will get easier for me next year. It's just scary to give the wrong answer. I get so embarrassed and turn red."

A moment later, Anna was off to her next class. Gwen and Lark headed to their lockers, chitchatting away. Lark was pleased with herself for letting Gwen's earlier comment easily roll off her shoulders. She did not give it more than a second thought; other than that, it was meaningless and simply not true. She recognized it was more a reflection of Gwen's own insecurities than anything personal. She realized maybe Gwen's teasing, though sharp, stemmed from feeling inadequate. The truth was, Lark was well prepared and confident in her grasp of the material. Lark finally gave herself permission to shine, and it felt liberating.

And in that moment, Lark had a realization that brought a smile to her face. Lark embraced the fact that she felt comfortable in her own skin and could control her reactions. Wisdom taught her many skills on how to do this effectively. The positive changes did not happen overnight and were not easy. In fact, making the changes came with lots of tears. However, Lark diligently practiced all she learned. She also gave herself grace about making progress. This patience helped Lark to thrive and be more confident. With this clarity, Gwen could no longer push her buttons. Lark was able to recognize her newfound strength to stand tall and proud. Perhaps this confidence had been hiding in plain sight all along. Lark just had to look in the right direction, inside herself, and turn on the lights.

The simple act of choosing how to respond became a catalyst for her personal growth and transformation. It dawned on her that Gwen, her oldest friend, had unknowingly done her a tremendous favor by challenging her, giving her the chance to thrive and transform. Lark suddenly felt a surge of appreciation for Gwen, understanding that true friends sometimes push each other in order to grow. She smiled, grateful for the unexpected gift of transformation and a deeper understanding of this friendship. *Wow, what a good friend Gwen turned out to be,* she thought, and she was grateful. Gwen unknowingly helped Lark to find her true voice and speak up for herself with dignity. This was a huge growth moment for Lark.

It was finally time for lunch, and Lark was ravenous. She headed toward the cafeteria, almost in slow motion. Lark was mindful of her breathing and each deliberate step. She felt her feet taking the steps, her book bag on her back, and the lunch bag in her hands. She felt the joyful anticipation of eating her favorite lunch, the usual peanut butter and jelly.

As she arrived at the doorway, she stopped and surveyed the large room. It was as if everything was quiet and came to a complete stop, like time stood still. This moment was just for her pleasure and appreciation. She saw all the different friend groups gathered around the tables. She noticed the windows were wide open to allow the warm breeze to fill the room. She noticed the people online purchasing lunch and the teachers taking their break. As she glanced to the left, she saw something that made her heart smile and filled her body with complete joy. Lark took a mental snapshot of this scene to remember forever.

They were all there! All her friends sitting together at one lunch table, happy and smiling. She saw the largest table in the cafeteria, and it was filled with her friends! Lark was over the moon with delight. She saw Gwen, Nikki, Ashley, Carly, Molly, Anna, and Alex. Jonah was there too, as one of his classes had a change of schedule. They were all talking and laughing. Lark was simply amazed. This was her dream. It was her deepest wish to expand her circle of friends and have everyone get along. Today was proof that her dream came true.

In that rare, wonderful moment, she felt Wisdom by her side. She felt her love and encouragement. Lark trusted this knowing with every fiber of her being, and it felt peaceful. She heard Wisdom whisper into her ear, "I wonder what you will create next?" Lark smiled to herself and then went over to the table to join her friends for lunch.

Chapter 44:

Another Dream, Another Teacher

It was finally evening, and Lark was able to escape to the backyard for a few quiet moments for herself. She enjoyed looking up into the sky to admire the velvet black sky. She noticed the bright, silvery moon and twinkling stars. She wondered what else was out there... *Is Wisdom there with all those stars?*

Lark had a shawl around her shoulders to keep herself warm as the evenings were frequently cool. Lark felt like Wisdom tonight. She had the elemental amulet tucked inside her sweater. She took it out from hiding and let it dangle around her neck, close to her heart. She wanted the amulet to absorb the energy rays of the full moon. She remembered Wisdom reminding her to regularly connect to the elements of nature, earth, air, water, and fire. She was encouraged to revere all of nature and continue to learn all she could to preserve the environment for future generations. She felt a sense of deep gratitude as she held the pendant in her hands. It was like having a part of Wisdom with her now and always.

To honor Wisdom, Lark dropped her thinking mind into her heart and let her energetic field expand. She felt a sense of oneness with her environment. This was a blissful, expansive feeling that was getting easier to do each time. Lark started to reflect on the incredible day and all her wise insights. She felt proud of herself and liked who she was becoming. As a matter of fact, she loved herself. She loved her life.

Just then, her thoughts drifted to her last encounter with Wisdom. She memorized those moments, her words, and Wisdom's soft, gentle embrace. She felt safe and at ease. She recalled her last words from that day as well. "You have graduated. School is out for the summer. Go play and have fun. You are a teacher in your own right. You are a wise soul, a wonderful daughter, a terrific sister, and friend, to all who know you. Share your love generously, as we are all here to love each other. The more we love, the more we get."

A tear rolled slowly down her face, not from sadness but from gratitude. She wondered what would be next. How would she practice all she learned and continue to grow without Wisdom's direct guidance? So many questions filled her mind with curiosity and a sense of wonder.

Lark felt a cold breeze on her back. It was getting late and now rather chilly. She thought it was probably time to go inside. She said goodnight to her family, headed upstairs, and closed her bedroom door. She was happy to have more time before sleep time. She wanted to journal everything from today. She knew this was going to be a long entry and got herself comfortable. She captured everything from the day as best as she could remember. Her favorite part was seeing all her friends sitting together, chatting away in the lunchroom. All her desires, heartache, and tears created this beautiful scene.

Throughout this journey, Lark knew she had created something wonderful. She heroically fostered the creation of new friendships. These new bonds were not just for her but for the benefit of all her friends. The friendships and sense of belonging that blossomed were a direct result of her open heart and willingness to be vulnerable. It became clear that nurturing these connections was an accomplishment worthy of celebration.

When Lark was done, her hand was hurting from so much writing. She wanted to capture every detail and realization from the incredible day. She was pleased with her determined efforts. She proudly wrapped her red, leather-bound journal with the ribbon, placed the amulet into its box, and carefully put both items into their hiding place.

Finally, it was bedtime! Lark was exhausted and ready for sleep. By the time she got into bed, she heard the wind whipping loudly outside her bedroom window. Wow, the weather changed fast. It was lovely just a while ago. Soon afterwards, she heard the sound of large raindrops pelting on the roof. It was pouring outside, and Lark loved it! She relished being lulled to sleep by the sound of a rainstorm. That would certainly transport her to dreamland in no time.

Lark was now all snuggled up in her bed with soft covers keeping her warm. She took delight in listening to the raindrops hitting the roof and windows. The sound of the wind, thunder, and flashes of lightning made it even better.

Within minutes, she was fast asleep. The thunder and lightning got even stronger, more powerful, which only deepened her slumber. Hours go by, then the storm intensifies with wind and rain. Lark is peacefully sleeping. She is in dreamland and back in the Sanctuary of Life.

Wisdom appears to Lark in her dream. Lark is very much aware she is dreaming. She is overjoyed to be with Wisdom once again. Wisdom reminds Lark of her most recent message.

"Trust that I live within your heart and mind. I am always here for you, but I am no longer needed in your daily life. You are a fine student and have learned well. You are implementing all I have taught with grace and dedication. It is time for you to fly free, apply my wisdom accordingly, and be who you were born to be.

"Remember, when the student is ready, the teacher will appear. It is now time for me to graciously step back and let you take the lead. You are ready for your next chapter."

In her dream, Lark truly understood why Wisdom originally appeared. She was a student ready for a teacher, and her teacher was eager for a special student. Lark embodied Wisdom's wisdom. Throughout their time together, Lark slowly became a teacher for others. Some of Lark's students included Grace, Mom, Jonah, and Gwen.

Wisdom gives Lark a hug and a kiss on the forehead and once again vanishes into thin air, a blue mist. Lark is sad but understands why Wisdom first appeared and why she now must leave.

Lark feels herself stirring in her bed and is feeling melancholy. She is restless, rolls over, and falls back asleep. As she falls into another comfortable, deep sleep, another dream begins. It's a wonderful dream about the Sanctuary of Life. But this dream is different, oh so very different. The Sanctuary of Life looks totally different. It is more colorful, filled with flowers and animated with life forms.

And then there she is, a beautiful, majestic teacher in a long, flowing robe. Quietly, she says, "Hello, Lark, my name is WONDER!"

THE END

Epilogue

A New Beginning

When Lark awoke the following morning, she found that the storm had finally ended. Outside, birds sang together in cheerful harmony, filling the air with their joyful melodies. The mood in her room was bright and uplifting, and she felt a deep sense of happiness and contentment. All was well in her world. Sunlight streamed through her window, bathing everything in warm, golden light. It was a vivid change from the fierce storm of the previous night. Lark felt a wave of eager anticipation for the day ahead, excited for the possibilities that summer would bring. School was out, and all her friends were planning to gather at the beach to celebrate the beginning of summer break.

Preparing for the day, Lark made her way to the bathroom to wash up. She stood before the mirror, brushing her long, thick brown hair as she always did. Suddenly, she noticed something out of the ordinary. Her heart skipped a beat with surprise, and she leaned in closer to examine her reflection. There, gleaming in the light, was a single, long strand of blue hair. The sight sent a rush of memories flooding through her mind, and a wide smile spread across her face. As she gazed at the blue strand of hair in the mirror, a surreal realization dawned on her. And Lark remembered everything…

Reflections

Reflections

Reflections

Continue the Journey

Visit:

WiseMindHypnosis.com/books

The journey does not end here.

On the website, you will discover a growing collection of beautiful companion resources created to extend your time in the Sanctuary of Life.

As a reader of *Walk with Wisdom*, you are invited to visit a special page created just for you, featuring downloadable resources inspired by Lark's journey with Wisdom.

One of the first gifts waiting for you is **A Wise Mind Reset**, a simple collection of eight daily mindfulness practices designed to help you reconnect with calm, clarity, and your own inner wisdom.

From time to time, new resources may appear as well, including reflection pages, creative coloring sheets, and perhaps even a few more glimpses into Lark's continuing adventures.

If this story touched your heart, a thoughtful review helps other readers discover it too.

Thank you for being part of the journey.

Your support truly makes a difference.